THE
DANCE
TREE

Kiran Millwood Hargrave (b.1990) is an award-winning poet, playwright, and novelist. *The Mercies*, her first novel for adults, became an instant *Sunday Times* bestseller. It won a Betty Trask Award, and was named amongst the NYT 100 Most Notable Books of 2020. Her bestselling works for children include *The Girl of Ink & Stars* and *Julia and the Shark*, have won or been short-and long-listed for numerous awards including the Waterstones Children's Gift of the Year, the Waterstones Children's Book Prize, the British Book Awards Children's Book of the Year, Costa Children's Book Award, the Blue Peter Best Story Award and, twice, the CILIP Carnegie Medal. Kiran lives in Oxford with her husband, the artist Tom de Freston, and their rescue cats, Luna and Marly.

Also by Kiran Millwood Hargrave

Books for adults

The Mercies

Books for children

The Girl of Ink and Stars
The Island at the End of Everything
The Way Past Winter
The Deathless Girls
A Secret of Birds & Bone
Julia and the Shark

THE DANCE TREE

Kiran Millwood Hargrave

PICADOR

First published 2022 by Picador
an imprint of Pan Macmillan
The Smithson, 6 Briset Street, London ECIM 5NR
EU representative: Macmillan Publishers Ireland Ltd, 1st Floor,
The Liffey Trust Centre, 117–126 Sheriff Street Upper,
Dublin 1, DOI YC43
Associated companies throughout the world
www.panmacmillan.com

ISBN 978-1-5290-0516-5

1 3 5 7 9 8 6 4 2

A CIP catalogue record for this book is available from the British Library.

Typeset by Palimpsest Book Production Limited,
Falkirk, Stirlingshire
Printed and bound by CPI Group (UK) Ltd, Croydon, CR0 4YY

Visit **www.picador.com** to read more about all our books
and to buy them. You will also find features, author interviews and
news of any author events, and you can sign up for e-newsletters
so that you're always first to hear about our new releases.

For Katie and Daisy, who held hope for us when it was
too heavy to carry alone.

Their fragile bodies are like the strongest gusts of wind, and the paths of creation, innumerable as they are, tell us that nothing and nobody is expendable.

FROM
The Beehive Metaphor
BY JUAN ANTONIO RAMÍREZ

Sometimes the body experiences a revelation because it has abandoned every other possibility.

FROM
Fugitive Pieces
BY ANNE MICHAELS

When I saw this spectacle, I wanted to live for
A moment for a moment. However inelegant it was,

It was what it might have been to be alive, but tenderly.

One thing. One thing. One thing:

Tell me there is
A meadow, afterward.

FROM
'A Meadow'
BY LUCIE BROCK-BROIDO

Strasbourg, 1518

None dancing

She heard there was bread in the square. It's possible it's a lie, or that the loaves are so blighted as to be inedible, but Frau Troffea doesn't care. The hope is nourishing as anything she's had in her throat these past months. She went mushroom-picking with the others, laid traps to skin hares in the forests like Gyptians. Nothing. Even the animals are starved out after the Hungry Winter, this scorched summer. She brought home an un-nested bird and cooked it right on the ashes of their fire, chewed through its soft, shattering bones, chafing her gums until her mouth filled with iron and salt.

Her husband doesn't know how she suffers, has never seemed to know hunger. He grows sinewy, muscles like ropes wrapping his arms. But she has it inside her like a child, and it grows and sucks and swells her belly, until she cramps with carrying the full weight of its gnawing emptiness.

She has started chewing off-cuts of leather. She has started sucking the ends of her hair, and contemplating the stray dogs with new attention. She has started seeing white lights hang before her in the air. Lately she can stir them about with her finger.

But Frau Troffea has not yet lost her mind, and as she stumbles through her city, she comes up with a plan. If the bread is burnt, she can soak it in the river until it softens. If it is rotted, perhaps others will have left it. If there is not bread, or if it is all gone, she can fill her pockets with stones and walk into the water, as some have done. Women have been seen throwing their babies in so they can feed their other children. She would have done the same, had her children lived past infancy. The son that did is long hanged as a traitor. Samuel, one of hundreds sentenced in the place of their leader Joss Fritz, who melts into the Black Forest after each attempted revolt easy as snow.

The almshouses are overrun, the graveyards too. The end of the world is coming, from the streets to the churches they proclaim it. Geiler, the Trumpet of Strasbourg Cathedral, is eight years dead but his words are daubed on walls, echoed from the pulpits of the cathedral: *There is not one among us who can be saved*. The comet that dragged its fiery tail over the turn of the century and damned them is lifted from its crater and placed on an altar, but too late.

She prays as she walks, though her rosary is long gone, the clay beads cracking between her teeth like bird bones.

Frau Troffea swirls a thread of light through her fingers, soft as lambswool. Sweat runs down her lip, and her back, soaks the reeking cloth of her dress. The sun has seared the soles of her feet where she fell asleep outside a tavern at midday. The drink – it is new for her, and something they can ill afford, but the ruined wheat is good enough for beer – that alone is plentiful. Her husband has not come looking for her all night. Her feet are chafing on the cobbles, and it is good to feel them again, the blisters making way for new skin.

Her route takes her through the horse market, built when Strasbourg had a different centre so that it would stand at the edges. Now there are complaints from the cathedral of the smell, but Frau Troffea likes it: sour and strong enough to coat her tongue. She opens her mouth, fills her lungs.

It has grown like an unwieldy beast, this city. In her youth it was fat off wealth, and so the fleas came crawling. Trade is long diminished but still there are new faces every day, dark faces amongst them like the devils were already here, flooding the hospital with their filth. The Holy Roman Empire is locked in battle with the Ottoman Turks, engaged in a struggle for their very souls. She cannot read but knows there are pamphlets about them, the Turks who threaten their empire, their homes. They are the enemy but they come anyway, claiming to flee the same hordes that fight for them.

Frau Troffea is vigilant against such lies.

She spends her days watchful for the infidels, sees them even in church though there holy incense burns thick enough to make your jaw lock. She checks her body each night for bites and signs of incubi, finds only bones grown harder beneath her melting flesh.

The market square is listless and sways before her. She searches the closed-up stalls, the dusty ground, the grates clogged with muck dried hard by heat. She smells the sweet and the shit of it, of her city, baking under the relentless, blessed, accursed sun. Her head is full of it as she searches, hands raking the dust, thick handfuls of dirt. She murmurs a prayer like an incantation, as though God would drop loaves from the sky. But nothing falls except heat on her back, her calves, the burnt soles of her feet, and she wonders again why her husband has not come looking for her.

She is crying, but she is not ashamed. The tendrils of light swarm about her like flies, heavenly and revelling, ravelling her in their soft threads and weave. Her hands are full of earth and excrement, her fingernails itch and she wants to peel them off.

The light tickles her beneath the chin.

Frau Troffea tilts her head back, looks at the sun until her eyes fill with white. The light swirls about her like a cloud, buffeting her gentle as a wind-knocked sail. She picks up her foot, then the other. Her hips sway. She parts her lips in ecstasy.

Beneath the blue and burning sky, Frau Troffea lifts up her hands, and begins to dance.

One

Lisbet arches her foot, braces it against the wooden bed frame until the cramp subsides. Her eyes are sticky with sleep: she scrapes it away. She could lie here another hour in this early quiet, but this is precious time, and confined. Today Henne's sister Agnethe will return from the mountains, and all will be changed.

Henne lies with his back to her, his cotton undershirt dampened to translucence, his skin pink at the neck, a scar puckered starlike beneath his hairline where an empiric cut out a mole that would not stop growing. She turns her head to watch his breath. She could press her hand between his shoulder-blades, feel the work of his breathing hum like the skeps — but it is impossible, a distance too far to span. In their earliest days, she touched him always: her hands on his forehead, plucking chaff from his hair, stealing kisses behind his mother's back. Those tendernesses are past, now.

Her toes curl themselves again and she levers herself upright with a hiss. They have long discarded the sheet, are sweating into straw like horses, and a trickle works its way down her back. She wants to pull off her nightgown, walk through the forest to the river and roll in its mud like a pig.

7

She heaves herself to her feet, crosses to the window. A few bees drowse past the shutters, and she wonders if they recognise her out of her silk and wicker, can smell her sweat sweet with the honey they give.

The light itself seems bunched and thick with heat. Agnethe will return from her penance into a dismal summer. No air comes to stir the skin-stretched shutters, nothing moves at all except the bees and the pain in her leg, unfurling like thorns along its length. She catches her lip between her teeth, bites just hard enough to hurt, to turn the focus of her pain from there, to there. Inside her, the child stirs, and she watches the shadows flicker beneath her nightdress like minnows. *Still there? Good.*

She clasps her hands beneath the mound of it, lately grown too large to encircle at its widest point. Two months left. She has never got this far before, this large. She strokes her thumb against the taut skin and paces until it is no longer like walking on hot shards of glass. She manages eight turns of the room before the mattress rustles.

'Lisbet?'

She paces.

'Lisbet. Stop.'

'It's hot.'

She can only make out the glint of his eye, his teeth when he talks.

'A beer?'

'No.'

'You should lie down. Rest.'

She grinds her teeth. She tried that in her earliest pregnancies, though his mother argued, wanted her up and moving before her confinement, to speed it along and be strong. Henne overruled his mother's wish the first and second times, and Lisbet spent the latter days lying in their bed like a noblewoman, or else sitting at the kitchen table while he fussed and soothed her, feeding her milk dumplings drizzled in honey with his fingers.

They were hopeful, then, and even after the sixth they'd heard worse from the women at church. And now they are five years on from the milk dumplings and she has nothing living to show.

Sophey blames her, Lisbet can tell. She repeatedly calls Lisbet a slattern even though she is dedicated to the bees, telling her daughter-in-law how she worked the fields before birthing Heinrich, milked cows before Agnethe.

'This is why Henne has strong shoulders, and Nethe strong arms.'

Agnethe. Nethe. The name is almost mystical to Lisbet, mythical as those strong arms, or the jaw she is said to share with her brother. Soon enough Lisbet will see if it is all true. Sophey and Henne's mentions of Agnethe in the first years were so sparse they were easily swept aside, and any questions Lisbet asked were brushed off too. Lisbet always had the sense of entering a room another, dearer person had just exited, as though Henne went searching for a wife to fill the space at their table Agnethe had left. Ever a harbinger: her birth circling the comet's, her arrival stalking Agnethe's departure, her bloods chasing her mother's madness. A bee butts the shutter. She taps back.

Even Ida, so good at making Lisbet feel like she belonged from the first moment of her arrival, will only edge around the boundaries of the truth about Agnethe, giving her no answer beyond the facts. 'She has been at a nunnery, in Mont Sainte-Odile, paying penance.'

'But you were friends,' Lisbet would push, with a sensation like pressing on a bruise, braced for envy at the thought of Ida loving another friend as dearly as she loves Lisbet. 'You must know what sent her?'

9

But Ida, for all her wide eyes and childlike gaiety, is a master equivocator, and always led Lisbet past the topic and onto the new, more pleasurable grounds of gossip – Herr Furmann's latest indiscretion, Sebastian Brant's gambling debts – until Lisbet forgot why she cared, and Agnethe was once more only a shadow pinned to her back, glimpsed less and less.

Seven years' penance. Lisbet has tried to sound out the depths of such a sentence, weigh its particular gravity. She wonders how things will change, now another body will be in the house. Agnethe's is not the presence Lisbet has prayed all these years for. They were certain a child would arrive well before Agnethe's penance was through, maybe two or three as happened for Ida, their small faces scrubbed clean, their tiny fingernails full of wax from learning the bees. Lisbet closes her eyes against the vision, a sound escaping her, each lost child an excavation into her body and her heart. Into the gap she has portioned off at the table will step a full-grown woman, washed of some sin no one will name.

Henne sits up with a groan. She can see him rubbing his eyes in the low, slatted light, his skin cream in the darkness.

'Go back to sleep,' she says, harsher than intended.

He throws off the tangle of the sheet from about his ankles, and stands, becoming more solid in the gloom. She has always liked his sturdiness, the square block of him firm from his work at the forest, the tracery of scars from the bees at his wrists, from before they knew and trusted him. She desires him still, though he does his duty after every failed birth with his eyes closed. Now, he sees her watching him and turns away to dress.

She opens the shutters, wafting the bee back towards free air. The trees cover everything, edging up to the boundary of their scraped-out farm, where roots must be hacked and cleared in an endless battle. Already there is light above them, purplish as the streaks on her belly. Dawn arrives right into their room, though there is never time to watch it come.

Heaviness lands on her shoulders: Henne's arm, arranging a shawl. It is the most he has touched her in days, weeks perhaps. He withdraws just as fast. She shrugs it off, catching it and bundling it over a chair.

'Too hot.'

He sighs. There was a time when he found even her complaints charming. He would chuckle, call her schatzi, sweet one. Hadn't she been standing at this window, newly married and complaining of the cold, the first time he put a baby in her? If she stands here long enough perhaps he will remember, will hold her. She hears him pissing into the pot. The baby shifts.

She waits until he is done before turning, her belly knocking the window frame. 'I'm going to walk.'

He holds the pisspot. 'I'll come.'

She shakes her head, already slipping on her thinnest dress, stinking from constant wear. She feels the familiar hum inside her, the desire to go to the bees and her tree, to be alone there with her babies before the day begins. 'What if Agnethe arrives?'

His shoulders stiffen: she hears the hitch in his breath. He is worried about his sister's return. In their earlier days perhaps she could have asked him why. Now there is such a chasm between them she dare only skirt the pit of it.

'She will not be here for hours. It is treacherous to descend the mountain before light, and the abbey is a day's ride.'

He has pulled on his clogs before she has forced hers over swollen toes. When she presses the puff of her ankle, the mark stays like her body is fresh clay recently pulled from the ground. He opens the door and they move silently through the dark house, and out into the yard.

Lisbet feels the air stick to her like dust, and she follows

Henne with reluctance. He empties the pisspot, and has brought the last of the stale bread from the kitchen. He throws it to the chickens as they pass the coop.

The dogs lie slumped in the centre of the dirt yard. The small one, Fluh, is new and fierce and yaps like she is caught in a bait trap every time she sees Lisbet. Ulf, the wolfhound with matted fur, she minds less. He came to them as a pup, not long after she did, and does not jump up at her, or bite at her skirts.

Fluh scuffs the dirt around her, burrowing deeper in, but Ulf heaves himself to his feet and trots to catch up with them as they open the gate, pass the buzzing cones of the skeps with their wakening bees, and enter the forest.

The ground is all shadows, and Lisbet lifts her feet as though wading. The flies gather around her ears, but she cannot bear to let down her hair in the soupy heat. No sound but them breaking crisp leaves, dried early off the trees, and her breath already ragged.

Henne is walking a little ahead, turned slightly sideways to fit down the narrow path. He does not ask which way they should go: he leads and she follows behind. His hand trails and she wonders if he will mind her taking it. But then he lowers it to Ulf's head, and she rests her own on her belly instead.

They push upwards to the bluff, the closest thing to a view in this furrowed part of the world. She imagines them pressed down as seeds beneath His thumb, planted irreparably deep, and walks faster, overtaking Henne. On clearer mornings, when the wind pushes aside the miasma that hovers over Strasbourg most days, she can see every notch on Notre Dame's spire.

'Lisbet?' Henne is beside her, his hip butting hers. 'Slow down.'

She begins to tell him she is fine, but a wash of faintness sluices down her back, blessedly cold.

'Careful.' Finally, he loops his hand about her waist. She leans against him until the path stops leaping with little sparks. Still he holds her, and she closes her eyes. A sigh escapes her lips, and he releases her as though she had screamed. She stumbles, catches herself. 'Come, home.'

They are still more than a dozen paces from the summit. She used to run up it in the first months of their marriage, and be back before Sophey noticed her gone and her chores left untended. She feels lumpen and stretched, wishes she could have come alone, taken her time, gone to the tree. But now the sun is up and Sophey will be too, readying for Agnethe's return. Lisbet lets Henne lead the way back to the farm without complaint. At the skeps she moves to put her hand on the gate, but he nudges her on.

'I'll see to it.'

'They need fresh water—'

'I know,' he says with another flash of temper. 'They are my bees, Lisbet.'

Not yours, she thinks, *not mine*.

●

Already Henne is looking beyond her, to his tasks, to his day, so intent that he does not even notice the woman in their dusty yard, until Lisbet catches his arm. Her head is so full of Agnethe she lends the visitor a head or two in height, broadens her shoulders, places Henne's mouth and jaw over the fine features already breaking into a smile at the sight of them.

But then she steps towards them, golden hair catching the early light, a basket clasped in her slim hands, and it is Ida.

'Good morning, Frau Plater.'

'Herr Wiler.' Ida returns Henne's curt nod, but her eyes

13

are fixed beyond him, on Lisbet. No one looks so directly at her as Ida does, and it is another reason to love her. Henne continues to the skep yard. Their shared childhood should lend them some ease with one another, but instead there is something hard between them, a pit in soft fruit. Perhaps it is Plater himself – Ida's husband is as loathed as Ida is adored.

Ida kisses Lisbet's flushed cheeks, her breath sweet with wild mint and her lips soft and dry.

'How are you this morning?' asks Ida, eyes performing their now-familiar flick from Lisbet's belly to her face.

'Well enough,' says Lisbet, and the worry line pinching between Ida's eyebrows loosens. There have been so many days when all Lisbet could answer with were tears, that she takes each day of discomfort as a triumph.

'Good,' says Ida, and presses her miraculously cool hand to Lisbet's. 'See what I have brought you.'

She leads Lisbet to the woodpile Henne has stacked and left to dry in the steaming yard, and Lisbet sinks gratefully down while Ida perches beside, balancing the basket between them. She pulls back the cloth with a flourish, revealing a sack full of flour, white as fresh snow.

'A gift,' says Ida, 'because the rye didn't suit you.'

'I can't accept—'

'Feel it,' says Ida, her eyes shining with delight.

'My hands are dirty,' says Lisbet, though in truth these days even scrubbed clean her hands are a state, covered in bee stings, swollen with heat. She doesn't want to place them beside Ida's, so slender and neat-nailed as a newborn's. But Ida seizes her hot fingers and scoops a handful of flour into Lisbet's palm. It is soft as petals, light and fine as dust.

'My father double-milled it for you especially,' says Ida.

To her humiliation, tears start in Lisbet's eyes, and she swallows the lump filling her throat.

'Silly goose,' says Ida, laughing and wiping Lisbet's cheeks. 'You'll remember I was just the same, my final months. Like a rain cloud. Anything we can do to help comfort you is a joy to us. And in this heat I cannot imagine how you feel.'

'I am well enough,' says Lisbet sharply, pouring the flour carefully back into its sack, returning to the phrase that is all she can offer when her friend asks how she is.

Lisbet is careful not to complain, in case God hears and decides to take this baby from her too. It is one of the many bargains she has made with herself, balancing them atop each other as precariously as the basket between them. Ida has no such qualms: she has carried each of her children without so much as a cramp or a bleed, tempts fate and the Devil both without a second thought. But she is not Lisbet, who lives with the blunt evidence of her own accursedness, the litany learnt by heart: comet, Mutti, babies. So much wreckage. So much blood.

'Of course you are,' says Ida, nudging Lisbet from her self-pity. 'You must use this with your freshest water, and look – my father has given you a twist of salt.'

'It is too much.'

'Nothing is too much for you, Bet, for this baby. He will be here and safe and soon.'

Lisbet bites the insides of her cheeks hard. She hates when Ida says such things. She does not know so – no one but God does.

'And you must make sure the bread is only for you,' Ida chatters on. 'Not for Henne or Sophey.'

'Or Agnethe,' says Lisbet. 'I'll have a job keeping it from all of them.'

Ida's knuckles on the basket whiten. 'She is home today?' she asks lightly, though Lisbet knows she knows the answer.

'This afternoon,' says Lisbet. 'Was it part of your purpose in coming so early? To see her?'

15

'Of course not,' says Ida, flushing prettily. 'You know we are not friends.'

'I do not know anything, for you will not tell me.'

'There is nothing to tell.'

'Is it so terrible?' says Lisbet. She knows she sounds wanton but she doesn't care. It is her last chance to know about Agnethe before she meets her. 'What she did?'

'I have told you a hundred times,' says Ida, already in control of herself, her hands loosening on the wicker, her cheeks pale once more. 'I know nothing of Ne— Agnethe's sin. It is wiped clear now, anyway. Seven years' penance – she is blameless once more. You must not ask her.'

Lisbet sighs and shifts. She doesn't wish to fight with Ida, not with her gift beside her and the sun heating the wood beneath them as fast as her brow.

'Thank you,' she says. 'Please thank Matthias, and Herr Plater.'

Ida snorts. 'You think my husband had anything to do with this? His duties keep him in Strasbourg most weeks.'

Ida is not sorry about this, and Lisbet cannot blame her. Plater was announced the council's enforcer after the last revolt, responsible for the harsher sides of the Twenty-One's dealings in the city and its surrounds. With their own eyes Ida and Lisbet have witnessed broken doors in the slums on their almsgivings, and the gaol beside the river is expanded twice over. Lisbet is not alone in noticing Plater takes pleasure in his dark work.

'Which reminds me,' says Ida. 'He will call on you today.'

'Plater?'

'Yes,' says Ida. 'He told my father so.'

'When?'

'This afternoon.'

'Perhaps he wishes to see the penitent.'

Something flashes across Ida's face. 'She would do well to stay out of his way.'

'What do you mean?'

'Tell Heinrich, won't you? To expect him.'

'Of course,' says Lisbet. When Ida closes like this she is tight as a locked box. There is no budging her. Before her friend can rise, Lisbet seizes her hand as Ida had hers. 'You know you can speak with me, about anything—'

'This looks restful.'

Ida's hand closes convulsively on Lisbet's. They turn to squint into the light. Backed by brightness, Sophey Wiler's narrow body slices into angles, nearly vanishing at her waist, at the place where her hands meet her hips. A frown line cleaves her face in two like a scar.

'Frau Wiler,' says Ida, jumping to her feet. 'How are—'

'Busy,' says Sophey. 'What are you doing here so early?'

'She brought me a gift,' says Lisbet, unable to rise from the low log pile. Too late she remembers Ida's instruction not to share the fine flour, but already Sophey is holding a knotted hand out for the basket. Ida meekly hands it over, and Sophey sniffs at the contents.

'Won't your children be missing their mother?'

'I was just taking my leave,' says Ida. She is as cowed by Sophey as anyone – no one is immune to her force. Sophey turns without another word, and strides to the kitchen.

'She is always so rude to you,' says Lisbet.

'She is rude to everyone,' shrugs Ida. 'And today is an anxious day. Even Sophey Wiler must be nervous to receive her returned daughter.'

'I suppose.'

She pulls Lisbet gently to her feet, kisses her once more on her cheek, and pats her belly gently. 'Grow well.'

'Go well,' says Lisbet in return, and watches her slight-shouldered friend hurry from the yard. Beyond her, she can see Henne among the skeps, moving from hive to hive, a smoking tray in his hand like a priest's censer. He is too far for her to smell the rosemary, but she carries it anyway, on her own clothes and hair. The tug in her chest is physical, as though her longing is a thread pulled between her and the hives. Her affinity for the bees is preternatural, and when she is at her duties she feels a rearrangement of herself, like stars fallen into constellations of good fortune. Even Sophey sees it, though she would never say so.

The first time she saw the farm she thought it quaint, with its three solid structures forming an open-faced square aimed at the skeps and the forest beyond. She imagined children tumbling into the dust of the well-kept yard, hanging from her skirts. Noise all about her, tears and laughter: the delicious sounds of life and need.

Since visiting the almshouses she knows they live in what passes for great comfort for these parts. Bees, a kitchen, and three rooms besides. But their farm feels both empty and cramped and even in the full glare of the sun, dim somehow. Hemmed in. Only the bees and her tree offer joy: one given her by Henne, the other a gift to herself.

'Lisbet!' Sophey's voice is a summons and a command. Lisbet sighs and turns her back on the bees, the deserted yard, and goes inside.

Two

Sophey stands like a prophet with a staff, bristle broom in hand. She holds it out to Lisbet.

'The room needs sweeping.'

There is no need to ask which she means. There is Henne's room, Sophey's room, the kitchen, and the room. Agnethe's room. It has been kept closed, like a tomb, and Lisbet has seen the door rolled back only a couple of times in her half-decade in the house. Once, to free a blackbird that flew through the shutters and seemed intent on breaking its neck, and another when Plater came to levy tax on their doors and windows, counting them so ponderously she wondered if he was paid by the minute. They can hardly spare the space, but there is an unspoken agreement that Agnethe's room is to be ignored, as though the door were a wall, wiped smooth until its resident returned from the mountains.

Lisbet takes the broom uncertainly.

'I'll see to the loaves,' says Sophey, already turning away. 'Don't forget to beat the sheets.'

Standing on the threshold, smelling the stale air, watching the dust swirl in the gaps from the shutters, it looks to Lisbet as though Agnethe has only stepped out that moment. The sheets are crumpled, the pillow indented, the stool in the corner of the room not quite aligned, as though knocked slightly as its occupant rose. Beside it, a broad bowl of the sort Sophey sent her to market to buy in the earliest months of Lisbet's arrival. Perhaps it is all tainted by Agnethe's sin, and each of her items must wait out the seven years' penance, before they too can be lifted and washed clean.

The bowl has a fine skim of dust, the water long dried to vapour. But as Lisbet lifts it, she thinks she catches the ghost of a scent, herbal and sweet as Ida's breath. Beside it is a comb of yellowed bone, still thickly matted with long blonde hairs, shining and brittle. Lisbet wipes out the bowl and sets it back in its place, pulls hair from the comb and opens the shutters to drop the coarse tangle outside. They share their view with Agnethe: true east, trees. Made bright by the light, the room loses its careless abandonment, and becomes something more maudlin.

Lisbet strips back the sheets, fingers gritty with dust, and sweeps the floor, finding small soft feathers from the blackbird, empty snail shells, their glistening trails buffed to a shine by the dry heat. She wipes them away, pockets the feathers and shells. She replaces the pillow, turning it so the indent is hidden, and as she does so something under the fabric shifts and crinkles. Lisbet searches the seams of the pillowcase, but they are sewn shut with fine stitches of the sort neither she nor Sophey can manage at the moment with their swollen fingers.

She can hear Sophey and Henne speaking in the kitchen. She slides her fingernail against the thread, but it is closed flush into the cloth. She pulls gently, then harder, and the neat thread gives. Lisbet hooks her finger inside, sifting through the straw until she feels something rough knotted through something soft. She pulls it out, and onto the sheets falls a lock of blonde hair, plaited with an undyed silk ribbon.

Lisbet holds it in the centre of her palm, sun cleaving light and shadow. It is almost weightless, rendered as coarse as the strands she pulled from the comb. But though the colour is a match for that tangle, and even for Henne's hair, Lisbet feels certain it is neither of the Wiler siblings'. The way it is tied, kept, concealed: all of it tender and illicit as the ribbons Lisbet has arranged at the dance tree.

'Lisbet?'

She startles, nearly dropping the token, and folds it carefully into her skirts as she turns to where Henne is leaning on the door jamb, stoppering it up as surely as a door.

'I'm hungry,' he says, voice distorting as he yawns. He has fine teeth, lined up straight and solid as gravestones. Lisbet tongues the gaps in her gums, ten black holes. For almost every baby lost, a molar rocked itself loose and was pulled by the empiric.

'Coming,' she says, and listens to the thumping tread of him, the hushing scrape of the bench on old rushes. In her haste she has disarrayed the fine alignment of the token, and she straightens it as best she can, before sliding it back into its place, so Agnethe will find all as she left it.

•

The returned penitent arrives in the early afternoon. She is tall as her brother, tall as the stooped horse she has ridden since dawn from the abbey at the crest of Mont Sainte-Odile, a distance only thrice as far from their farm as Strasbourg itself, but of such fame and notoriety Lisbet feels she stands in the presence of a being from another world.

Agnethe Wiler's appearance does little to amend this fantasy. Aside from her height, which she wears without apology, there is the matter of her head, which is shaved pale as a peeled onion, and covered in a great many nicks and scars from repeated shearing, ranging from old skin brown as preserved rind to new pink. There is even, at the coarse collar of her tunic, a fresh bloom of red. Her hands, when she has dismounted and folded them before her, head bowed to her mother, are similarly scarred, and her face, now lifted to the sun by Sophey's twisted fingers, is hollow beneath the cheeks as if whittled clean away.

And yet she is handsome still, Lisbet cannot deny it. Henne's features are worn more smoothly on her, and even her eyes with their plucked-out lashes, the lids pink and crusted, only serve to show their blue more purely, like pearls presented on the plump tongue of an oyster. Had she hair as blonde and long as Ida's, she could perhaps match her for beauty. As it is, she stands apart, the strangest woman Lisbet has ever seen.

'Are you hungry?' asks Sophey, by way of greeting the daughter she has not seen for over half a decade. Agnethe nods, supplication in her every gesture, though Lisbet cannot think her meek. She radiates strength, though she tries to suppress it.

Nothing is hidden, that shall not be made manifest.

It was one of Geiler's favourite passages, parroted by Sophey and lobbed like a spear at Lisbet whenever a chicken is taken by a fox, when the farm cat fitted and died in Lisbet's arms. But Lisbet sees a new meaning to it looking at Agnethe: not an accusation, but a statement of intent.

Sophey turns without another word, goes inside. Henne steps forward and embraces his sister briefly, bumping his jaw against her concave cheek, before taking the reins of the panting horse and leading it into the shade of the coop, to the long trough where the old mule is drinking. Lisbet and Agnethe watch his progress, neither willing to break the skin of the silence settling between them. Lisbet supposes the mule will go to the slaughter at last, now the horse is returned to them. The ancient animal has swollen knees, and sores on its back that will not close however much Lisbet coaxes them with honey.

She glances at her sister-in-law. Her eyes are even more startling up close, and her gaze is clear and direct. Lisbet's tongue stirs dryly.

'Hello, sister,' says Agnethe, and her voice is low and hoarse with disuse. 'I hope you are well?'

Lisbet nods, knows she should return the enquiry, but it feels impotent in the face of Agnethe's scarred and naked head, her gaunt cheeks, and then Henne is stepping between them and they follow him inside.

There are eggs steaming on the scrubbed wood of the table, their shells speckled. Lisbet's stomach growls at the sight, and at the smell of the bread fast proven in the sun and baked by Sophey that morning with Ida's gift. Henne takes his seat, and Lisbet drops gratefully onto the bench, before remembering that two of them must now share it.

She slides along, skirt catching on the splinters rent by the long-dead tabby mouser. She tugs it free, and Agnethe sits carefully beside her, back straight as a rod. Lisbet's belly means there is a clear foot of air between them and the table, but Agnethe doesn't seem to mind, only bends her long, sinewed neck to pray. Lisbet sees older, deeper scars, disappearing down the back of her smock, radiating from her spine like cut wings. Henne coughs, and Lisbet too clasps her hands, and Sophey leads them to their *Amen*.

Once they are portioned their bread, their egg, Lisbet must try to match Sophey for pace. She could eat double, thrice her helping, could eat the whole of Henne's heaped plate, but Sophey's grim delight in her gluttony slows her. She tears the crusty bread into pieces, to measure her consumption. Beside

23

her, Agnethe picks up the still steaming egg, holds it as though it were cool as a river stone and peels, careful at the membrane, the egg emerging whole and perfect. Lisbet knows it must hurt her, can see her pale fingertips darkening.

'That's a new trick,' says Sophey. 'You were never gentle before. Did they teach you to peel eggs on the mountain?'

Agnethe smiles smally, her eyes fixed on her work, though Lisbet notices her slide a jagged shard of shell beneath her fingernail.

Sophey snorts. 'Taught you silence and all. Time was she never shut up.'

Agnethe presses her fingernail down and Lisbet sees blood rise to rim it, but her expression does not change.

'Well then,' says Sophey into the quiet. 'Well.'

She cracks open her own egg, and Lisbet follows a beat behind, finding the yolk chalky and pale. They are lucky the hens had any to give – their offerings are more and more meagre lately. She thinks longingly of the twist of salt Ida brought, but Sophey has it stowed with their coin and the length of silk kept once for Agnethe's dowry and now for some unknown purpose.

Agnethe's touch is hesitant as she pulls apart the bread. She places it in her mouth quickly, as though it might be snatched from her. Lisbet hears a low rumble of pleasure from Agnethe's long throat. She stuffs bread into her own mouth. It is as good as it smells.

'This flour is finer than we are used to,' Henne remarks. 'In honour of Agnethe's return?'

'A gift,' says Lisbet. 'From Ida.'

A choking sound from beside her. Lisbet turns to see Agnethe clamp a hand over her mouth, and shove herself roughly back from the table, almost overbalancing the bench and Lisbet with it.

'Nethe,' says Sophey, a warning. Agnethe lowers her hand, and with all their eyes upon her, chews until the bread must be mush, and finally, with great effort, swallows.

Sophey nods, seemingly satisfied. Lisbet's heart is beating absurdly, as though it had been her that Sophey's hard gaze pinioned to the bench.

They continue to eat in silence. Henne's face is forcibly vacant, but Lisbet can read him well enough to recognise tension in the slight hunch of his shoulders. She has forgotten her resolution to eat slowly, and her plate is half empty before Agnethe pushes hers away.

'Did they allow you to waste food at the abbey?' says Sophey sharply, but Agnethe shows no sign she has heard beyond lifting the egg to her lips and taking tiny bites. When Sophey's attention has again turned to her own meal, Agnethe palms the remainder of the bread, and quick as a blink places it on her lap, out of sight of her mother. In another blink, she passes it sideways to Lisbet, who accepts the still steaming crust gratefully.

She nudges her knee against Agnethe's in thanks, the two of them allies. Agnethe's leg is cool and firm as marble against hers, but then she withdraws, ending the contact as fast as Lisbet began it.

She rises to tidy the table, and Lisbet comes with her, taking Henne's plate and carrying it to the door to throw the crumbs outside. She nudges it open with her elbow, and it snags. She pushes harder, and an exclamation comes from the other side.

The obstacle is removed suddenly, and Lisbet feels herself tip. She braces for the fall, resigned already to pain, to blood, to the loosening ties of her belly, to another ribbon in the tree, noticing as she does how there is the sound of wood clattering, how the man – for it was a man's voice that exclaimed – moves aside to avoid being crushed by her mass, and then how cold, thin fingers with the strength of wire grasp her under the armpit and around the ribs, and knock a shocked gasp from her throat.

Agnethe pulls her upright and back, yanking the bench toward her with an ankle, and lowering Lisbet gently onto it. Her breath is ragged, and she pulls Lisbet's skirts straight where they have ridden up, exposing the dark down of her calves. It all took the measure of seconds, the plate Agnethe dropped in her haste to rescue Lisbet continuing to clatter and roll.

'That was quite the welcome.'

A heavy foot stops the plate's progress with a definitive thump. Lisbet knows him by his voice, by his sturdy boots, thick-soled and calfskin-soft, sent from the outer reaches of the Empire, and by his smell: leather from his jerkin, worn even in the hottest days, inscribed with the crest worn by those in service of the Twenty-One, and smoke from his pipe, and sweat. She smells it on Ida sometimes, though she knows her friend washes with a fanatical diligence every time they lie together, as though she could scrub his scourge from her skin.

Henne rises from the table. 'Plater.'

Lisbet bites her cheek – she had forgot to warn her husband of his visit.

'Wiler,' says Plater. He is a tall man in his boots, matching Henne and Agnethe for height, though slighter than either, with an almost girlishly lovely mouth, and thick hair the colour of copper. It is beautiful hair, and on his daughter works a mesmeric charm of the kind that makes strangers stop her in the street, but it adds an unnatural gleam to Plater that seems almost devilish.

'Frau Wiler,' he nods to Sophey, 'Frau Wiler,' and to Lisbet, who drops her eyes, feeling as always the hatred she part

26

inherited from Ida and part grew herself. The room has contracted with him inside.

'And . . .' He lingers on the pause, and Lisbet becomes suddenly aware of how still Agnethe is, like a hare in the sights of a fox. She is not even trembling, but she is close enough to Lisbet that she can hear the hitch in her breath when Plater turns his green-eyed gaze on her, steps into the room. 'Fräulein Wiler, returned from the mountains.'

A soft sound comes from Agnethe, so low Lisbet is the only one to hear it, and again she is minded of a hare, the sudden snuffing out of breath when the jaws snap shut.

'She is not practised in her voice,' says Sophey. Perhaps it is in defence of her daughter, but the less charitable part of Lisbet thinks it is more out of deference to the council's man. Sophey is as Ida marked rude to all, but authority – and the only authority she considers above her own is God's and so the Church and the Twenty-One's – makes her as close to meek as a woman of such steel can be.

'Of course,' says Plater. His attention is so focused on Agnethe, Lisbet is surprised she does not sink to her knees under its weight. There is something repulsive in his gaze. Lisbet would call it lecherous were it not tempered with distaste. His eyes rake over Agnethe's scarred head, her collarbones, her hands, balled into fists at her sides. The effect of him is almost supernatural, he so glows with menace. The incomprehensible thought of Ida with such a man hits her anew. 'You are nearly cured?'

'Nearly?' says Lisbet, startled out of her silence. 'Seven years is spent.'

'She must pray in the cathedral,' says Plater. 'It was an original term – a final supplication in her home city.'

Agnethe gives a tight nod. 'I had not forgot,' she says, voice strained.

'It speaks!' says Plater. 'So the priests can expect you soon?'

'Tomorrow,' says Agnethe.

'You can be assured she will complete her penance,' says Henne hotly. 'We know the law, we would have ensured it.'

'He only means you did not have to trouble yourself with attending us in person,' says Sophey with a sharp glance at her son.

'That is not why I am here,' says Plater, with exaggerated surprise as though to suggest Agnethe is so far below his notice as to be invisible, as though he had not stared at her like prey since his arrival. 'A cup of beer if you will, Fräulein Wiler.'

'Then why are you here?' says Henne, and Sophey hisses a warning. Henne treats Plater as the boy he skinned his knees with in childhood, and not as he should: as the man who speaks with the power of the Twenty-One. Henne refuses to forget Plater is the son of a labourer, set apart only by his willingness to dirty his hands in exchange for perfumed water to wash them clean again.

'A letter, Herr Wiler,' says Plater, producing it, sealed, from his breast pocket. Lisbet can see the parchment is limp, stained by his sweat. 'Do you wish to step outside?'

'This is my mother's farm,' says Henne. 'If she wishes to hear it she should.'

'Would you like me to read it to you?'

'I was schooled in my letters same as you,' says Henne, and strides around the table to snatch the missive, ripping the seal in his haste. Lisbet peers at the writing, though of course she cannot read beyond his name – Heinrich Wiler – written at the top in neat, slanting cursive, and recognises the seal is their wax, left undyed and unmixed: the richest, rawest gold. It is always with pride she spies their products at use in the church, or else by the Twenty-One themselves. Sebastian Brant, the city's syndic, sends for it specially. It is a high honour, though from Henne's tangible bristle Lisbet knows the letter does not bring good news.

'A summons, in fact,' says Plater, his delight in their dismay barely concealed. He takes the cup of beer from Agnethe without thanks, and she fast withdraws her hand.

'To court?' says Sophey in confusion.

'To Heidelberg,' says Henne. 'To defend our rights to our land.'

Heidelberg. It is a court of sorts, where the Church has a papal seat and universities besides. Several days' ride, and not somewhere they have ever had cause to go.

'To answer claims your bees steal from the land, which is none but God's alone.'

'We all belong to God,' says Henne, and Lisbet places a gentle hand on his taut waist. 'So what is the bound of this claim?'

Plater gestures around them, slopping beer on the floor, to the neatly fenced skeps stretching from yard to forest, at the shed and the chicken coop, the house made even more ramshackle by his attentions. 'Where are your wildflowers, Herr Wiler? Where is the nectar that feeds your bees, makes your wax so sweet?'

'The forest,' says Henne, 'as they ever were. We have permissions, as others have to graze livestock in fields—'

'Have you been to the forest of late? It may have escaped your notice, but the summer is vicious this year.' Lisbet tightens her hold on Henne's side. 'In the wilds, flowers wilt or do not grow at all. And to the east, at the monastery, are two dozen acres of cornflowers and poppies watered daily.'

Now Lisbet understands, clear as though she has read the letter herself. It is an old claim, made every two years or so, that everything from their bees to their honey is stolen from the monks at Altorf. In fact, the monks themselves are thieves, diverting the river so their fields escape drought, and thus depriving all those downstream.

'That was settled,' says Henne. 'My wife accounted for the extra skeps. She herself won the forest bees for our hives.'

'This is not about the bees,' says Plater. 'Are you sure you do not wish me to read it to you?'

Lisbet redoubles her efforts on Henne's shirt but he steps away from her. 'I understand perfectly. But there are no nets, no fence that can hold such a creature. It is my bees that fetch from where they can, make what we harvest, and my hands that press the wax, not the monks'.'

'And they claim that output is only possible due to their part,' says Plater. 'And so you must go to Heidelberg to sign a contract admitting as much.'

'I will not.'

'You may take any petition to Heidelberg,' says Plater, his voice bored now that it is clear Henne has mastered himself, and will not threaten violence. 'But I do not think you will find much success. I think it wise to ready yourself for a share of your skeps to go to the monastery.'

'But they are ours!' says Lisbet, unable to swallow the outburst. Panic dapples her vision.

'None but God's,' says Plater coolly. 'As your husband himself said. And the monastery sits higher in God's estimation than any farm. Heidelberg will be a reminder of that.'

'You have grown so large in your own esteem,' says Henne, 'it is a wonder you can fit through the doors anymore.'

'Heinrich,' says Sophey, appalled. Plater's smirk does not falter, but something dark slides behind his eyes.

'You were ever cocksure, Heinrich Wiler,' he says smoothly, an arrow drawn back against a bow. 'Perhaps you forget who you are speaking to? And perhaps you forget where you stand, on borrowed ground, with stolen bees, a barren wife and a sinner for a sister – in other words, on quicksand. And this,' he leans in and taps the letter, shaking now in Henne's clenched fist, 'will hopefully remind you of your position in life.'

A barren wife. A sinner for a sister. The mould-bloom of Lisbet's panic sharpens into hate. She wants her husband to shove the man through the door, to stamp on his smirking face until he spits teeth into the dust. She herself would do it, to death. But Henne does not defend her, nor Agnethe, and Lisbet's mouth fills with bitterness.

'My father bought this land, and I work the bees. You and your council have no claim here,' says Henne.

'Take your woes to Heidelberg.'

'I shall.'

'You shall not!' cries Sophey, and Plater snorts.

'You can inform me if that is your plan and I will send word for them to expect you. You have a day to make your decision. I will not keep the Twenty-One waiting beyond that. Brant is personally concerned by the matter.'

He throws the empty cup to the table and leaves as abruptly as he entered. As though on reflex, Agnethe steadies the rolling cup, and Henne slams the door behind him.

'Henne,' says Sophey weakly, 'what shall we do?'

But Henne only takes his knapsack from its hook, and strides from the room. Sophey trails him, leaving Agnethe and Lisbet in their stunned silence.

Agnethe collapses onto the bench beside Lisbet. Her whole body is trembling, and Lisbet wonders what it is about Plater that makes her so afraid. Does she too love the bees, as Lisbet does, feels the threat to them as a threat to her own person, her own happiness? The thought sparks apprehension, a possessiveness she reminds herself she has no right to feel.

Then she spies Agnethe's face, the hard-set line of her jaw, and there is no terror there. Instead, her eyes shine with anger. It strikes Lisbet that perhaps she was wrong – that perhaps Agnethe is no hare, but rather the fox.

Three

Blood thuds in Lisbet's ears. She used to be careful of such high feeling in her carryings, but it is impossible to quell her fury, her fear. She picks up the broom and her hand trembles.

'I'll see to that,' says Agnethe, her face emptied. 'Sit.'

'I do not need to sit,' says Lisbet, leaning on the table. Agnethe takes the broom firmly from her. Though Lisbet cannot stop her she remains on her feet, an act of defiance, as Agnethe sweeps up the broken pieces of the plate and throws them onto the banked fire. The heat flares briefly, like a demon dog licking their faces.

'Was he always this cruel?' asks Lisbet.

Agnethe doesn't look at her. 'He grew into it.'

'Ida remains herself,' says Lisbet, though she feels the same spike of ownership as she had about the bees. 'Ever kind, ever constant.'

Agnethe sweeps the floor vigorously, hands white against the handle. Lisbet watches her a moment.

'I'll wager this is not the welcome you had in mind.'

A sharp snort. 'It is exactly as I expected.'

It is said with just enough wryness, and Lisbet allows herself a smile despite the wretched news. She takes up a scrubbing brush, skimming crumbs from the table onto the floor for Agnethe to sweep.

'He is set on going to Heidelberg.' Sophey stands in the doorway, looking at them both accusingly as if it were them who ordered it.

'What other option has he?' says Lisbet, her hands cramped about the brush. 'We cannot lose the farm.'

'We would not lose the farm,' snaps Sophey. 'Only the bees.'

Lisbet throws the brush down with a clatter, nerves singing with strain. 'The bees are the farm, our livelihood.'

'Before you arrived,' says Sophey, 'we had less than half the skeps, and the rest beets. It was good enough.'

'I know what you had,' mutters Lisbet. She is a frayed length of twine, unravelling. Agnethe's return, Plater's visit, and the baby hanging from her ribs have broken her patience down to nothing. The bees are her anchor in this place, in her life where she drifts without a child to keep her steady. They alone – their care, their needs, their inscrutable patterns and wildness – keep her sane. To lose the bees, after so much loss, would be to lose her mind.

'He must go, Mutter,' says Agnethe. 'You cannot give up all you have built.'

'You of all people should know,' says Sophey with a snap of anger, 'that to set against the Twenty-One is to set against God. And see where that got you.'

Agnethe goes very still, as she had in Plater's presence. Lisbet guesses it is a trick she mastered at the abbey. She imagines this tall, marked woman moving through dark halls in high mountain air, learning to turn herself invisible. Is that how to account for sin? To attempt to scrub yourself from the world alongside it? Certainly Sophey and Henne have acted as though Agnethe did not exist in these seven years, and it was easy enough for Lisbet to join them in this fiction. She has not spared so much as a prayer for Agnethe. Lisbet remembers the bread, the strong hands holding her up, and feels a thump of protectiveness toward her new-found sister. She will know her. She will show her she sees her.

'Agnethe is right,' she says. 'There is no choice. We must fight it.'

Sophey sucks air through her gapped gums as Henne returns with his knapsack slung over his shoulder, and his high pattens strapped over his shins, shedding dirt.

'Do not leave now,' she says. 'If you are to go, we must prepare bread and blessings for the altar at Heidelberg, and tomorrow you can pray with Agnethe at the cathedral.'

'There is no time—'

'There is always time for prayer.' Sophey softens almost instantly, and places her hand on his shoulder. It sits curled on the expanse of mended cloth, twisted with sore bones and rough flesh. 'If you must go, please go with a full day's light ahead.'

'I'll be travelling all hours,' says Henne. 'We have not the coin for taverns and rest houses.'

'Then you shall sleep in churches,' says Sophey firmly. 'Joss Fritz is coming south, everyone says so. It is not safe in the dark.'

Though not two years ago priests were stabbed by rebels in a church, and though Henne is more likely to join the revolt with its mission against the Twenty-One than meet it, he grunts his assent, and slings his knapsack onto the freshly scrubbed table.

'Tomorrow then,' he says, as though it was his plan all along. 'First light, Agnethe?'

'You must to the mill,' says Sophey, 'to tell Plater. Perhaps—'

'Agnethe can wait in the cart,' says Henne impatiently.

'And me,' says Lisbet, desperate to be out of the stifling

house and away from Sophey's agitation. If they are going to the Metz mill she can see Ida. 'I will come too.'

Henne sits to discard his pattens, unstrapping them from his clogs. 'Lisbet can take some candles to the market, some sealing wax. I'll prepare them now.'

'I can do it——' starts Lisbet, mind already soothed by the thought of the pressing shed, the thick encasing smell of wax and honey, but Henne is out the door. Sophey rounds on her at once.

'He risks all for us,' she says. 'And you would wave him off gladly?' Her hand cuts the air, stopping Lisbet's interruption before it has begun. 'You hear as well as I do the warnings at church. They hang the rebels at a rate of hundreds and still there are more. It is as Geiler foretold. In this heat everything is damned.'

She speaks as though Lisbet does not know it, has not heard with her own ears word of Sophey's beloved Geiler's now infamous sermon that rot will grow from rot ever since the comet smashed a year's corn in Eninsheim. Their corn, Lisbet's father's field, the same night Lisbet was born. The field never yielded again. All this, Sophey doesn't know.

Whatever Sophey thinks, Lisbet does listen to Pater Hansen at church. More than that, she sees it with her own eyes when she and Ida travel the slums. Stink and sickness, and so many babies, sallow-skinned and barely crying. Pater Hansen tells them in the city women drown their babies, and Lisbet dreams herself with a net, hauling them to safety.

'Which is exactly why we must keep our bees,' says Lisbet with a courage she doubts she'd possess had she not a witness in Agnethe. 'They alone are unsullied by the heat, or else we'd be at the mercy of the weather like any other farmer.'

'Like my husband?' spits Sophey. 'You think you are so much better, turning us from cabbages and beets to bees. But

36

nothing is worth losing a son for. If you were a mother you'd understand.'

The breath stops in Lisbet's chest. Her face flushes hotly and she feels she will be sick on the fresh-swept floor. She shoves past Agnethe, standing blameless beside the door, and walks as fast as her belly will allow to the forest.

Both women call after her, Agnethe soft and Sophey angry, but Lisbet's blood is a roar in her ears and nausea rocks her belly. She does not trust herself not to cry, or scream, and there is only one place where she can do both without judgement or notice.

The skeps hum quietly, the bees stilled by the heavy air. The pressing shed's door is closed and the bowls are recently filled, and she is glad for once not to have to tend them. A needle enters precisely under her ribs and darns in time with her breath as she crosses the boundary of the wood, and within a few steps the trees have thickened. She finds a smooth-trunked paper tree, its bark peeling in feathery strips, and leans her palms against it so she can vomit without falling. She heaves until there is nothing left inside her, nothing but the baby and her thumping heart.

Lightheaded, she presses her forehead to the bark. It is warm as her blood, and she clasps her sweating palms beneath her belly, trying to take the strain from her back. Her anger feels enormous and smothering as smoke. *If you were a mother . . .*

But I am, she tells herself. *Many times over.* She loves each lost child though they are not here, though all she had of them was blood or else bloodless bodies — *is that not enough?* She knows Sophey has lost children, that most women do, that Ida is rare in her constant safe carryings. But if there are other mothers with empty arms, Lisbet has not met them, and so has not met anyone who understands what it is to carry the weight of so much absence.

Inside, the baby flickers. She used to think of them as fish, swimming through her depths, but now she wishes for trees, thick-rooted and strong. She rubs her ribs, and pushes herself upright.

She should go back to the house. She knows the route to her tree like her own palms, could do it blindfolded as well as in the dark, but the forests have grown more dangerous with such desperation in the city. Other tenants of the Twenty-One are not offered the chance to go to Heidelberg and argue their claims, and the evictions watched over by Plater and his ilk increase apace. Still, to give up the forest would be to give up her tree, and that is not worth contemplating. With the fierce sun diluted to a dapple on her shoulders, she pushes on.

Her path is invisible to all but her, and undesirable. The trees are thick and licked in thorns, the ground kept boggy by underground streams that swell to rivers in the rainy months. There are better areas for shelter near the city road, more easily sought, and this is why her sanctuary is so protected, enshrined.

She feels like a bee, sowing its maps into the air, a bird weaving its way home, stopping to listen now and again for approaching footsteps, for any sign at all she is not alone. For she must be, here. When her clogs sink into the familiar mossy ground she feels her heart lift. She pushes aside the brambles she places at the border to discourage animals, and enters the small clearing. It is quiet and shadowed as a church.

There at the centre is a thick-trunked linden with a stage built into its branches. A dance tree. The platform she mended sits in the highest branches, jutting like a land-wrecked boat. All around it are her babies' ribbons, twelve lengths of cotton ripped from the first infant's smock she ever sewed, dyed in the brightest colours she could muster from beetroot and beetle wings.

The bees brought her here. It is another thing to love them for. When Henne was in Colmar delivering wax, and she pregnant a third time, full of grief and hope, she'd mistaken a trail of them for their own. Believing them to be deserters of Henne's hard-won hives, she followed them into the forest with a sack and a stick of burning rosemary, ready to bring them home again. She'd fought through the brambles and found them here, a wild colony living in a hollow branch that skewered the rotting platform.

She'd recognised it instantly for what it was: a dance tree. A doom tree. A relic of the pagans who had their churches open under God. Mutti told her some still stood, and in her latter days sent Lisbet out across the comet-cursed field to search the copses edging their land in the hopes of finding one. Mutti had lost hope in empirics and prayers by then, reaching for some ancient magic to cure the constant ache of her feet, the blood pooling beneath the skin like a malignant bruise.

Lisbet failed. But here, too late for Mutti, she has found one. Now the branch that held the bees is empty, stopped up with tarred sticks to prevent them returning, and that colony blows about their skep yard, bringing the sweetest wax. Henne must not fail in Heidelberg. It would break her heart.

The ground is scattered with leaves and her gifts. She brings the babies magpie offerings and places them at the base of the tree: pleasingly patterned stones, found feathers, flowers pressed and weighted with pebbles. She used to be superstitious about it, making deals and promises with each token – *If I find a seven-petalled flower, this baby will stay. If I can match this stone's white band with another, my baby will live.* But repetition can ruin such resolution, and now she places no especial importance upon the way and what she lays in the shadows.

Today she fixes the feathers found in Agnethe's room in the

bark of the tree. They are fluffy and soft as baby hairs. She clears the ground of fallen twigs and leaves, placing the empty snail shells down. The hush of the canopy overhead makes it silent as a church, and she bows her head as she approaches the altar of its trunk, rests a hand lightly there. It is miraculously cool, and she pulls her hand away with great effort.

The steep, ladderlike steps are dark. They would be cold under her feet, lichen and moss and age making them slick. She would be stupid to climb so large, even with the dragged branches and planks laid across to make the platform steady again. She'd come the day she was certain this baby was inside her, two missed bloods, stood with her head pressed to the mended railing, praying.

She allows herself to lie on the platform for hours after each tied ribbon, but now there is only time to circle the trunk. It is enough to remind her that Sophey, for all her conviction and resentment, cannot take the simple truth of those ribbons from her, of the place she has kept aside in her heart.

•

The next day seems to dawn hotter than any other. Henne whistles tunelessly, intent on the road, packed hard and unforgiving by weeks of sun, its potholes treacherous. The mule and horse struggle to match their paces, and the cart lists constantly to the left, towards the tall trees. Agnethe sits stiffly on Lisbet's other side, the siblings immoveable and solid as gateposts. Between them, Lisbet sways, belly pressing hard on her bladder, already regretting her resolution to see Henne on his way.

In the wide bed of the cart is a bundle of carefully wrapped candles, enough to light a modest church for a week. Beside it is a package of bread, baked with much of the remainder of Ida's gift, dried strips of lean bacon, a waxed cloth covering it all, though there is no sign of rain. Sophey had bit her lip hard seeing them off, almost as though she would cry, and Lisbet searched herself and realised that she felt nothing close to tears. Apprehension perhaps: but it is all for the bees, and the baby that spent a fractious night stirring her insides like cud.

The Metz mill sits halfway between Strasbourg and their farm. The forest is better managed here, though the roots constantly snake to the river, threatening to choke the water to a crawl. It is fastest to reach through the trees, a journey Lisbet has made so many times she could do it blindfolded. But as is the same for any settlement built near the Black Forest, where feet may pass, a cart cannot. This is why it offers safety for Joss Fritz and his rebels, for Lisbet and her dance tree, and why it takes double the miles to travel by horse than by foot.

Lisbet will be glad of a glimpse of Ida, of her ordered house and rose-cheeked children, the smell of fresh-baked bread that rises always from the timbers of the Metz mill. If the city is lately even more of a nightmare, the mill is like something from a children's story, sitting in the fork of the road between church and city, solid and square, clean and neat. Lisbet always leaves with her dark hair coated in a light film of white.

Agnethe's straight back stiffens further as the lines of the roof come into view, and the fetch-and-carry sound of the millwheel in the river rises over the clop of the horse's hooves.

Outside the door, Ilse sits in the dirt with a doll. A serious, watchful girl of six, with her father's hair and mother's large eyes and mouth, she is the sole daughter in a sea of sons, as Lisbet had been. She stands as the cart approaches, dusting herself down.

'Good morning, Ilse,' says Lisbet, as neither Henne nor Nethe offer a greeting. 'Will you fetch your father?'

She waits until the girl goes inside, releasing a snatch of childish voices from behind the door, before turning to Henne.

'Could you not raise a smile for the child at least?'

Henne's jaw juts mulishly. At her other side, Agnethe stares straight ahead, her hands jammed beneath her armpits, her expression so similar to her brother's Lisbet would laugh if their countenances weren't so grave.

The door opens and Ida comes out, her face unguarded, a smudge of flour on her cheek and her thick blonde hair uncovered. She startles at the sight of them, and immediately retreats, calling an apology before reappearing with a scarf covering her head, as her husband demands.

'My apologies, Herr Wiler.' Ida's voice is higher than usual. Her hands tremble. She is nervous, and will not meet Lisbet's eye. 'Ilse mentioned only Lisbet.'

'And was meant to fetch your husband,' smiles Lisbet. 'But no matter, I had hoped to see you.'

Henne shrugs. 'It is all well with me, Frau Plater. I have seen your hair many times as a child.'

'Quite so,' smiles Ida, but her brightness falters when she turns her attention to Agnethe. 'Hello, Agnethe.'

There is a charge like the moments before a thunderstorm: that unbearable ache when the air itself strains to break apart. Lisbet can hear the dry click of Agnethe swallowing, and when she looks into her sister-in-law's face, it holds such loathing it makes her flinch. Plater grips Ida's wrist and pulls her behind him, eyes fixed on Henne.

'You took your time,' says Plater, as his wife stands massaging her wrist.

'A day, you said,' says Henne. 'It is the morning.'

'Well observed.'

Lisbet is only dimly aware of their exchange. All her

attention is on Ida, on her sore wrist and downcast eyes, and on Agnethe, her hooded hostility, which seems less focused on Plater than on his wife. While Plater and Henne jibe feebly, there is a real and silent struggle occurring between Ida and Agnethe, and Lisbet cannot fathom why.

Henne climbs down from the cart to unharness the horse, strapping his pack to its flank.

'It is a wasted journey,' sighs Plater with false pity. 'But I admire your belief.'

'Goodbye, wife, sister,' says Henne, ignoring Plater. He hesitates before mounting the horse, his foot already in the stirrup. He looks from Lisbet, to Agnethe, and his gaze is not what Lisbet is used to – it is softer, pleading almost. 'Agnethe—' he begins, and then seems to think better of it. He swings himself up.

'I thought you were to pray at the cathedral,' says Lisbet.

'Tell my mother I did so.'

And then he is gone, kicking the horse into an instant gallop, the creature that bore his sister from the mountains now carrying him to a city where their futures will be decided. Lisbet cannot feel the true weight of the moment, for the ache in her bladder has reached a new pitch, and she slides along the cart's bench.

'Are you to town?' asks Plater. 'I will ride with you. The council must be informed their possession of the bees will be delayed a few days.'

'There will be no such possession,' snaps Lisbet, before mastering herself. 'Ida, might I have a drink?'

'Of course,' says Ida, flinging herself into grateful movement, approaching the cart and holding out her hand to help Lisbet step down. 'Agnethe, would you like—'

But Plater hisses, a curt and warning sound, and Ida leaves her sentence unfinished, leading her friend inside. Lisbet waves briefly at the boys strewn around the room before walking immediately through the cool and ordered house to the pit behind.

'So that was your rush,' says Ida, leaning on the door jamb as Lisbet squats and sighs in relief.

'I do not know how you managed three babies before your father dug you this,' says Lisbet, throwing a handful of dirt into the pit. 'The forest is too far off from here.'

'I did not always make it to the forest,' laughs Ida, turning to lift the dough she is working and brush the table free of flour. It is so plentiful here she does not even scoop it up to save for later: another benefit of being the miller's daughter. At her feet Ilse is showing her brother Alef how to tie a knot, and Martin watches and dribbles in a corner while the infant, Rolf, sleeps strapped on his board on the table.

Lisbet trails her fingers over his cheek, soft as a feather, and resists the urge to pluck him up and smell him. She imagines the scent of milk on his skin, woodsmoke folded into his neat muslin, the give of his warm legs between her thumbs. Want needles her chest.

The children take no more notice of Lisbet than Ida takes of them, and Lisbet feels a stab of jealousy. How it must be to bear child after child, so many you can stand to let them play unguarded, sleep unmolested. How it must be to never lose a child before they even breathed. No wonder Ida's face is so bright and clear, no matter how tired she gets. Such worry breeds age in you like nothing else. Lisbet sees it in her own greying hair, stark against the dark strands, feels it in her chest: a weight Ida will never carry. When a child does not live, it fills your arms with such emptiness they ache.

Lisbet smooths the thoughts from her face, and smiles at Ida, who brings her a bowl of water for her hands and face, and a cup of light beer. It is impossible to resent such a woman her houseful of children, especially with a husband like Plater, and Lisbet does not try.

'What was that?' asks Lisbet, splashing her cheeks. 'Between you and Agnethe?'

Ida shrugs tightly. 'We haven't seen each other in years. We are strangers now.'

'Agnethe and I are more strangers,' says Lisbet, 'and she did not look at me so.'

Ida is quiet, knocking the air from the dough with precise, practised punches. When her mother lived, they'd made a business of it, a mill and bakery both. But Plater does not like his wife to make other men's bread. Only his own.

'So Henne must go to Heidelberg?' asks Ida.

Lisbet nods, and with great effort puts down her cup. She does not want to leave this cool room, thick with the smell of babies and flour, and go out into the heat, to the city. But she has already left Agnethe long enough with her tormentor.

'I pray his journey will be successful.'

'It must be,' says Lisbet, a little harsher than intended. Prayers are not enough, if they do not work. Sometimes Ida seems not to understand this.

Rolf squalls, and Ida lifts him distractedly to her breast, shrugging down her sleeve in a well-practised motion, her shoulder creamy and plump, her breast veined blue. Lisbet's own are the same, but even now she cannot be certain the child she carries will ever drink from her.

Ida props Rolf on her hip and picks up the dirty bowl, the cup, continues to knead the dough while he feeds. She is so natural, so effortless with the children it makes Lisbet's heart twist. Had even one of her children lived, she doubts she would have such ease. And what a life here, despite her husband, with fresh-milled flour daily, a well to draw cool water from, and more than that: Ida herself. The person she is, so beautiful and kind. If Lisbet did not love her, she would hate her.

'Must you go to the city?' says Ida.

'We have candles to trade, melting as we speak I would wager.'

'I wish I had the flour to give you for them here, but you know Alef will not allow us to sell from the mill anymore.'

'I know.'

'Are you sure you would not like to stay? Hold Rolf?'

She nods down at the suckling infant, but Lisbet doesn't even allow herself to imagine his warm weight in her arms. She grips the edge of the table, smooth and hard and nothing like a child. 'I promised to accompany Agnethe to the cathedral.'

'For what purpose?' asks Ida, again with a feigned lightness.

'She must pray there to complete her penance.'

'And then it will be at an end,' says Ida, and there is a sudden drop in her voice, an envy almost. Rolf has turned his face from her nipple, showing it large and dark pink as the inside of a flower. His mouth works as he searches for it.

'Are you all right, Ida?'

Her friend looks down almost absently to her whimpering child, and stoppers up his mouth with her breast again.

'Of course,' says Ida, kissing her cheek. Lisbet smells the baby, the milk, and nearly swoons. 'Until church, then.'

Four

Though Plater is a narrower man than Henne, he spreads himself across the bench of the cart so Lisbet must practically sit atop her sister-in-law, Agnethe's hard hip digging into her fleshy thigh. Agnethe had leapt from the cart the moment Lisbet emerged from the house, with the pretence of helping her up, but Lisbet guesses it was to avoid having to sit beside Plater. He wears gloves despite the heat, his forehead sweating, and the smoke-and-leather smell of him is stifling as the incense burned in church.

As they fork right to the city, the forest begins to fall back like a retreating army. At the crossroads there is a cage suspended from a post, empty and glinting. The metal would be scalding under skin. Lisbet saw a woman in it once, bridle about her face like a vice.

Agnethe twists in her seat to watch it, and Lisbet feels her trembling. Her lips move.

'What are you praying for, Agnethe?' says Plater. 'Surely not the sinners?'

Agnethe turns her face away.

The road takes on a gentle slope, and they lean back in the cart while the mule puffs and wheezes, its hooves skittering slightly on the packed dust. The candles shift in the back, and Agnethe puts out her arm to hold the protective cloth in place. Lisbet sniffs the air, checking for signs the wax is melting in the heat. She wishes she could force the mule to quicken its pace, but Plater has taken the reins as though it were his own cart.

'There will be a thief there soon enough,' continues Plater, though they have left the cage behind them. 'A woman, caught taking nails from a church door. A church! The depravity of this city.'

Lisbet's stomach twists. She imagines her, this woman, who for some reason has her mother's face in the worst, final days of her sickness, with ragged fingernails prising metal from wood, splinters beneath her nails, like Agnethe and the egg shell.

'You are lucky, Agnethe Wiler, I said it even then,' says Plater. 'To be sent to the mountains. There is a tighter grip on sinners, now. Sebastian Brant has a firm hold of the council, and agrees we must instil the fear of God back into their hearts, or else they will not obey.'

He speaks as though he is a part of the Twenty-One, not only their hired brute. Beside her, Agnethe is stone again. Lisbet holds her breath and her tongue, wondering if this is the moment she will at last learn Agnethe's transgressions. But Plater speaks only in allusions.

As they reach the lip of the hill they see the spires of Notre Dame, and Plater crosses himself. Lisbet and Agnethe mimic him. The first time Lisbet saw them, she wept at how the world held such beauty, such grandeur. She had never seen the like near her father's fields, where only trees stood higher than their farm, and their church was cramped and draughty, housing animals in the bleakest winters. She felt Henne had pulled her from a pit, loosed from her the misfortune that trailed her like a dog.

And now there are stories of farmers bringing their herds onto the cool, hallowed stone to save them boiling in their pens. Though the cathedral's spires stand high enough to spike the sky, it does not take long for her sights to be brought low once more.

The smell comes like a cloud from the river that cuts east of Strasbourg. It is brown and sluggish beneath the sun, and as they near the city proper, the smell grows solid, grows guts and breath. Lisbet comes this way most weeks with Ida, making for the slums that line the outer edges of the city, and yet the smell is always a slap. She scrunches her lip below her nose, and Agnethe retches quietly into her sleeve. Only Plater seems unmoved.

'Do you find it much changed, Fräulein? I suspect the air was of a different sort in the mountains.'

Lisbet wishes he would stop talking, yet she would dearly like to know the answers to his questions. She herself has seen the descent of the city, already in motion when she arrived, but surely worsened for her proximity. She came by Henne's side in this very cart, with this very mule drawing her into her new life. The signs of the previous year's Hungry Winter were everywhere, small crosses marking the spots on the cobbles where men and women froze to death in the streets.

There has been more and worse since, the returning war wounded mouldering in the almshouses, their eyes empty and mouths full of stories of the Turks. But the most brutal stories are of those unlucky enough to die unburied, their spirits returning to the forests and fields, legions of fury screaming toward their kin, shrieking justice. Lisbet can believe it: devils walking the earth. The whole of Strasbourg in free fall toward this hellish summer.

They begin to pass the hovels, slumped structures of wood

49

and thatch, bound with rotted rope or else left open and unpeeled to the elements. Herr Lehmann and his wife are sleeping slumped in their doorway: Lisbet knows that inside are eight children, knows they will have sucked the meat from the scrawny chicken she brought five days ago, long boiled its paltry bones to mush.

It has not always been like this, as Sophey takes great care to tell her. The city sat high in the Pope's estimation, had been gifted funds to build upon its fortunes as Heidelberg did. But then Lisbet arrived, and with her, signs suggesting damnation. More and worse Hungry Winters, blighted summers, plagues and sweats and starvation. Only Sophey seems to see it clearly —the rot at the core of her, like spilt salt or a fishbone in the throat: a bad omen. In the fields of her father's farm, furrowed by the comet's fall, it felt safer to be so, though her mother saw it too, prayed for her daughter until she lost her reason and her will. Lisbet flicks the thoughts from her like lice. Not with the child inside her. She must not linger in those dark and waterlogged places.

The outlook doesn't improve as they near the labyrinth of the city centre. The miasma is heavy as fog, the sunlight mired to a feverish yellow that taints all it touches. Lisbet shudders as they descend through it. Sometimes there is an edge of sweetness from a private church, or else freshness from a baker, but those scents all are jumbled together, like threads of gold in stinking rope. Only the cathedral seems unblemished, its pure honey stone shining over the low roof-tops surrounding them.

She straightens her back as Plater navigates the mule through the outskirts into the main market square. Notre Dame looms at the far side, and the air is awash with flies numerous as crows over her father's fields. It is busy as ever, bodies packing in from all sides, but the stalls are empty. She sees no meat anywhere, just meagre rye and shrivelled salsify. Only firewood is plentiful, and no one is buying that with the heat, the forests so nearby.

Plater yanks the mule to a halt. He throws down the reins, and jumps lightly into the packed dust, looking around as though he owns all he surveys. A crowd of boys jostles, palms upstretched, and Plater shoves them aside, as though he was not once one of them.

'I wish you well with your prayers,' says Plater, before shouldering away in the direction of the city hall. Lisbet feels Agnethe wilt with relief.

While Agnethe fetches out the candles, Lisbet hands a coin to the smallest boy, telling him to watch the cart. She recognises him as Herr Lehmann's eldest, Daniel. The others disperse, cursing, and Daniel stands proudly by the mule's head, his hand on the reins. His fingers are all bone, his pinched face hollow at the cheeks. Herr Lehmann sells his children's teeth to merchants and empirics, despite Ida's entreaties not to.

She recovers herself. 'Come then, to Mathias first, else the candles will melt.'

Lisbet's dress is too long and drags in the muck. She sees no animals, and wonders, not briefly enough, where all the shit has come from.

They reach Mathias, wide as his daughter is narrow, stooped now and with long nails on his little fingers that he uses to scoop up the flour and show the fineness of the grain. His stall alone is well stocked – a benefit of Plater's influence as well as his own hard work. He doesn't watch them approach, his attention turned towards a gathering of people at the centre of the square. Even when they halt before his stall, his watery blue eyes are turned away.

'Herr Metz?' Lisbet says gently. He used to be a quick man, but in the years Lisbet has known him he has dulled, the sharpness of his brain wearing smooth as a grindstone. Though his body remains strong, his sight and mind are failing both.

He turns his filmy eyes upon her. 'Lisbet?' He sounds dazed.

'Yes, Herr Metz, it's me. I've brought a candle, if we might have two sacks of flour?'

'Yes, yes,' he says, lifting his hand to pat her gently on the shoulder and bring her into focus before he bends to the knotted sacks. But as he does so, his fingers tighten. His eyes are wide. When Lisbet follows his gaze though, it is only Agnethe, standing uncertain with the bundle of wax in her arms.

'You . . .' he gasps, 'you.'

Agnethe takes another small step toward him, and holds out the bundle. He takes her hand, slowly and carefully as Lisbet might trap a wayward bee, and draws her even closer, so his rusting eyes can lock her in their gaze. To Lisbet's surprise, they fill and spill over.

Mathias takes the candles and lets go of Agnethe's wrist, and it falls limply to her side. He turns away, wiping his cheeks, but there was no mistaking the tears.

'You are returned,' he says, the shake clear in his voice. 'Did they treat you well?'

'Yes,' says Agnethe, and Lisbet notices how her voice is thick with emotion, too.

'Good,' he says, unwrapping the bundle as briskly as his stiff fingers will allow. 'Have you . . .' He trails off, and shakes his head as though dislodging a fly. 'You can take three.'

'Three?' says Lisbet.

'Three sacks,' says Mathias, 'with my blessings.'

Lisbet cannot understand what is passing between them, but she will not decline his kindness. 'We must to the cathedral first,' she says. 'Thank you, Mathias. We will collect them on our return.'

'I prayed,' he says. His eyes are still bright. 'Every day. I pray still.'

'Thank you,' says Agnethe. She looks as though she will reach out to him, but instead she turns to Lisbet, and motions for them to mount the cathedral steps.

At the stone basin set outside and filled daily with fresh water, they wash their hands. Lisbet wonders if the farmers anoint their animals before crossing the dark cave of the cathedral threshold. Agnethe rubs the dusty, lukewarm water over her scarred head. She is drawing looks and mutters, her baldness marking her out as a penitent, but she seems not to notice, or at least not to care. Perhaps she was always a woman who was stared at: with her handsomeness and her height Lisbet can believe it.

Into the blessed cool of the cathedral they step, side by side like newly bound lovers. The smell of shit dissipates, replaced with incense made from a tree that grows in the deserts of the place their empire fights for even now. Somewhere far away that is hotter, Pater Hansen says, than even this summer, so hot the Turks' blood bubbles and runs black as their hearts, darker than their skin. Lisbet sees such men and women more and more often in Strasbourg, though they mostly keep to their quarter of the city. They do not look like demons to her, any more than her mother looked possessed when the priest declared her so.

The light is softer here, like being underwater, the sun's glare dispersed to a glow through the rose window. Someone, somewhere, is crying, and the stone walls bat the sound about like a cat with a mouse in its paws. Lisbet looks around, searching for the source, but Agnethe seems to hear nothing, see nothing but the gilded cross hung over the altar, the flooded light of a hundred candles. She walks towards them as though in a dream. Lisbet trips after her, pride blooming in her chest.

These are their candles for the most part — the bees who hum in their hives worked this wax into existence. It is a miracle greater than anything she hears of in church — this everyday transformation, like water into wine. But that thought in itself is blasphemy.

Agnethe falls to her knees on the stone, the dome of her head tilted back, her arms draped out at her sides in supplication. Lisbet has never seen someone pray in such a pose. When she bends her neck to speak to God, she feels the aim is to make herself as small as possible, turning inwards to find some tiny voice that perhaps sometimes she believes is from heaven, but is more often her mother's. She fails even at carrying God inside her like others seem to. But Agnethe prays like in the holy stories, as though God is everywhere, and she is showing herself as broadly and as boldly as she can.

Lisbet searches for a priest or warden, some figure of authority who will surely come and clip Agnethe's exuberance, but she sees no vestments, only hungry faces. She lowers herself, the smooth stone cool enough to be felt through her skirts. She has not prayed in the cathedral for years, and knows she should pay her respects, if not to Him then to the place, the old stone and high windows, the glass and the scents pressing down on her like a heavy palm.

She clasps her hands in the attitude of prayer, but all her attention is for Agnethe. Her lips move fast, as though she cannot possibly fit all she has to say inside her head, inside the time she has left on this earth. Her eyelids are nearly closed, but a line of white shows shining in the candle light, and beneath them Lisbet can see movement, as though she is a child caught in dreams.

Soon Lisbet's knees are aching, and her back and her neck, and she knows she will have a job standing, but Agnethe gives no sign of stopping her prayer. Her stance has drawn more looks, more mutters, but Agnethe has not noticed. She is entirely elsewhere.

At last, Lisbet admits defeat. She does not know how long this final act of penance will last, and her legs are starting to tingle and spasm. She heaves herself upright using the pew, the wood groaning with the effort of holding her, her skirts catching beneath her feet. She hears a small tear: her hem, giving. She wants suddenly, foolishly, to cry. This is her mother's skirt, let out again and again during her mother's repeated carryings until it would only be good for a belly Lisbet was certain she would never be able to grow. At last she fills it, and she misses her mother with the sharpness of a child waking in darkness.

She turns from Agnethe, from the altar, from their bees' candles transmogrifying the building into a celestial space aglow with gold, and stumbles back into the blunt sunlight. At the doorway, she looks back at her sister-in-law, made tiny by distance. From here, she looks as though she is aflame, and Lisbet shudders.

She thinks to return to Mathias, to start the process of transferring the sacks to the cart, but a shout pulls her attention. A child is running, laughing, followed by another, toward a crowd of perhaps fifty people at the square's edge. For such a gathering, they seem oddly silent. Lisbet squints. There is dust rising from the crowd's centre. The children reach the outermost edges and vanish amongst the larger bodies. Checking again over her shoulder that Agnethe has not moved, Lisbet traces the children's steps.

She shoulders through, imagining a Gyptian in scandalous dress, or perhaps even a bear brought from the north and poked into a jig. But the feel of the crowd is wrong: there are no lewd calls, no drums beating. Only a muttering, a solemn witnessing.

She ignores the irritable comments as she forces her way forward, arms scooped around her belly. She hears something above the noise of the crowd, a sort of dragging, scuffling sound, a sob.

At last she is close enough to see what has drawn the onlookers. A rough semicircle of space is gouged out of the centre, like an eye, and at the heart of the eye is the dust, thrown up in huffing clouds that fall heavily in the windless air.

For a moment, she is eight again, and watching dust in her father's parched fields take shape, grow hands and feet and teeth as it gallops towards her. She is twelve, and the blood from her mother's feet stains her hands. She is fifteen, and at a dance, her hands in Henne's and her heart loud in her chest. Lisbet recovers herself. This is no dust spirit, no dancing lovers, but a woman.

Lisbet could perhaps call her a dancer but she looks as though she is being hauled between two devilish ropes caught about her limbs. Her arms wave and swat aside the stolid air, whirling about her head. Her hair flies across her face and Lisbet can see nothing of her features except her mouth, gaping in an *o* of sorrow, or terror. Her legs hop and her feet lift, beating the ground into its dusty flurries, but there is no rhythm to her movements.

As she spins, flecks of spit land on the ground, marking it with brown streaks. It speckles the faces of those opposite. Something dark lands on Lisbet's skirts: a red spot. It is blood, she sees now: the woman is bleeding from her soles. Her shoes are soaked through with it, and as she stamps and jumps and sways she weeps and moans, gleaming streaks of tears and snot stringing in her filthy hair, the slack circle of her mouth shockingly red.

'Please,' says a man beside Lisbet. 'Please, Magret. Stop.'

Lisbet sees him reach out to the woman, but this is no ordinary disobedience. The woman looks possessed.

Lisbet crosses herself, lowering her voice to a whisper so as not to break the silence of the watchers, and leans in to the woman beside her.

'What is happening?'

The woman's hair is full of rat tails and her breath is hot against Lisbet's cheek.

'Three days, she's been dancing.'

'Three *days*? Why does no one stop her?'

The woman jerks her head at the man who now kneels in the dirt, beseeching. 'Her husband's tried. Lots of us have. He gets her home, she sleeps an hour, comes back.'

'Have the priests been called?'

'Of course. They think she's a drunk.'

'Isn't she?' says Lisbet.

The woman narrows her eyes. 'I've never seen a drunk dance till they bleed. Three days, I said. Three. And not a drop of water or beer or otherwise passed her lips. They're calling her a saint.'

'Who are?' says Lisbet. 'She looks a devil.'

The woman shrugs, losing interest. 'The Twenty-One will decide.'

She points at two men standing across from them. Lisbet can see the taller one in profile: a straight nose, a pronounced chin. Copper hair. She feels disgusted resignation. Plater, again.

'Here at the Twenty-One's bidding,' says the woman, her voice a whisper. 'They won't let this go on much longer. More people come each day to gawk.'

'I didn't know about her,' says Lisbet.

'Still here though, aren't you?' The woman licks her sun-cracked lips. Her tongue is purplish and swollen.

Lisbet looks at the dancer. Her head has tipped back, like

Agnethe's in the cathedral, her face blotched as though burned. Her eyes are open and rolling, her throat convulsing around irreconciled words. Lisbet wants to wrap her in a blanket and rock her. The dancer's hands flutter.

'Please, Magret,' moans her husband. He is sobbing. 'Please God. Stop.'

Lisbet's baby kicks. Faintness shudders through her, and in answer, she turns and pushes back through the crowd using her elbows, propelling herself to the edge until she breaks out and gulps air, though it is sour and gritty. The stain on her skirt seems to have spread.

Mathias is still at his stall, and his pale eyes flick to her though she is not certain his sight reaches so far. She tries to regain her breath, to tidy her hair, scraping back the strands that have plastered themselves to her forehead. The woman's hair seemed to have a will of its own, vipers taken root in her scalp. She feels her mother's hair in her palms.

'Are you all right, Lisbet?'

She jumps, but it is only Agnethe beside her, her hand hovering uncertainly over her shoulder.

Lisbet nods, recovering herself.

'What is it?' frowns Agnethe, and turns her blue gaze to the crowd. Lisbet does not want to have to explain, have to wait while Agnethe goes and sees for herself what is at the centre of the gathering. She wants to leave. She pulls desperately on Agnethe's sleeve.

'Nothing,' she says. 'Someone making a spectacle. Please, can we leave?'

'Are you unwell?'

'Yes,' says Lisbet. 'Please.'

'Of course,' says Agnethe. She turns briskly from the crowd, and Lisbet follows her back to Mathias' stall. Agnethe shoulders two of the sacks without effort.

Mathias leans into Lisbet. 'It isn't natural,' he says. 'I've seen her here the past week. Every day the same.'

Lisbet squints at him, catching up. 'The dancer?'

'Strange, is it not?'

'What's strange?' Agnethe has returned, but before Mathias can answer Lisbet speaks.

'It is done, Agnethe's penitence. She prayed at the cathedral.'

Mathias' misty eyes shine, and he seems to chew his tongue to repress some strong emotion. 'Your prayer was peaceable?'

'It was,' says Agnethe, though to Lisbet it had looked anything but.

'It is done, then,' says Mathias in mimicry of Lisbet. 'It is lifted. How do you feel?'

Agnethe bends to the final sack, scooping it into her arms, and offers him a sad smile before walking to the cart. Lisbet waves farewell to Ida's father, and contemplates the climb into the cart with dismay. Her legs still tremble from kneeling on the stone, and she braces herself against the wooden sides.

'It's all right, Frau,' says a small voice. Daniel, loosing the mule's bridle. His nose is running and she resists the urge to wipe it with her skirts. He scrambles into the seat and holds out a sticky hand to her, pulling her up, skinny legs shaking.

'Thank you,' says Lisbet, as he jumps down.

'Wait.' Agnethe turns to the sacks, opens one. 'Take some.' She jerks her head at the boy, who is hovering uncertainly. 'Come on.'

He doesn't wait to be asked again, and plunges his hands into the sack. He scoops up a mound, and another, and, as if worried she will change her mind, scurries off with it, making a tray of his jerkin. Lisbet thinks too late to shout after him, offer a ride, but he is already out of calling distance. Stray flour sifts through to the ground, making a tracery of his path, and she hopes he will have some left by the time he reaches home.

One dancing

The story of her birth is the story of a comet. At the moment Gepa Bauer's mother felt the first pain of her coming, her papa saw it, a burning star ripping the dark sky for three days while her mother laboured on all fours like a beast, her husband and sons sleeping in the barn because they were scared of her pain, of the blood, of the wise woman who came with sweet mallow and iron tongs. To the east, the comet found a farmer's field and scorched it fully, furrowed so deep those who were there said it was like a tunnel to Hell carved in the soil. As it tore the ground, Gepa was born feet first and the agony broke her mother's mind.

From that day she was the omen, the bad sign looked for in the fields when the crops failed. She was loved despite these calamities, but at eight her mind followed her mother's, and both of them were cast onto the Church's mercy. In an almshouse with twenty-four other women, she at last found friends, all of them cursed, all of them damned, and together they could link hands and dance to music no one else could hear. When they danced, they were one body with many hands and many feet, one breath in their chests and one pulse in their wrists.

When the last of their mothers died, they left the city Gepa was born in, and went to another city, a bigger city, full of churches and men that could pay to keep her in her wrong mind and in good shoes. She and her friends were peeled apart, by marriage or children or disease, and suddenly it was years later, whole seasons of starvation and pox and sex, and she was alone in the city, and she did not know her name.

She calls on her mother and her mother comes, her face wiped smooth as it was when they tipped her into the mass grave, and her mother takes her hand, and her mother leads her to the market square where oftentimes she and her friends would hold hands and weave through the crowds lifting purses and blowing kisses, their hair fresh braided and fragrant.

She stands in the square, before the Notre Dame. Her good shoes are in pieces, and she kicks them from her feet. Her hair is stringy and stinking. Ahead is a cluster of people though it is late and the church candles are no longer lit, and she pushes forward until she sees a woman. The woman is dancing to music no one else can hear, and her feet are two white comets in the dark, dragging deep tracks in the dust.

Her mother moves her closer, so she sees the woman's hands fluttering and empty, gesturing her on. She reaches out and takes hold, and the woman's pulse starts to beat in her wrist, her breath filling her chest. She hears the music lift and sweep them together, close as a kiss, and by the time the priests come to take the woman away, it is too late. The woman has already passed the music on to her, and she holds it, bright and burning as a fallen star, strewing its pieces to any who will take her hand.

Five

'Was she a dancer?'

Lisbet looks at Agnethe, astonished. They have ridden in silence through the twisted streets of the city, Agnethe expert at the reins, and are now on the road home.

'Who?'

'The woman you did not want me to see,' says Agnethe lightly. She glances at Lisbet and laughs, a surprisingly girlish sound. 'I have a head or two on you in height. I could see well enough it was no simple madwoman in that crowd.'

'It was,' says Lisbet defensively. 'A madwoman. She was dancing, maybe, but it was not a usual dance.'

'I could see that much,' says Agnethe. 'But she moved as though to music.'

'Yes,' says Lisbet. She feels ashamed, oddly guilty. 'I was not concealing it from you. I did feel unwell.'

'I could see that, too.'

They are approaching the metal cage, and this time Agnethe has no need to avert her eyes. Her head tilts back as they ride beneath it.

Lisbet feels a desperate need to make amends, to offer some information. 'Plater was watching her.'

Agnethe's hands clench on the reins. 'Poor woman, to have his attention.'

'The Twenty-One ordered it. She has been there three days. That's what Mathias said.'

Agnethe frowns. 'Dancing all that time?'

'What do you make of it?' asks Lisbet.

Agnethe seems hesitant. 'I have seen fevers, holy trances. Never dancing, but chanting, or else complete stillness.'

Lisbet feels a trill of excitement. 'At the abbey?'

Agnethe gives a noncommittal grunt.

'What does it mean?'

'Any number of things. The sisters called them abandonments – whether to God or the Devil was a matter of opinion and rested much on their view of you. They cast judgements like stones, thrown without care or calculation.'

Lisbet is amazed to hear her speak in such a way about holy orders, and thrilled too. 'Were they cruel to you?'

'Cruel?' Agnethe sounds amazed. 'It is not so simple. As a penitent, pain is salvation. Perhaps it looks cruel, what was inflicted on me bodily, but they did it to save my soul.'

'Do you believe that?' asks Lisbet, because something in Agnethe's tone suggests insincerity, even humour.

'I must believe it, or it was seven years for naught.'

They fall back to their silence until the cage is out of sight over the hill behind them.

'It was a shock, to see how the skep yard has grown,' says Agnethe. 'Henne did well, to marry you.'

Lisbet flushes with pleasure. 'I enjoy my duties.'

Agnethe gives her a sideways glance, and Lisbet flushes harder at her misunderstanding. 'With the bees.'

Agnethe lets out a hoot of laughter, an unguarded sound. 'How did you meet?'

'A dance,' says Lisbet. She has not had cause to recount

their meeting since Ida asked many years ago. She is surprised to find the memory unfaded, full colour in her mind. 'Near my father's fields. Henne was in town to trade.'

'Which town?'

'Eninsheim.'

'Of the comet?'

Lisbet's throat tightens. 'Yes.'

Agnethe doesn't press. 'I hope he is a good husband to you.'

'He is.' Lisbet answers without consideration, and in the ensuing silence she thinks again, thinks deeper. Next to Plater, Henne seems a saint. But he has grown so cold to her, careless of her feelings. He does not hide that he thought her, with her broad hips and field-fed complexion, a good carrier. He does not hide that he is dismayed to be wrong.

They pass the Metz mill and reach the forest road. The shadows slide over them, and in the dimness Agnethe seems to find courage. 'What have they said about me?'

'Nothing,' says Lisbet, startled. 'You mean Sophey, Henne?'

'All of them,' says Agnethe, her light tone failing to belie her urgency. 'What have they told you?'

'That you have been at the abbey at Mont Sainte-Odile.'

'Did they tell you why I was sent there?'

'No,' says Lisbet truthfully. 'They spoke of you hardly at all.'

As soon as the words are out she wishes she could reel them back in, but it is too late. Agnethe lets out a small exhale.

'I didn't mean—'

'It's all right,' she says.

'They missed you.'

'You are not a skilled liar,' says Agnethe gently. 'And nor should you be. It's all right,' she says, glancing again at Lisbet's stricken face. 'I expected as much.'

'Ida sometimes spoke of you,' says Lisbet, but it has the opposite effect to what she'd hoped.

'She should not,' says Agnethe sharply. 'I doubt her husband tolerates talk of sinners.'

'I don't think her husband tolerates much at all.'

Agnethe snorts. 'I think you are right.'

There follows another silence. It feels to Lisbet that she skirts a chasm, a darkness that draws her nauseatingly closer. To fall in would be fatal, and irresistible. The question is formed fully in her mind, but again it is Agnethe who breaks the quiet.

'And what of you, sister?'

'Me?'

Agnethe nods at her belly. 'Has it been a safe carrying?'

Lisbet feels her throat close. 'Thus far.'

'I pray for a safe birth, too,' says Agnethe. 'Though I doubt you need my prayers. You look strong. I am sure you will be a good mother.'

It is all Lisbet can do to keep from creasing over and rocking. She turns her face towards the forest.

'I have said something wrong,' says Agnethe. 'Please forgive me, I'm out of practice with speaking, especially of such things. There was none of that at the abbey, as you can imagine.'

Lisbet shakes her head, but to her horror the tears she held back in the city are falling now, dripping off her chin. The trees melt into a grey-green haze and she feels the cart draw to a stop. A strong-fingered hand takes hers. She is worried Agnethe will ask her questions. It is what Ida would do, desperate to know what is wrong, to fix it, but Agnethe only sits, her hand in Lisbet's, and waits.

At last, Lisbet wipes the wetness from her cheeks.

'I'm sorry,' she says. 'The heat, and the dancer. The bees. I am worried for our future.'

'Yes,' says Agnethe. 'And for your child's, of course.'

'I am hopeful of it – their future. But . . . you must not suppose. That there will be a child.'

'It is wise to be cautious, but you have no reason to be afraid.'

Lisbet's laugh is more of a hiccup. 'I have a dozen reasons.' She thinks of her tree, of the ribbons, and it seems a very small comfort in that moment, a miserly display. She can almost hear Agnethe's thoughts, arriving suddenly at understanding. The hand in hers twines more tightly.

'A dozen?' Agnethe's voice is strained.

'You think it foolish to count?'

'Of course not. Lisbet, I am sorry. Where are they rested? Might I see the graves?'

'There are none,' says Lisbet, her own voice cracking. 'None lived long enough to warrant a burial.'

'But you must have marked them, no matter their age,' says Agnethe, and Lisbet looks up at her, shocked. Henne never thought to suggest it, nor Sophey. Even the ones with small fingers, lidded eyes, perfect-pale and froggish, slipped from her too soon – they were grotesque to her husband and mother-in-law, unblessed, taken from her and buried unmarked and unremarked-upon. But Agnethe seems to understand: they were there, they existed. Lisbet remembers the lock of hair, kept careful and curled in Agnethe's pillow.

'Yes,' she says. 'I did.'

'You must show me when we are back at the farm.'

'They are not there,' she says. 'Henne wouldn't . . . they were not babies, yet. They did not breathe.'

'They would not mark them?'

'Nor seem to remember,' says Lisbet. 'Except that I failed.'

Agnethe's face becomes shadowed. 'I know this feeling. But it is no failure, to love. No failing.'

She sounds suddenly angry, and Lisbet feels emboldened by her raw emotion. 'You understand.'

'Of course.'

'You have felt it?' So this is the secret, the sin: Agnethe has had a child, perhaps even lost it before birth. Already she is drawing Agnethe tight to her chest, keen to share stories. Already she has pulled her from the cart, through the forest, to the dance tree.

But Agnethe looses her hand, and picks up the reins. With a soft cluck of her tongue, they are moving out of the cooling shadows and into the glare. The harsh brightness reveals the bones of Agnethe's cheeks and brow, just like her mother's. It is ridiculous to be cowed by the structure of Agnethe's face, but Lisbet is, and she does not ask more. Her vision of leading Agnethe to the dance tree flickers and dies.

•

'Three days? You are certain?' Sophey's hard face has taken on a blade-like intensity. 'Why?'

Lisbet shrugs. She doesn't want Sophey to see how much the dancer dismayed her. 'A madwoman.' Even the word sticks in her throat like a bone.

'But the Twenty-One's men were there?'

'Plater,' clarifies Lisbet.

Sophey crosses herself. 'He is everywhere. Did Henne see?'

Lisbet hesitates, but Agnethe saves her from the lie. 'He left as soon as he'd prayed.'

'Good,' says Sophey. 'He does not need such a sight to cloud his mind.'

'Do you think they will punish her for something so simple as dancing?' says Agnethe.

'They are right to do whatever restores calm,' says Sophey. 'We can ill afford a further slide into disorder.'

'She harms no one,' says Agnethe.

'She makes a spectacle,' snaps Sophey, slicing her hand through the air. 'You have been sheltered, on your mountain. There have been famines, droughts, revolts. Priests murdered at prayer. The whole city is tipping, and Geiler said—'

'Geiler is long dead,' says Agnethe, and Sophey glares.

'And yet he knew where we were going. He said we must guard our minds as well as our souls. The Twenty-One are right to rid the square of her.'

'It is not certain she is damned,' says Lisbet, glancing between them. 'Some spoke as though she may be blessed.'

'The priests will decide,' says Sophey, seeming to regain some mastery over herself. 'It will be at an end soon enough.'

'At the abbey,' says Agnethe, 'when one started a mania, others often followed.'

Sophey spits. 'Do not speak of such things. Of madness as infection. We are not all so weak-minded as you, Agnethe.'

'You call me weak, when I have borne all that has been done to me?'

Sophey crosses to Agnethe and pinches her beneath the arm.

'Stop,' she mouths. The women spin away from each other, Agnethe rising just slow enough for Lisbet to catch the furrow of anger across her brow before she goes outside, pushing aside the panting dogs.

Lisbet does not want to be alone with Sophey. She points at the grey water bucket. 'I'll change that.'

Without waiting for assent Lisbet lifts it as swift as her belly will allow, slopping a little on the floor. She tosses the dirty cloth back onto the scrubbed table and Sophey hisses but Lisbet doesn't break her stride, following her sister-in-law out into the delirious mid-afternoon sun.

There is no sign of Agnethe. The dogs are resting their

heads on their paws, and twitch their eyebrows at her. It is so hot Fluh barely gives true venom to her growl. Lisbet pours some of the water into the trough and Ulf heaves himself up and lopes over to drink, leaning a little against her thigh. She can smell the meaty stench of his fur, knows it will get worse without Henne here to comb it out. She will have to.

She lets him rest against her a moment longer, before crossing the yard and moving around the outhouse to the marked-off realm of the skeps. The bees are at work in the boiling air, legs fat with pollen the priests say they stole. But her bees are no thieves.

The bees. They are their own. It was the first lesson they taught her, even as she coaxed them to the skeps. They are not dumb beasts: they have their own mind even if it is the mind of the king bee. This is why they are spoken of so often in church, their obedience, their duty. Geiler himself preached that as the bee flies into the sky, they are the soul entering heaven. But Lisbet knows what only those who tend to them know. That wildness is the key to their success, that freedom sweetens their honey. That you cannot truly keep bees. You can only make them want to stay.

The pressing shed is windowless and hot, thick with honey scent. It has been added to over the years, expanded as the number of their skeps did. She fetches bowls specially made for the bees. They are shallow, flat-bottomed, hollowed unevenly to allow the water to sit in little pools. It was Lisbet who suggested this shape, to make it easier for the bees to land and drink without drowning. Henne never minded the losses, too few to make a difference to the hive, but Lisbet couldn't stand the tiny bodies upturned, the minute hooks of their feet exposed and their little souls stilled.

She pours the remaining wastewater into the bowls, then takes the nectar on the shelf, bound up in wax cloth so it will not stick. She breaks two combs off from the discard, leaves the mask on its hook. She doesn't bother with the gloves either, using her bare finger to stir the nectar into the water of one bowl, then the other. It is soft from the heat, and disperses easily in the water. The smell fixes to her nostrils.

She wipes her finger dry and, lifting the bowls, goes back outside to the gate that marks the skep yard boundary. A few bees straggle across her path, one landing on her wrist a moment before lifting away. The first bowl she places beside the gate, walks with the second to the other end. The skeps seem to shift and rustle, the hum inside barely a whisper.

She thinks of the baby inside her, its workings formed, small heart and lungs and a white, white soul, and as she places the second bowl, she feels a kick, deliberate and hard, against her spine. Tears start in her eyes and she gasps with the pain and relief of it. She straightens, her closed fist low on her back, and knocks gently in reply.

The yard is still empty, Agnethe vanished and Sophey inside, both dwelling on the dancer. Lisbet wants to scrub the sight clean from her eyes. She checks once more the door is closed, that Sophey does not watch her leave. Snapping her fingers for Ulf to stay behind, she enters the shadows.

Sophey does not know what she speaks of, when she says spectacle. She has never invited enough confidences to know about Lisbet's mother, how when Lisbet started her bloods, Mutti lost her mind. Only Mutti and Lisbet drew the line between these two events, and so now she alone must shoulder the knowledge that her mother's unmaking was tied to her becoming.

It began with the pits, Mutti digging great gouges from the ground with her hands, scrabbling in the fine stones that marred their land until her fingernails tore. When their father asked what she was doing, she said she was digging a grave. She would not say for who.

They kept it hidden as long as they could. But then she took to walking to market barefoot, arriving ragged and wide-eyed. An empiric was sought, and brought vinegar and witch hazel, poultices and blades. By turns he bled and salved and shaved her, until Lisbet came to believe no sickness could be worse than such cures.

Abandonments, Agnethe called them. It seemed less an abandon and more a staving in of her mother's reason, an assault on all she was. How those people in the square can stand and jeer, gawp and laugh at the sight of someone wrenched from their sense – the cruelty of it stops Lisbet's breath.

There were still good days with Mutti, and it is these Lisbet recalls as she walks to her dance tree. They were the days her father and brothers were out working, and Lisbet was left to cook or sweep. She would instead climb into her mother's bed and take her swollen feet into her lap, and rub them while Mutti told her about her sister, Petta, and her life before the farm. About the dance tree they called a doom tree, sitting in judgement in the centre of their village. About the river she would swim in, the thunderstorms so strong it made her hair stand on end. *And that was not easily done, those days*, Mutti'd say ruefully, rubbing the bristles on her head, survivors of the empiric's shears.

Lisbet reaches the brambles, pushes them carefully aside, and steps into the calm embrace of the clearing. Mutti would have loved it here. Her longing to find a dance tree one last time intensified in her final weeks until it was nearly all she spoke of. Most of all, she would tell Lisbet that to be a woman was a brutal, beautiful thing. Sometimes she would crush Lisbet hard to her chest when she said so, and those were the times Lisbet guessed the grave was for her, or Mutti, or maybe them both. That she wished to take her to the church of her childhood to absolve her of some sin not yet committed. That Mutti wanted to spare her the same sadness she clearly felt.

How many of you were daughters, Lisbet asks the ribbons, *how many sons?* She used to dream of girls, as many as Mutti had boys, that she could tell about her mother and so create a chain between them, woman to woman, and Mutti would not be lost. But she thinks that now an ignorant, indulgent thought: now she wants only for her child to have breath in its body.

And then, there is a sound. A sigh, a sob. She feels a charge pass through her, like the thunderstorms her mother spoke of. She looks up at the branches, but they are still, and silent.

'Mutti?' she asks the air. 'Mutti, are you there?'

The sound again, closer now. But it does not come from the air, or the tree, or the ribbons, or from her own fast-beating heart.

There, again. There, again. She waits. It minds her of the dancer in the city, the huff of air forced out as though from bellows, stoking the fire of her mania.

Fear, cold and griping, twists Lisbet's stomach as the bramble bushes part. A woman weeping like her heart were rent, dragging her bare hands through the thorns so as to draw blood. Lisbet knows already the shaved head, the broad shoulders.

Agnethe stops abruptly. Her face is pinched and pale, with two spots of colour high in her cheeks. Her eyes are swollen, her nose running, and Lisbet remembers Henne's description of a victim of a swarm: bloated and waxy-skinned, mottled.

'Lisbet.' Agnethe croaks her name. Seeming to come to herself, she snatches her hands away from the brambles, clamping them beneath her armpits. 'What—'

Her gaze drifts up, her tear-streaked cheeks shining.

Lisbet's heartbeat stoppers her throat. She knows what

Agnethe will see — a squat, broad linden, fluttering with dried leaves and torn scraps of fabric, the platform as haphazard as a ruin — and it is so different from what Lisbet sees it feels a betrayal. She wishes she could grow herself large and engulfing as a fog, hide the dance tree from sight. It is hers, and her babies', and she does not want to share, to explain.

Agnethe steps closer, head tilted back, eyes wide. The sight seems to have shocked her from her weeping. 'What is this?'

Lisbet cannot swallow her heart. It is too high, too loud, as it always feels here, so close to the memories of her could-have-been-children. But Agnethe seems not to require an answer. She approaches softly, picking up her feet like a child eluding the cracks in the floor that will gobble them to Hell. She reaches one of Lisbet's gifts, a pebble that sat pleasing in Lisbet's palm and that she wrapped with thread in a pattern like lace, and squats beside it.

'Don't—' starts Lisbet. She has a superstition, a horror of moving them once they are settled. But Agnethe makes no attempt to shift it. She only looks at it intently.

Lisbet can see the deep gouges on her hands, the blood bright against her pale skin. Agnethe rises so fast it makes Lisbet gasp, and her heart dislodges, her voice coming out clear. 'You're bleeding.'

'What is this place?'

Lisbet shifts, her feet aching. 'A tree.'

'I see that,' says Agnethe, a faint smile on her lips. Again, she is all Henne. 'The ribbons, the tokens. It is like some pagan shrine.'

Lisbet trembles, her knees softening so she must reach out again to the trunk to steady herself. 'It is no such thing.'

'I'm not accusing,' says Agnethe, holding out her bloodied palms. 'Only asking. What is it, Lisbet? Did you do all this?'

Lisbet chews her lip. She feels afraid, as she was taught to be afraid in childhood, of words like pagan, like wise, like woman, like witch. But Agnethe comes closer, and her face is open curiosity and hunger. 'It is beautiful. The ribbons. And that –' she points to the platform, 'did you do that?'

Lisbet nods at last, and allows herself a smile when Agnethe whistles admiringly. 'Why?'

The lump swells again, and Lisbet drops her gaze to her belly, hands coming reflexively to cup under it.

'A dozen,' says Agnethe softly. 'If I counted, there would be a dozen ribbons. It is your tree. For them.'

'And for myself,' says Lisbet. 'Somewhere safe.'

Agnethe nods. 'It's beautiful,' she says again. Her arms twitch, and she looks as though she will embrace Lisbet. Instead she comes to stand closer.

'Your hands,' says Lisbet.

Agnethe looks down distractedly. 'Oh.'

'You should wash them.'

Agnethe reaches out to Lisbet, and she resists pulling away. Her hand is swollen with its scars, slick with blood, and Lisbet can smell her damp, dank breath, like stale water, as though Agnethe has come drowned from the river to find her. 'Lisbet . . .'

Lisbet waits. Agnethe is about to tell her something, perhaps in exchange for her own confidences. She turns to look at her sister-in-law, but she is searching the ground, the tree, and will not return her gaze. Lisbet feels something slipping away, reaches out to grab it. 'You can tell—'

'Can I come here?'

'What?'

'To this place,' says Agnethe. 'When it all . . .' She gestures at her head, and Lisbet understands, the need for solitude, for quiet. 'I doubt church tomorrow will offer much escape.'

So she had noticed the looks, the whispers in the city. Lisbet is learning not to discount her sister-in-law — that even when she seems elsewhere, she is watchful. Even when she seems stone, she feels everything.

'I won't touch anything,' she hurries on, mistaking Lisbet's silence. 'But I understand, of course, if you want to keep it for yourself, for your . . .' She gestures at the ribbons.

Lisbet hesitates, but how can she deny this bleeding, wet-cheeked woman? 'Yes, Agnethe.'

Agnethe seems to wilt with relief. 'Nethe. It's what my friends used to call me. What Henne used to call me.'

There is a swarm of sadness there, packed close but containing immense, humming depths. *Nethe*. It suits her better, the precise, percussive hit of it.

Lisbet nods. 'Yes, Nethe. Come whenever you need.'

Six

Their church is a low affair, more wood and daub than stone, remnants of the old kinds of worship chiselled away at its edges so the whole place has an unfinished air. Pater Hansen, their priest, matches it well. He is old, and stooped, and has a worn grandeur to him, high cheekbones and silver eyes, his skin folded like melted wax. Some priests dress as though they were princes, but Pater Hansen wears the same vestments every year, patched and darned, the precious thread dulling, and this wins him respect among his congregation, and derision from those better-heeled.

Lisbet knows she should not judge a vessel of God by the scent of him, but she does. With a baby inside her she can smell everything to the point of exhaustion, and Pater Hansen is all beeswax, and incense oil, and old, old sweat. Humanity and divinity – as it should be, she supposes.

Ida is in the front pew, her daughter and sons beside her. The mere sight of her head neat in its scarf, the familiar frizz of flaxen hair about her temples and the curve of her cheek when she dips her head to her hands is a comfort to Lisbet, who could barely sleep last night for dreams of her mother, for waking fret over the bees and their fate.

But for the first time, Lisbet feels she has an ally at the farm. Other than Ida and the bees, she has been without company the six years she's shared Henne's home, but after their visit to town, their happening across each other at the dance tree, she and Nethe seem to be drawing closer together.

And Nethe needs a friend even more than Lisbet. The tension between Ida and Agnethe is clear, and her appearance at church caused something as close to a ruckus as the over-heated congregation could muster. From Lisbet's accomplished eavesdropping, no one seems to know the charges that sent Nethe to the abbey, only the fact of her sin and subsequent penance. Herr Furmann, the main benefactor of the church and with the ear of the Twenty-One themselves, approached Nethe before the service, all scented silk and waving wrists, but Nethe sidestepped him, edging closer to Lisbet, who used her bulk to shield her from further advances.

She understands their curiosity – there is little to talk on other than the weather, the certain descent of Strasbourg into a deeper circle of Hell. Even the war against the Turks has lost its sheen, made dull by constant attrition. Pater Hansen's final remarks do not help Agnethe's plight, for they take on a wholly different bent from his usual guttering out.

'A word on the occurrences in the market square,' he says, dragging his eyes from the pulpit to affix somewhere above and to the left of their heads. Lisbet is slow to understand what he is referring to, but Sophey goes rigid, her jaw set. 'I know there has been some talk on the woman dancing. I wish to reassure you that it is an instance of womanly weakness only. We know they do occur—'

His eyes drift cloudily over Agnethe, who looks deter-minedly back.

'– and the Twenty-One are keen to settle the facts of it.'

At this, Plater stands as though Hansen had called him by

name. The priest blinks, his mouth open to continue, but Plater turns his back on the pulpit and takes up the priest's thread without a moment's deference.

'The matter is already at an end,' says Plater, 'but it is true the council is against superstitious talk spreading. A woman took up dancing about a week ago, in a conspicuous spot beside the cathedral. She remained there every day and most nights, stopping only to fall into a sleep of sorts, whereupon she was taken home. But she returned each day, and following careful observation our syndic Sebastian Brant and the Twenty-One decided she must be taken to Drefelhausen.'

'To the shrine?' says Herr Furmann, the only man in the church who outranks Plater in influence.

'To the shrine of St Vitus, yes,' says Plater, clearly irritated to be interrupted.

'So she honours the saint? It was a holy mania?'

Nethe said in the abbey such judgements between holy mania or demonic possession rested on whether someone was liked or not. Lisbet eyes her, wondering what effect such a pronouncement will have on her. But Nethe has turned to stone again.

'The Twenty-One believe it to be so,' says Plater. 'She must seek to avail herself of some sin, though why she chose such a hysterical fashion speaks to her character. She will be washed in the saint's shrine, and that will be the end of it.'

Plater sits, and Pater Hansen is left to dither his way through a dismissal, before descending from the pulpit and being immediately accosted by Herr Furmann.

'That's that,' says Sophey, satisfied. 'Come then.'

But neither Lisbet nor Nethe move. Herr Furmann has drawn Plater into his discussion with the priest. Lisbet suspects Nethe too is hoping to catch some of what the men are saying, but they are obscured by bodies leaving the church. Ida rises from between her daughter and husband, and starts to make her way to them. Nethe stands suddenly and follows her mother from the church without a backwards glance.

Ida reaches Lisbet, and helps her to her feet. 'Herr Furmann seems disturbed.'

'The dancer was disturbing.'

Ida looks at her sharply. 'You saw her? Was it as they said, then?'

'It was,' sighs Lisbet, shifting to relieve her back a little. 'But it is at an end now.'

'Are you sure you are well, Bet?' asks Ida. 'I can go alone to the almshouses.'

'Well enough,' says Lisbet, not careful enough to hide her irritation. 'Please don't talk to me like Henne.'

Ida smiles. 'I would never presume to.'

'You know,' laughs Lisbet, as they start down the steps to Ida's cart and horse. There is no sign of Sophey and Nethe, already hurrying home. 'Like I am ailing.'

'I can see you are not,' says Ida, readjusting the baskets in the bed of the cart, full of fresh-baked bread, some beets and mushrooms, cool clay pitchers half topped with milk Lisbet can smell is already on the turn in the heat. Slender givings, even by the Twenty-One's standards. Lisbet has long suspected Plater pockets most of the alms allowance he is given by the council to pass on to his wife.

'But you are so large. It is good –' she catches at Lisbet's hand again, 'a good thing. But I know it is heavy.'

The road to the city is busy with pilgrims and churchgoers, toing and froing from Notre Dame, and hawkers selling them cheap tallow candles and oat cakes. It was not always so, she remembers. The Holy Day used to be observed tightly, the whole city caught in amber and prayers, but the rot Geiler preached of spread fast. Now there are tales of monks running gambling dens, priests frequenting taverns. If they cannot trust the clergy to sanctify it, how can the rest of them, with farms to run and mouths to feed, be expected to?

Ida leans into her gently. 'You are quiet today.'

'Thinking,' murmurs Lisbet.

'Careful,' says Ida teasingly. 'You'll have a frown line deep as Pater Hansen's.'

Lisbet tries to summon a laugh and cannot. She feels very heavy, as Ida said, and a little sad.

'Come, Bet,' says Ida. 'What's wrong?'

Lisbet knows Ida will not cease her questioning. She has a mother's intuition, is used to coaxing troubles from sullen children. Lisbet sighs, and shrugs. 'You are missing Henne?'

'No,' says Lisbet, so quickly it shames her. Ida arches her brow, steering the horse through the narrowing streets that skirt the city.

'The bees are well?'

Lisbet does smile at that. Ida understands better than any her obsession. 'Yes. For now. If our petition does not succeed—'

'It will. What then?' Ida shoots her another sharp look. 'Do not keep the secret, it'll age you faster than a sin.'

'It's Nethe,' says Lisbet, and feels Ida draw away slightly.

'You call her Nethe now?'

'This is why I did not wish to say.'

'What do you mean?' says Ida, and though her voice is light there is a sting in it, a bee's hook left in honeycomb. 'What about her? Is she well?'

Lisbet hesitates. 'The day we saw the dancer. I found her wandering in the woods. She was distressed.'

'By the dancer?'

'No. Something Sophey said.'

She looks at her friend. Ida's profile is beautiful, Lisbet has always thought so, though Ida thinks her nose too big, her chin too soft. She wonders whether to share the whole truth. But how to explain about the dance tree here? It feels a blasphemy.

'It must have been strange in the mountains. She was never going to come back the same.'

'I suppose not,' says Lisbet, but Ida seems distracted.

'Here we are.'

Their arrival at the slums usually warrants a flurry of activity, of grasping hands and gratefulness that Lisbet cringes against. But as they stop outside Herr Lehmann's house, they see the door tied closed with rope. Ida frowns and jumps lightly down from the cart, peering through the rotted wood.

'No one?' asks Lisbet.

Ida goes to the next hovel, and the next, but though there are hawkers milling about the cart, there is no sign of their usual greeters. Ida goes back to Herr Lehmann's door and knocks. Lisbet climbs down and looks through the collapsing shutters.

'Hello?' A thin voice works its way through the door, and Lisbet recognises their eldest girl.

'Hilde?' says Ida. 'We're here with bread, and milk.'

'I can't open the door from this side.'

Lisbet tugs on the knot.

'No,' says Hilde, hearing what she is doing. 'They said to leave it closed.'

'Where are your parents?' asks Lisbet.

'The city,' says Daniel, coming to join his sister. 'Gone to see the dancers.'

'The dancer is gone,' says Ida. 'Taken to the shrine.'

'All of them?' asks Hilde, and her little brother Gunne says something inaudible and excited.

'There is only one,' says Ida. 'Lisbet saw her.'

'No,' says Hilde, her mouth pressed so close to the door

Lisbet can see her gapped mouth, smell her rancid breath. 'There are more.'

'Hundreds!' says Gunne, knocking his sister aside and hooking his chin through the gap.

'Not hundreds,' laughs Ida, pressing her thumb sweetly to his chin.

'Not far off,' says Daniel. 'Mutter and Pater have gone to look.'

'Can we go?' says Gunne. 'Can you take us?'

Ida clucks her tongue. 'There's no sense in seeing that. Just some women dancing. What shall I do with the basket?'

When they have passed through the Lehmanns' rations and turned their backs on the hovel, Ida looks at Lisbet slyly. 'I suppose we could go.'

Lisbet snorts. 'What happened to "just some women dancing"?'

'We might want to join in.'

'That's not funny,' says Lisbet. 'You didn't see her. If they're like the first was—'

She swallows her sentence. She doesn't have the words, doesn't want to voice it, nor the familiarity she felt, the recognition bred from years by her mother's bedside. 'It's hardly a dance. It's ugly, Ida.'

'But it's something happening,' says Ida, sounding petulant as a child. 'Please, all I have at home is my father.'

'And your boys, your girl.'

'Joys, always,' says Ida dryly. 'We can have time together this way. And it's my cart, so you have to come.'

It is impossible to dissuade her, and it is easier for Lisbet to sit in the cart than to stand her ground. Soon they are over the familiar bridge, and into the market square. It is full of the emptied congregation of Notre Dame, of street preachers and beggars. They distribute the last of the food within moments, but when they look about for the promised hundreds caught in mania, there is no sign.

'See,' says Lisbet, relieved. 'Rumours. Can we go?' It is hotter here with the press of people, Lisbet thinks she could stir the air like stew. But Ida pays a man to watch the cart, and asks him where the dancers are.

'There.' He points in the direction of the horse market. 'There's a stage, now. Another at the tanners' guild.'

'A stage?' Ida's voice is bright with excitement, and Lisbet feels her throat tighten. 'They've closed the guilds?'

The man nods. 'Nowhere else to put them. The physicians say the only thing is to leave them to it.'

Ida spins to Lisbet and takes hold of her hand. 'For them to cease trading in the guilds – this is grave, Lisbet!'

Her voice however is not, and her grip is too tight. Lisbet tries to prise her fingers free, but Ida is pulling her towards the horse market, and Lisbet must be intent upon her feet, avoiding the worst of the muck.

She likes the horse market. It has a green scent, like the fields at her father's farm, and the snickering horses have kind eyes and smell of hay and home. But as they reach the bounds, the smell is all human. Sweat and dank breath, and Lisbet hears jeering, and beneath it, drumming.

'Ida—' She pulls free as the crush starts to tighten, and Ida is snatched away by the current of the crowd.

Lisbet is carried along too. Without her friend's hand, she feels unmoored, and it is all she can do to stay upright, her belly wrapped in her arms, the smell and the heat and the sound unbearable. And then she is borne through the bottleneck of the gate and the stage is before her, and it is worse than she could have imagined if she had allowed herself to imagine it at all.

There are not hundreds, maybe three dozen, but it is impossible to count them precisely, moving as they do without rhythm or pattern, held to the stage by hands that bat and slap them from the edges of the platform. The stage stands at head height, so the dancers seem to float over the crowd, demonic angels swooping and spinning. They are all women, all loose-haired and wide-eyed, all wheeling and skipping. Their clogs lie abandoned, strewn across the stage, feet already bloody, sending speckles flying like mist over the new-laid planks, which still hold the smell of the forest.

Lisbet sways, nearly falls, but in this crowd it would be fatal. She forces herself to plant her feet, juts out her elbows to protect her belly. Mixed throughout the dancers are men, broad and bearded, and clearly not possessed by whatever music has seized the women. Lisbet watches as one snatches a woman about the waist and swings her around in a wild circle, knocking another dancer to the floor. The fallen woman leaps up immediately, limping slightly as she hops.

'Leave her. Please God, leave her,' says Lisbet to herself, an incantation spoken loud enough for a woman beside her to take notice.

'They are the council's men,' she says, without taking her eyes off the dancers. 'Ordered to keep them dancing.'

'They think that is the cure?' says Lisbet. Her vision is blurring, catching on the women's feet and hair, dragging like a fish on a hook.

The woman shrugs. 'Musicians are coming soon. They hope to play the mania out of them.'

'Surely music will only make them dance harder.'

Lisbet loses her footing again as more people push through the gate and propel her towards the stage. She feels caught in a net, moving as though in a nightmare towards the stage with its devilish load. Her foot sinks into horseshit, she feels the grain of it seep into her clogs and the smell of it made fresh again. Hands are upstretched to the stage, grasping the dancers' feet, snatching for tokens of cloth and hair, as though they are living saints. Lisbet clings to her belly like a raft as she is brought to the stage.

This close, they are suddenly less frightening, their faces transported. They make no sound but heavy breath, their eyes skimming the crowd like stones, skipping the jeering faces, lifted to somewhere else. A woman of Sophey's age with a curve to her back looms over Lisbet and bends like a girl, her arms thrown out, head tipped back in ecstasy, a gold chain encircling her wrist. Her bare feet lift and stamp: she smiles, showing pink gums. She is heedless of the crowd baying and jeering, is only her body and its limits, entirely of her flesh and outside it.

Lisbet imagines letting her mind drift, her body move in a way it hasn't since she was a child in the fields, running with her brothers. Her skin smooth and unblemished, her heart unscarred. One of the men catches the old woman's wrist and jerks her left and right, her head cracking on its stalk, and a grimace crosses her wrinkled face. Her eyes scrunch as she is whirled away, the man braying as he swings her.

Something in Lisbet snaps like a trap. She bares her teeth and pushes back through the crowd, through the gate, away from the women and the men and the stage, away as far and as fast as she can until a stitch tugs at her side and she must stop, panting. She heels her palms into her eyes, hard enough to make sparks skid across her lids. A hand grasps her shoulder and for a moment she thinks it is one of the hired men hearing her thoughts and ready to force her onto the stage. She cries out and pushes away, and Ida's voice exclaims her name.

'Sorry,' says Lisbet, catching her friend's arm. 'I thought—'

'No,' says Ida, and her face seems shadowed. 'I don't blame you.'

She looks back at the stage, at the women whirling upon it, and shudders. 'They look so . . . extraordinary. Filled with light, or feathers. Don't you think? Radiant . . .' Ida lifts her face to the sun, beatific. Her gold hair slips its scarf, and shines a halo about her pale face. She looks almost ecstatic, and it terrifies Lisbet, who snatches the scarf before it slides to the ground, and flings it at her friend.

'I'm going.'

'So soon?'

'The bees,' she answers tightly. 'You know they are constant work, and with Henne gone . . .'

She starts to stride away, her heart beating hard, ears ringing. Madness, mania, abandon – all this she can just about hold, just about tolerate. But the rapture she'd seen on Ida's face nauseates her, not least because she'd almost allowed herself to feel it too, watching the old woman dance like a girl. It is not a game, to lose your mind. Lisbet hasn't told Ida about Mutti, beyond that she is dead, and now Lisbet is doubly glad of it. She would hate Ida for her reaction to the dancers if she had.

Ida catches her easily, falls into step beside her and Lisbet wishes she were not so large, so lumpen, wishes she could leave it all like the woman on the stage, lifted out of the stink and sound.

'Slow,' says Ida softly. 'Careful, Bet.'

Lisbet wants to cry. It is too hot, and she is done. Even with Ida beside her, she feels entirely alone. 'I'll walk.'

'Of course you won't,' says Ida, slipping her arm through Lisbet's. But as they move against the crowd, away from the beating heels and spinning women, Lisbet sees her friend look back often, until the dancers are out of sight.

•

'More,' Lisbet tells them the instant she comes through the door. Sophey is at the fire, stirring stew and looking weary, older even than she had when they left for church that morning. 'There are more of them. Dozens. All women.'

Sophey raises her arm impatiently, cutting off Nethe's words at the inhale. 'You saw them?'

Lisbet nods, dipping her hands into the bucket and running the rag over her neck. 'Ida and me both. The entire horse market is given over. The guilds too.'

'Ida saw them?' asks Nethe.

'Yes, and she was horrified,' lies Lisbet. 'Of course.' She shudders at the memory, the crowds, the men grabbing and spinning the women. Ida's shining face.

'Don't you go strange,' snaps Sophey. 'I've enough foolishness from this one.'

'But it means something, now,' says Nethe with the tone of a dropped conversation taken up again. 'Now there are more dancers. I said more would follow, and see? They are.'

'The Twenty-One are bringing in musicians,' says Lisbet despite Sophey's warning glance. She knows her mother-in-law wants her silent, but she needs to speak it. 'To play out the devils.'

'They are daft with heat is all,' says Sophey, crossing herself. Nethe and Lisbet follow. 'And thirst and more dancing will not cure it. Geiler would agree. I will have no more talk on it.'

She sets down her cup, sitting with difficulty, her coarse fingers out in front of her. They are curled as though about a churn, and from the strain in the ropes of her knuckles Lisbet knows she is trying to straighten them. 'Such mania means prayers, and prayers mean candles. We have work to do.'

Forty-seven dancing

In Frau Clementz's thirty-second year, there came a fervour for angels. Men, her husband and eldest son among them, heard angels whispering in the rotten crops, and plucked up scythes and marched to the Church's stores, demanding grain. They saw angels in the whorls of the huge wooden doors, and broke them down. They felt angels in their throats, and her son Arnd swore he saw an angel running gold beneath his papa's skin.

Most of them were killed of course, angels slipping from their cut-down bodies and dispersing in the air like smoke. Frau Clementz herself saw it when they hanged her husband, the gold threads Arnd spoke of severing and the last essence of the angels flying from him. He pissed himself and she hoped the angels would not see this, his final human failing.

Arnd was angry, after. She could not reach him in his anger, his rage. When the next Bundschuh came, he was first out of the door though she threw herself around his waist, threatened harm on herself, his brothers, anything to keep from having to watch another man she loved hang before a screeching crowd. Still he went, and again he returned free and unharmed, their rebellion beaten. And angry, so angry he was like a hot coal in her house. He brought her a gold bracelet, a thing so fine it was as though it was woven, and bound it still warm around her wrist. He said he took it from a priest. He said it reminded him of the angels beneath Papa's skin.

The third time, a man named Joss Fritz came to their church, and the priest himself let him speak. He was a thin man, with a quiet voice, and yet there was power to him. Arnd thought him the second coming though that itself was blasphemy. This time Frau Clementz did not even try to stop his going.

Now Arnd is hanged, and her other sons are married, her back is curved as a question and the angels have returned to her. She sees them in the shadows of her empty house, in the dusty jars that once held preserves, in the well long dried up. She sees them in the guilds, in the market. They do not come near her, of course. No one does.

She wears the bracelet though this summer as she walks after the shadows, all the way to the guild, and sees angels scattering among dancing women. She sees them threaded in the hair of one, wrapped around the jaundiced limbs of another.

She closes her eyes, and hears them humming to her. She listens as a man with big, rough hands like her husband's spins her. She feels the bracelet break, and she does not much mind. Because when Frau Clementz holds her arms up to the sun, she sees angels glint gold beneath her skin.

Seven

Lisbet feeds Ulf and Fluh, and pours the last of the stagnant water in the bucket over their backs. They are steaming, tongues obscenely pink through their yellowed teeth, and she smooths Ulf's haunches, works free burrs, the dog standing still for her as she cracks fleas between her fingernails.

The bees are out and wafting on the air. She does not mind the work ahead – welcomes it in fact. She collects rosemary, places it into the smoking tray, hooks the bucket onto her elbow and, pulling her collar up her neck, goes to the first skep.

The bees rise from their places, like the flies clogging the forest shadows, and she places her hand lightly upon the top of the first hive. A couple settle, lift, settle, spreading the soft breeze of their wings over her skin, whispering across her fingers.

They'd terrified her those early days. When Lisbet first came to her new home, she thought the skep yard looked like a graveyard, the skeps headstones. But during her third pregnancy, perhaps recognising her sadness, her need, Henne took her to the yard early, dressed her in the thick cotton robe and wicker mask he never bothered with. It was cooler that summer, but still she could barely breathe, barely see.

'I will show you one, and then you do the same, so they know we are family.'

She rolled her eyes at the thought the bees would know such a thing, but she was under the mask. He went to the closest skep, and lifted the light wicker cone. A small, fast shape whipped across her line of sight, carved into pieces by the wicker. Underneath was the hive, a square block of hollowed-out wood, and more bees spiralled out from the slats in the front.

'Don't worry,' said Henne, his voice a hum low as the bees, 'just breathe.'

She wanted to say it is hard in the mask, beneath the sun, but instead she did as he told her.

'From here,' he said, and touched her just beneath her breasts, where her belly was just starting to swell. His hand was hot and close and large. She felt she would disintegrate beneath it, like honey in water.

As he unlatched the clasps, bees came to settle on his hands, but he kept his actions slow, in time with the tide of his breath. She watched for signs of swarming, but it was as he said: they didn't mind him at all. He lifted out the comb, dripping with honey and precious wax.

'It is not yet full,' he said. 'But in a few days it will be. Then you'll need to brush off any bees, like this—' He ran a finger flush along the comb, the dislodged bees landing on his bare fingers and taking off again, landing and at last returning to the hive. 'And then you take the combs inside.'

Henne replaced the comb, the wooden section he'd removed. He did up the clasps and lifted the wickerwork back over the hive.

'Your turn. Slow.'

Henne caught her about the waist. She felt him breathing against her nape, his heartbeat between her shoulder-blades, and joined her breath with his. She would do it perfectly, she decided, she would give him cause to be proud.

She lifted the cone, then moved slowly to the back of the hive, flexing her hands in their too-large gloves. Even through the truncation of the wicker the bees showed gold and black and solid. She flicked open the fingernail-sized clasps, biting down on her lip to remind herself to be slow, to not fumble and drop the wooden segment that peeled off into her hands.

The motion brought her down level with the inner workings of the hive. It looked like a diseased body, the malignant clumps of black bees like tortured growths, the sweet reek of honey and wax filling her nostrils. Several bees alighted on the wicker, and she imagined them plunging their stingers into her eyelids, leaving them puckered as the man Henne once told her about.

A dark shape washed over her face, and it took her a moment to realise it was Henne's hand, brushing aside the gathering bees.

'They like your pulse, schatzi. We'll make a beekeeper of you yet.'

He was right. Now it is easy as breath, easier than holding her husband. She may not be a good wife, a good daughter, a mother to living children, but this she has. The bees dance about her hands, their buzzing louder than her heart.

She wipes them gently from her skin and lifts the skep slowly, turning it so the combs are revealed, black with bees. She washes the rosemary smoke over them like a priest in church, and the bees fly from the combs as prayers to Heaven.

Waving away a few stragglers, she draws out the golden tablet, amazed as always by its easiness, the way it snaps in her hands and, loosened by the heat, throws up its thick scent. Henne says it is proof they do God's work, that the bees give to them so freely, that it is hardly toil at all to keep them, but Lisbet likes to think they would not yield so lightly for just anyone.

She inhales deeply as she places the first comb into her bucket, humming softly as the bees circle and settle and fly away again. She breaks a second and a third, lifting any caught bees from the bucket and letting them return to the hive. She leaves the rest of the combs so they can begin their work again, and moves to the next skep.

When she leaves the yard, all is as she found it, and she still hums to herself, to the baby, as she walks to the press housed in its rough shed. It is not so fine as the machines they have at the monastery, where counterweights lift and drop the thick slabs of oak, but she can manage. She arranges the trough below the press, checks the fine mesh is beneath the lowermost slab, and lays the tablets of comb onto the wood.

Bracing her elbow against the shelf Henne put up for this purpose, she hoists the other slab on top, and tightens the clamp so the wax cracks and squeezes. She breaks off a corner and wraps it in wax paper. The baby pushes out a shoulder or a foot, and she cups it. She could be here half a decade ago now, when all this was new to her and their third child was inside her. Years folded close as cloth.

The honey drips, and then pours, chasing the channels of the mesh, and she waits a while, counting heartbeats, until it settles to a steady stream. She tightens the clamp once more, picks up the smoking rosemary, and regretfully, without letting herself look back, goes outside.

'Frau Wiler?' The voice is all too familiar to Lisbet, and sets a rocking motion in her stomach, sickening as a rotten tooth.

'Herr Plater.'

'At work still I see,' says Plater, smoothing his jerkin. 'Henne's journey progresses apace?'

'So soon you come to visit us again. Can I help you?'

She does not invite him in. Let him stand in the sun. Already he is sweating: it streams down his cheeks and into his collar. His face is oddly hairless. His breath is sweet with clove and mint. He smiles wider, and Lisbet resists the urge to shove him, to kick him, to do violence to this man who threatens all they have.

'Straight to business, like your husband.'

She waits.

'He'll have missed the dancers,' he says. 'You've seen them?'

She gives him a tight nod.

'My wife said so. The Twenty-One want it quickly resolved. They called an emergency council, and both physicians and clergy are in agreement for the cure. They have ordered High Mass and emptied the city of hures and vagrants, built stages, ordered strong men to dance with the afflicted.'

'Yes,' says Lisbet, disapproval weighting her voice. 'They are rough with them.'

'They need to tire them,' says Plater. 'They are bringing musicians too.'

'All this I know,' says Lisbet.

'You have not let me reach my point.' He pauses, as though daring Lisbet to speak again. When he is satisfied she will not, he continues. 'You will accommodate the Church's musicians. One, perhaps two.' He holds up a hand to stifle her words before they can leave her mouth. 'You are not unique in this. All those with debts hereabouts must give up their spare space.'

'We have none.'

'Of course you do, with your husband away.' He crosses his arms, tilts his head appraisingly. 'Surely you will be glad of the company, three women alone and no man to protect them.'

'We need no protection.'

Plater clucks his tongue as though admonishing a dog. 'Come, Frau Wiler, you know these are dangerous times. The city emptied of sinners, where will they go?' He glances past the skeps, at the forest, and Lisbet cannot help but follow his gaze. The trees melt to black. 'It will help with your standing before the Church, the council.'

'We need no help,' snaps Lisbet. 'We are churchgoers, almsgivers.'

'But your bees feed from the monastery's wildflowers, and yet you will not pay your portion of profit to them.'

Lisbet's insides churn and fret. 'That is a matter for the court at Heidelberg.'

'Do not forget,' says Plater, 'under whose Heaven those courts run. The musicians will be here tomorrow.'

'Have we no choice?'

Plater is already walking towards his horse, his rough hands in his silk pockets. Fluh whimpers and leaps from his path.

Lisbet braces herself, and returns indoors. Sophey is at the table, her head in her gnarled hands.

'This heat,' she murmurs. 'When will it end?'

Lisbet waits until Sophey smooths back her hair, wipes the sweat from her temples. Her mother-in-law fixes her with her black eyes, the hollows beneath them large as knuckles.

'Plater was here.'

'Now?' Sophey rises, her knees clicking, murder in her eyes.

'He's gone,' says Lisbet. 'But he brought a message.'

'More from Heidelberg?'

'From the city, from the Twenty-One and the Church.'

'One and the same,' grunts Sophey. She is of the view that the clergy are too much concerned with the council. That there must be more separation in order for priests to be pure. 'What more do they want with us?'

Lisbet explains about their plans, about the exodus from the city, the stages and the musicians. Sophey winces.

'You should have called me.'

'He would not be dissuaded.'

'We'll see,' she says. 'I'll to the city now. Have you wax ready?'

'In the pressing shed. Where is Nethe?'

'Agnethe is praying, not to be disturbed.'

When Sophey is gone, Lisbet takes the wrapped edge of honeycomb from her pocket and knocks on Nethe's door.

'Nethe?'

She presses her ear to the wood, can hear murmurs.

'I brought you something.'

Nethe's prayer continues unabated.

'Do you wish to walk with me? We could go to the tree.' Lisbet sets the honeycomb down beside the door.

Curiosity is so sour in her throat she could gag on it. Even after she has walked to the dance tree and back, still it sits there: the curiosity and the honeycomb, both.

For the next few days, Nethe's piousness persists, and Lisbet does not see her, nor hear her except at night, when by pressing her ear to the wood of her door, she can hear the whisper and urgency of Nethe's voice, praying.

·

Ida moves against the tide of churchgoers, a furrow between her eyebrows. Plater is not at church, kept away from home with the commotion in the city, and Ida looks well on it, better rested. Lisbet opens her mouth to greet her, but Ida speaks not to her, but to her sister-in-law.

'Are you well?' Ida steps closer to Nethe and Nethe steps

97

back, as though it is a dance between them. Nethe had emerged from her room only that morning, hollow-cheeked and stinking, and washed in the trough they kept for the dogs. It is as though the stone Lisbet felt she'd chipped away at over the past week has recalcified and made Nethe back into Agnethe the penitent, the stranger.

'I am,' says Nethe, Henne's jut to her jaw. The tension thrums in Lisbet's ears. Ida's hand makes a movement, so small and impulsive Lisbet might have blinked and missed it.

Nethe turns and strides to the door, and to Lisbet's surprise Ida hurries after her. Lisbet raises an eyebrow at Sophey, but her mother-in-law is already following. Lisbet stands a moment as though caught in a net. Her head is all confusion at Ida's pursuit. She pushes herself heavily after them, out into the searing light.

Whatever the women were saying, Sophey has stopped it. She stands between them, planted as a fence. There are spots of colour high in Nethe's pale cheeks, and Ida is agitatedly plucking at an imaginary loose thread in her impeccable sleeve.

'Foolish,' Sophey spits. 'God damns you both.'

'You think I do not know that?' says Nethe, furious brightness in her eyes. She is breathing as though she has run a race. 'What do you think I have prayed for the past week?'

'What has happened?' says Lisbet, looking at Ida.

'Go now to your almsgiving, if you please, Frau Plater,' says Sophey, with her practised blend of venom and politeness.

'I—'

'Now.'

Ida obeys, meek as a daughter, making for the cart. Lisbet starts after her friend, but someone taps her firmly on the shoulder. 'Wiler, yes?'

'Yes,' says Lisbet confusedly, turning to see Herr Furmann looking at her with detached interest.

'You are in charge of the alms, with Frau Plater?'

'Yes she is,' says Sophey, with her usual mix of deference and defiance in the presence of the wealthy. 'Can we help, Herr Furmann?'

'I have several flagons of beer to offer.' He gestures at his horse and covered cart with iron spokes and polished leather seats. 'Times like these, any extra service is a pleasure.'

'Very kind,' says Sophey, though she knows well as Lisbet that men like this see generosity as down-payment against favour here or else in Heaven. 'We will move them to Frau Plater's cart now.'

'You'll never manage,' he scoffs. 'What about you?'

Nethe stands behind them, unavoidably strong-looking despite her week's self-imposed fast.

'Yes,' she says. 'Of course.'

She follows him, transfers the heavy clay pots from cart to cart as he watches and shouts occasional advice. When she is finished and Lisbet goes to swing herself up onto the cart beside Ida, Herr Furmann tuts. 'No, no, I want those pots returned. You will have to pour them into different vessels, whatever they have available. Can you manage that? Or you?' He glances between pregnant Lisbet and slender Ida, and then looks to Nethe again. 'You must go.'

All of the woman flinch, as though he's produced a whip.

'That is impossible, Herr Furmann,' says Sophey. 'Agnethe is needed at the farm.'

'It will be the work of a moment, a woman that size.' He waves aside her concern. 'And with such madness in the air, I would think you'd want to keep that one safe?' He points at Lisbet's belly, and Lisbet's mind clouds with shame, with anger. 'There are sixteen flagons in all. Do count them out and back in, won't you?'

If it were anyone else, Sophey would stand her ground. But instead she is forced to chew her tongue as Nethe, looking as though she goes to her death, climbs up beside Ida. Ida is straight-backed, staring ahead.

Herr Furmann swings himself up heavily onto his fine stallion. 'Be sure to tell your husband who made this donation, won't you, Frau Plater?' Ida jerks her head tautly, flicks the reins.

Sophey holds herself long enough for Herr Furmann to ride from the churchyard, and then presses her fists to her eyes.

'Imbecile!' she rages, and Lisbet doesn't know if it is aimed at her, Herr Furmann, or Sophey herself. Before Lisbet can respond her mother-in-law begins hurrying along the path home.

Lisbet doesn't even try to catch her. The exchange has set her body pitching, and instead she cuts through the forest. On her way to the dance tree she must cross the river. The heat has shrunk it to a stream, and it is warm enough to be uncomfortable as she wades across, the smell brackish as Nethe's breath. The skin at her wrist is blue with her blood, the channels swollen.

She steps clear of the water, trying to untangle what she has just witnessed.

She knows they were childhood friends: Henne and Nethe Wiler, Ida Metz, Alef Plater. But those ties were broken before Lisbet arrived. She sometimes wonders if a match would have been made between Henne and Ida, leaving Alef for Nethe had she not sinned and been sent away. The neatness of it punctured by Nethe's departure and, as all things were, by Lisbet's own arrival. Stepping into Nethe's space, into her shadow.

But what Lisbet saw outside the church was not the traces of friendship, but enmity, at least on Nethe's part. What cause would she have to hate Ida – what cause would anyone have?

It reminds Lisbet that before her arrival is an expanse of blankness that feels now like a conspiracy: a deliberate attempt to obfuscate, to keep her ignorant.

She searches the bank, letting her mind drift to this small task, loosing her confusion for the moment. She selects a pebble for its smoothness, its thin band of quartz, and walks through the murmuring forest to the dance tree. When she enters the clearing she sniffs the air like a dog, checking for intruders. But the tokens are there, the ribbons still tied, the platform bare.

Lisbet lays the pebble at the base of the trunk. It is warm from her hand, and she closes her eyes a moment, gives it the pulse of her blood before she lets go.

•

Sophey allows her absence to go unremarked, gesturing for her to pass the bucket of honey Lisbet has wrested from the trough. Her expression makes it clear she welcomes no discussion, and she flinches at every sound from outside, anxious for Agnethe's return. They spend the afternoon sweeping out Henne and Lisbet's room, opening the shutters wide in the hope the air might stir to some degree of freshness.

For all Sophey's complaints, she will not give anyone reason to call her an ungenerous host. She bakes a loaf with the last of Mathias' fine flour, mixes fresh honey into the dough. She tells Lisbet to keep two beeswax candles back from the order, and stores the tallow ones on a high shelf, out of sight.

It is dusk, and Lisbet is setting out water for the bees when she hears voices, Nethe and Ida returned from almsgiving. She starts towards the road, but the voices are angry, raised as hackles. Lisbet draws back into the shadow of the skeps, and sees Ida's horse halt at their boundary, Nethe stepping from the high cart, her face blotched red, and Ida tripping after, tears falling freely down her pale face.

'Agnethe, I swear by all my sons—'

'Don't speak to me of your sons,' spits Agnethe. 'Or of anything you have.'

'Please,' says Ida. 'I had no choice. Believe me.'

'There was a choice. Don't think your marriage saves you. There is no remedy for it.'

'Then so be it,' says Ida. 'Let me at least make amends with you.'

She grasps Nethe's hand then, and Nethe flinches but does not draw away. Even in the low light, Lisbet fancies she can see Nethe's indecision.

'Agnethe!' Sophey's voice is a vice, the door banging open before her.

Nethe pulls her hand from Ida's and walks quickly across the yard and past her mother, who slams the door behind them. Ida stands bewildered, her hands open. Lisbet steps from the skeps, opens the gate.

'Ida—'

Her friend jumps, bringing her hand to her mouth. 'Hiding, Lisbet?'

'Is all well?'

Ida laughs hollowly. Lisbet comes close so she can see her in the low burn of the last light, reaches out to thumb the tears from her friend's cheeks. Ida moves clear and presses the heels of her hands to her temples as though she would crush her own skull. 'It is too hot.'

Lisbet is unmoored by Ida's spikiness. 'What happened?'

Ida's shoulders slump. 'It is too much.'

Lisbet bites her cheek. 'You will not tell me?'

'I cannot,' says Ida simply. Lisbet waits hopefully, but when Ida speaks her voice is clearer, more direct. 'They are an army, now. It seems every woman in Strasbourg dances. The musicians will have to play all hours.'

'You think it will work?' says Lisbet.

'There will be an end, one way or another.' Ida looks full at her then, her eyes the shade of violets growing. 'Am I good, Bet?'

Lisbet grasps her. 'You are the best woman I know. What did Nethe say to you?'

Ida's hand goes slack in hers. She draws away, back to the cart. 'Good luck with your musicians, Lisbet.'

Eight

There are two of them. One is tall and blond and pale, a stalk of wheat. The other is short and broad and dark. A Turk. He speaks for them both.

'I am Eren,' he rests a slim hand on his tunic, 'and this is Frederich.' He has a soft voice, slightly inflected.

Sophey nods tightly, at a point to the left of him, and Lisbet wonders if she has ever been so close to a Turk before.

'Frau Wiler.' She indicates Lisbet. 'Frau Wiler.' She points to Nethe. 'Fräulein Wiler.'

Eren nods a greeting, and Frederich sweeps a low bow.

'We thank you for your hospitality.' Frederich looks as though he is holding back a laugh. 'It is good to have some-where to lay our heads before the city tomorrow.'

'Are you a drummer?' asks Nethe. She indicates the skin stretched over wood lashed at Frederich's hip.

'A piper.'

'He's joking,' says Eren, nudging his companion in the ribs. 'Do not speak to him, he's a fool.' There is affection in his voice, brotherly.

'Let me show you to your quarters,' says Sophey, pulling Nethe back. Lisbet notices she turns her head up as she speaks, addressing Frederich alone. Eren seems not to notice, or perhaps he is practised in not noticing. He bends to Ulf, who is butting at his legs, and Fluh, keen not to be left out, dashes over and nips at his fingers.

Sophey kicks the dog aside, and Fluh whimpers, feigning injury, lifting her paw. 'This way.'

They follow her without comment, but Eren bends and smooths back the fur at Fluh's side before he enters.

'A Turk,' says Nethe, as soon as they are out of earshot.

'I have eyes.'

'It is an insult,' says Sophey, emerging from the kitchen, blinking in the glare of the sun. 'An infidel.' Sophey snatches at the broom kept just inside the door, and begins sweeping out imagined muck from the men's boots. 'If we have any trouble, they're out, Papal decree or no.'

'I imagine we will barely see them,' says Lisbet. 'Didn't they say they start tomorrow? And they play until dark. We will all be abed.'

'Musicians. A foolish plan. Those physicians.'

Her muttering drops as there is the creak of a floorboard from within. The tall one, Frederich, stands by the table. Without his drum he seems even slighter.

'Might I take supper? We have travelled all day.'

Sophey pushes the broom into Nethe's hands and goes to see to their guests.

•

The first days the musicians make as much of an impression on the house as spiders. They find only traces of them, in the crumbs not swept from the table, the shadows that move under the door.

Lisbet is able to brush off their proximity like cobwebs, more bothered by the bees and the business of sharing a bedroom with Nethe. Her frantic praying has ceased, and she eats at every meal, but there is still a restlessness to her, an edge that makes Lisbet's own anxiety rise. Their distance has remained, the walls around her reinforced by what Lisbet had seen of her exchange with Ida. And, though it is churlish, the fact she has not asked to go to the dance tree even once makes Lisbet feel betrayed, as though she has opened that most sacred place to find it stomped over and forgotten.

Sophey is the worst affected by the strangers. The lines of her face are more deeply etched, the shadows under her eyes drape to her cheeks.

'I hope they do not expect us to launder their clothes,' she spits, as she scrubs the men's plates with a horsehair brush, and changes the water between. 'I will not touch them.'

Lisbet knows her mind is full of tales of Turks escaped from slavery and murdering their masters. But Eren is not a slave, and Lisbet is sure he is not vicious after seeing his daftness with the dogs – though Lisbet knows a man can stroke a dog and strike a wife.

At church there are stories: the woods are full of the undesirables the Twenty-One have removed from the city. Herr Furmann's goats were taken, herded in the night out into the forest, and dams have been found forced, rivers following new paths into the trees. Lisbet sees no evidence of them at the dance tree, protected as it is by the boggy ground and distance from the city, though she has taken to walking there only in the middle of the day, as though heat might keep malefactors at bay.

On the third night of the musicians, Nethe speaks her name. Lisbet lies still, waiting. She closes her eyes as Nethe shifts in the bed. She can smell her breath as she leans over her. Then the weight lifts as Nethe stands, and, before Lisbet can decide what to do, she slips from the room.

Lisbet listens carefully: Nethe is moving through the house, to the door. The dogs make no noise. Lisbet hesitates a moment. She feels for the lock of hair, but it is gone from Nethe's pillow. She heaves herself upright. She follows Nethe's path on bare feet, wincing as the door squeaks. Nethe has left the door to the yard propped open with the broom, spilling moonlight onto the table. The bread stands untouched: the musicians are not back yet.

Ulf's long nose is poked through the gap of the door. Lisbet creeps to him, places her hand over his muzzle to push him gently backwards. He licks her palm in long, rough tracks. His tongue is dry as sand, and she lifts the bucket, takes it outside with her, scanning the yard as she refills the dogs' trough. The night is smotheringly warm though the sky is clear, the stars pricking brightly at its fabric. A figure rounds the wall.

'Nethe,' she hisses, realising even as she says the name it is not her. They are too short, and as he lifts a hand in greeting Lisbet sees it is Eren.

Lisbet's hands go across herself: she is in her nightdress, an old tunic that is far from indecent, but frayed about the collar and cuffs, with a rip under the right armpit showing wiry black hair.

Something smoulders in his hand. A pipe, giving off sweet smoke. Eren has paused, and Ulf goes to greet him, his old tail creaking from side to side like a rusted hinge. Lisbet realises how she must look, clutching at her swollen body, and so she drops her head and moves back into the house. She knows Eren is waiting, giving her time to go to bed and avoid the encounter. But instead she lights a beeswax candle, takes up a knife, and slices the bread. The baby is shifting inside her, filling her throat with sourness, and she needs something to settle it.

The musician opens the door, moves aside the broom. He

pauses at the threshold, registering her presence. Backed by moonlight, he seems cut from shadow. She gestures at the chair across from her, places a slice of bread on a plate, slides it across with a wafer of honeycomb, the honey pooling onto the wooden slab.

He nods his gratitude, and unslings from his back a bundle: his instrument, she guesses, though she has not seen the like before. A drum she knows. A pipe. But this has a bowl and a neck, and strings hauled taut across them. The bowl is painted yellow, and she thinks of her tree, the ribbons gaudy in the green.

Eren sets the instrument down on the table beside his plate. Its strings thrum in response, a low hum of song. He winces and reaches out his hand to still them, raising his other in apology. His fingernails are white, crescents smooth on his dark skin, but when he turns his hand to her, she sees the calluses across his fingertips.

She is staring, and rises to fill a cup, sets it down in front of him. He nods his thanks, and bends his head to pray. Lisbet didn't know Turks prayed. She joins him, and then watches him out of the corner of her eye as they eat.

His shoulders are slim, but his body is broad, nudging his arms out from his sides as though someone were lifting him beneath the armpits. His face is long, and his eyebrows thick, black as his hair and beard. His skin is dark as the wood of the table, his hand resting still and light upon his cup as the other brings bread to his lips.

She dares a look at his face. His beard is clipped closer than Henne's or her father's, showing a straight jaw, high cheekbones and cheeks scooped in between. The moustache is fuller than an Alsace man's, and curls about his lips. She studies him as she would a hive, appraising, until he looks up from his empty plate, and smiles. His teeth are very straight.

'Thank you,' he murmurs, and Lisbet shrugs to say she only sliced the bread, poured the mead. 'Am I right that you are the beekeeper?'

She nods. 'And my husband.' Her voice is very small, but he hears her.

'Heinrich Wiler, a man with a head for business,' he says, smiles again at her surprise. 'Frederich asked about you in the city.'

'Me?'

He gestures at the room. 'The Wiler household. Herr Metz the miller is fond of you.'

She relaxes into her chair a little, cups her belly as the bread soothes her stomach. 'We are loyal customers. Where is . . .'

'Frederich is still in the city. My friend is fond of nights. As you are, it seems.'

'I couldn't sleep.' It feels an intimate detail, but she parts with it easily.

'My mother was the same, with my sisters.' He nods at her stomach. 'And even then it was not so hot.'

'Is the city . . .' She searches for the word, and he waits, does not rush in to guess at her meaning like Henne would. She wants to ask if it has changed, but he would not know it before.

'Are there many dancers?' she asks finally.

His hand trembles slightly: she would not have noticed it but for a drop of mead escaping his cup and slipping over his fine fingers. She imagines, absurdly, catching it in her mouth, and takes a sip of her own. It is made with the honey from her favourite hive, the dance tree bees.

'The guilds are full,' he says, swallowing. 'They've opened another stage, in the carpenters' guild, and yet more dance in the streets. There is talk of building a chapel at Saverne.'

'Another stage?' Lisbet frowns.

'Yes,' says Eren heavily. 'I've never seen the like. They dance until they fall down, and the authorities revive them with ale and watered wine, and they dance again.'

A silence then. She wonders if he is recalling, as she is, the sight. It is easy to double the stages, and double them again, until the world is full of naught but women with lank, loose hair, their arms outstretched, their feet torn and bloodied. She presses down on her belly.

'You have not played for dancers before?'

'Dancers, yes, at feasts and festivals. Dancers like this, who wheel and spin and will not stop?' He shakes his head. His brown eyes shine in the candlelight, which picks out his lashes and chases them up his forehead in long streaks. 'Never.'

'But it will work,' she says. 'The Twenty-One have decreed it.'

'They believe it will work.'

'You do not?'

'You are very interested in what I think.' His voice is soft, his face free of jest. His hands rest atop the table. The bread knife is a fingerlength from his thumb. Lisbet wonders briefly if she should be afraid of him.

'I should to bed. *Elinize saglik.*'

She stares at him, and he repeats the phrase.

'Health to your hands.' He gestures at the loaf. 'For the food.' She looks down at them, at their swollen knuckles, the place where a bee took fright and pierced. Nethe's fresh-scarred hands rear up at her through the dark.

'I mean thank you,' he says. 'You can cover that over. I doubt Frederich will be back tonight.'

He pushes himself up, and she rises with him, a habit bred into her by her father, who never would have stood for a Turk. She does not want him to go, just yet, to leave her alone in her exhaustion.

'Where is he? Your friend?'

She wants to hear him say it. To say that despite the Church's ban on such things, Frederich is in a whorehouse, perhaps lying with a woman at this moment as they stand across from each other, his drummer's hands pressing flesh hard enough to bruise. A throb of want passes through her, and she blushes with the shock of it, that part of her forgotten lately, as though she were smooth as polished wood.

Eren is watching her, a slight frown pinching his brow. 'Good night, Frau Wiler.'

He goes past her to her and Henne's room. She can track him with her ears, knowing the route so well, the creak of each floorboard, the grate of the door on the uneven planks. His tread is unfamiliar though, softer than Henne's steady thumping. But he does not creep, like her. He only steps lighter.

He has left his instrument on the table. She had forgot to ask him what it was. She taps a string, and it lets out another tuneless hum. She stills it as he did, the wood worn and warm under her fingers. Again she is minded of her platform, and of Nethe, who woke her in the first place. Is she in the forest, the city?

She sighs, and arches her back. The mead has soothed her and the baby both, and she rises to go to bed. Before she leaves she wraps the loaf in cloth, and props open the door with the broom, so Nethe will have an easy passage to bed.

Nine

Nethe is barely able to rise the next morning, her face pinched by tiredness. She did not return until just before dawn.

Lisbet brings a cup of mead to her, and a compress of herbs that Nethe presses to her head, pushing the drink away.

'What is all this?' says Nethe. Her hair is bristle-brush long now, growing in straight, thick spikes so the scars are nearly covered.

'Pity, only,' says Lisbet, but when Nethe arches her eyebrow she sinks down on the bed beside her. 'Where were you last night?'

Nethe's lips twitch. 'Walking.'

'Where?'

'Where is there to walk here?'

'Alone?'

'You are same as my mother,' says Nethe, throwing back the sheets, 'all questions and no care for the answers but to sate your curiosity.'

She starts to strip the sheets, and Lisbet helps her. 'That is not true,' says Lisbet, but it is a little. 'How was the city?'

'How should I know?'

'From your visit with Ida,' frowns Lisbet.

'Yes.' Nethe's lips twitch again – this time Lisbet is almost sure it is a smile. 'Yes of course.'

'Well?'

'I have never seen the like. The women dance so light and the stages are so high it is as though they float. The music makes a church of it.' Lisbet snorts in disbelief, and Nethe rounds on her. 'If a tree can be a church, why not a guild?'

'Do not,' warns Lisbet. She bundles the sheets and stomps outside to the waiting bucket and lye. How dare she? The stings on the webs of Lisbet's fingers throb as she takes a paddle to it, letting them soak before throwing the sheets over the mangle board.

Lisbet works the rolling pin, splashing her skirts, flinging the sheets back over to work them through again and again, until they are wrung out. Still she repeats the wringing, enjoying the ache in her lower back, the heaviness growing in her arms, the sweat coming hot behind her ears, the handle catching sometimes on her hip, sometimes her belly.

'You are a demon with that mangle.'

Lisbet gasps and straightens, fearing Plater returned. But this time Frederich is there, leaning against the side of the house, his long limbs arranged like an upright cricket's. His smirk is back, lending his face a lopsidedness that is not wholly unbecoming.

She smooths her hands dry on her dress, knowing the lye will eat at the dye and leave streaks, not caring. 'Good morning, Herr . . .' She realises she has no other name for him, waits for him to provide it. 'Frederich. Back so soon?'

He levers himself upright, pushing off the wall and loping closer. 'So soon? I have barely been here, Frau Wiler.' Her cheeks colour, and still he moves closer, pushes on. 'The city has many intrigues. Not that your farm is without them of course.'

Frederich yawns without covering his mouth, and Lisbet is minded of her mother clapping her own hand over Lisbet's wide lips. *The Devil enters there, and must be kept out.* A mouth, Lisbet decided young, is inherently duplicitous. It does not help she has a large mouth, and her lips sit apart when she thinks or sleeps. She tries to correct it, keeps her tongue latched to the gilled back of her mouth, but always it parts with some irrepressible impulse.

Frederich has no such qualms – she can count each gap in his gums. Lisbet shudders, casts around for another topic. 'Did you lose your drum?' She gestures at his hip.

'Aye, and my dignity. One is more easily replaced.'

'Do you need food?' she asks. 'There is bread, honey—'

He waves his hand. 'Sleep only. The one thing the city cannot provide.'

His coarseness dismays and delights her. She straightens her spine, thrusting her belly out to create some distance between them. 'You know where the bed is.'

His grin deepens. 'I do. Your bed, is it not?'

'And my husband's,' she says, gathering up the wrung-out sheets. They will need to breathe in the air to keep them from becoming stiff, and she wishes, for the hundredth time this summer, for even a whisper of a breeze. 'Dream well, Herr Frederich.'

She walks away to the clothing line, knowing he is watching, and does not turn until she hears the kitchen door swing shut. Heat stings her collarbones. She is foolish, to speak so with the drummer. But her belly protects her. She cups it, marvelling at its size, the exact proportion of it, like a planet or a piece of fruit, so exact. Part, and apart.

From inside the house she hears a snort. Nethe has recovered herself then. Nethe's laugh comes again, and Lisbet goes to the door, presses her ear against it. She can hear the burr of Frederich's voice, the echo of Nethe's. Is this the answer for Nethe's tiredness, for Frederich's absence? Her cheeks colour at the possibility. Were they together last night?

The thought is alluring, dangerous. It fits with Lisbet's theory about an illicit baby, that such behaviour was what Nethe was sent away for. She is foolish to risk punishment again.

Lisbet sighs, gathers the sheets. She desires Henne still, wants him now, this instant, though he is miles away in Heidelberg. But he would not touch her even if he were beside her, both of them abed. Not with the baby in her. She thinks of going to the pressing shed, sliding her fingers into herself. She has nearly forgotten that part of her existed, but now, suddenly, it is all she is, aching to the point of pain.

Ulf trots up to her, butts his nose into her palm, and it pulls her back. She wipes her hand clean, scratches his ears.

'Stupid dog.'

•

'Do you know a man named Plater?'

Lisbet is exhausted, the darkened well of the kitchen welcome. Her sore hands are sticky with honey, wax under her nails that she skims with a paring knife. Nethe and Sophey retired to bed hours ago, but Lisbet found herself making excuses to stay in the kitchen despite her tiredness. Now Eren has returned with a clay pot, wafting the scent of fennel and meat into the air. She sinks down across from him, suddenly starving, when he asks her with worry in his voice.

'Regrettably.'

'I thought you would not be gladly acquainted,' says Eren. 'He sent his regards.'

'And what else?' says Lisbet, nerves knotting her belly.

'Nothing,' says Eren soothingly, 'but he did say to apologise for the kind of guest he sent you.'

He says it lightly enough, but Lisbet knows his meaning.

'He is a brute,' says Lisbet. 'Disregard all he says.'

'But he sent us to you?' asks Eren, lifting the lid from the clay pot. It comes unwillingly, stuck fast with dough sealing the rim.

'Baeckeoffe?' she says wonderingly, leaning forward as far as her belly will allow to breathe it in. 'Did Sophey give you scraps?'

'This is from Mathias Metz,' says Eren, pushing the pot close to her. It is thick and brown as mud, and she can see white bones slipped clean from their flesh. 'He seems to care for you all.'

'He is my best friend's father,' says Lisbet, dunking her crust inside. 'She is married to Plater.'

The stew is still warm from the baker's oven, and she feels sweat spring up anew on her lip, shields her mouth to wipe it away. She pushes the clay pot back to him.

'You must have some.'

'It is not for me,' he says.

'Join me,' says Lisbet. 'I cannot eat alone.'

He ducks his head, and dips the corner of the bread into the stew. He is a careful eater. She had noticed this before, but now it is clearer with such a messy meal before them. There are no crumbs on his beard, and no stew drips to stain his shirt. He reaches forward and dips the bread again, and she mirrors him, marvelling at how easy their silence is. His wrist is roped with veins.

He sees her looking, and places his hand into his lap. 'Apologies, I am not a skilled sewer.'

She frowns. 'I do not . . .'

He holds up his arm, showing the small rip extending from

the edge of the cuff and upwards an inch or so. It is closed by straggly twine, too thick for the weave of the fabric, tearing larger holes. 'The strings sometimes catch,' he says. 'When I play.'

'What is it?' She indicates the stringed instrument.

'A lute. My father's, once. It is a little broad for my hand-span, hence the torn sleeve. But if I do not leave them down, it is my skin that catches.'

He pushes his cuff up higher, and she sees scars there, pale as the stitches are dark on his shirt, an echo in opposite colours. Black hairs stripe his forearm. Her heartbeat becomes apparent in her ears, and she forces a laugh.

'I must fix that for you, or else the thread will rip.'

'I would not think to ask you—'

'Please,' she says. 'It is no trouble.'

'Now?' he asks, and though she had not thought now at all, she nods.

He rises to change his shirt, and she listens to the sleeping house, the forest mute with another windless night, and brushes crumbs from her skirts. The smell of the stew is rich, and she wants to lift the earthenware pot to her lips and lap it up like a cat.

'Here.' He stands in a darker shirt, more worn even than the one he holds out, thin as skin. She takes it – it is still warm from his body – and crosses to the shelf where the box of thread and yarn and needles and patches is kept. She selects the palest thread, which she herself had drawn from a spindle for Henne's wedding shirt, and a bone needle fine as a hair.

When she returns to the table Eren has moved the pot further off, resealed it with the dough and placed it beside the fire so it will continue to steep and strengthen in flavour. Lisbet wonders who taught him such things, who taught him to stitch at all. Henne would never contemplate learning such work.

As she settles to sew, first unpicking his stitches with the sharp end of the spindle, she watches him from beneath her eyelashes. He has his lute on his lap, and is moving his fingers over it as though to play, hands hovering just above its surface. The distance constant, aching. Has he a wife, who showed him how to darn?

She takes up the shirt and folds over the torn fabric, lightly runs a stitch to bind the edges together to hide the tears. His lips are moving, his eyes half closed, away from her and this room, the music and song inside somewhere she can't reach. She starts to bring the new seams together with a stitch her mother taught her, fine as a whisper. Across, across, through and through, to mimic the weave of the fabric. Her fingers remember and act of their own accord, much as his do, both of them playing well-worn rhythms. She double knots in reverse, so the seam will lie close to his skin and not trouble him.

'That was fast,' he says, when she holds out the mended shirt. 'You are skilled, Frau Wiler.'

'Lisbet,' she says.

'Thank you.' He takes it, holds the work to the candlelight so the stitches show through like veins. 'It is better than new.'

She bows her head against the compliment, winding the thread back onto the spindle, thinking how Sophey will notice it gone and likely ask after it. What will Lisbet tell her? That she sat with the Turk and ate Mathias' gift, and he gave her the shirt still warm from his back?

'Does he threaten you?' He is watching her closely. 'Plater?'

'He threatens all.' Eren frowns and she gestures around them, at the house, the yard. 'The farm, the bees. We borrowed from the church in the bad years, as most of Alsace did. We have paid it back but they want it ten-fold, and skeps besides.'

He nods slowly. 'It was so for us.'

'Your family?'

'Me and my wife, yes.'

She waits but he doesn't offer anything further.

'If Plater gives you trouble, I think I could scare him if you wished.'

'You?' Lisbet cannot hold her laugh.

'Oh yes.' Eren affects a deeper tone. 'Don't you know we Turks are demons, black-hearted as our skin.'

She laughs again, tighter, the needle warm in her hand. He has drawn his brow low over his eyes, made his lips a tight line, the candlelight finding new funnels of darkness in his face. Then he sits back, wipes his slim fingers over his eyes as though to smooth away the expression.

'You do not believe it?' he asks, himself again.

Lisbet shakes her head, drops the needle into the box, rises to put it away.

'You are alone in Strasbourg,' says Eren. He lifts his thick hair where it curls about his ear. The skin there is red and scraped.

'Someone hit you?'

He waves his hand. 'Glancingly. But you are not afraid of me?'

'My father had labourers.'

'Slaves?' asks Eren.

'Labourers. They were like you.'

'Musicians?' There is something taut in his voice.

'No, Turks.'

He takes a swallow of beer. The silence becomes sharper, but then he sets his cup gently down. 'Will you have to give Plater what he asks?'

'This is merry.'

The door has been pushed open and she had not noticed. Frederich stands yawning on the threshold, the recovered drum at his hip, and behind him the moon sits large and white as a peeled onion. She has sat with Eren deep into the night and not noticed that, either.

'Something smells good,' says Frederich, stepping towards the resealed pot and rocking back slightly on his heels.

'You are drunk,' says Eren lightly. 'To bed.'

'In my cups, dear friend,' says Frederich, a little too loud, and Lisbet shushes him.

'He is playing the fool,' says Eren, and lifts a chair softly, places it behind Frederich's calves. The drummer sits with a huff, and the chair creaks like old bones.

Frederich holds his finger to his lips, his bony shoulders raised so he has the manner of a naughty child. He reaches for the pot, and Eren playfully slaps his hand, places bread into it instead. Frederich chews obediently, reaching into his pocket and showing a crumpled, sealed letter to Lisbet.

'For you,' he says, spraying crumbs. It puts her in mind of the edict Herr Plater delivered, and she is loath to take it until she recognises Henne's blunt, cramped hand.

Her husband holds a quill like a child at his letters, pink tongue precise between his teeth, a frown creasing the sun-branded lines of his forehead. It always makes her queasy, this habit of concentration. Even at the point of his release, as he is dark and huge above her in bed, there is always the glint of his wet mouth, his tongue poked out like a worm winkled from the fresh-turned earth of a grave.

'This is from your husband,' says Frederich, his voice too loud again. 'The miller gave it me.'

Eren rests his hand on his friend's arm, dark fingers slim and encasing Frederich's shoulder. Frederich snorts, and repeats his announcement, in a mock whisper.

Frederich stretches his arm out, but before she can take hold of it, before she can do anything but feel the brittle, yellow quality of the parchment, he lifts it away. He is trying to make a game of it, and Lisbet feels her cheeks colour.

Eren plucks the letter from Frederich's hand and passes it to her. The parchment is skin warm from being pressed in Frederich's tunic, and she runs her fingers over its fold. The quality is bad, still bearing score marks from its flensing. She stares dumbly down at the shapes she knows are words, but she cannot read so much as her name. She only knows Henne's.

'Would you like to be left alone to read it, Frau Wiler?' Eren is watching her. His dark eyes are large in the candlelight, and the smile is gone from his beard. She looks back, and wishes she were alone with him again. She shakes her head.

Frederich belches. 'Begging your pardon.'

He pushes up, and with the skill of an expert drunk manoeuvres himself carefully around the table, and stoops through the door.

'I hope it is good news,' says Eren.

'I cannot read it. Sophey has some letters.'

'I can, if you would like.' She looks up at him, surprised. Something in his face contracts. 'We do read, where I am from.'

'Forgive me, of course.' Her cheeks are warm again, and she presses her clammy fingertips to them.

'Nothing to forgive.'

'Is it common? For musicians I mean.'

Eren shakes his head once, slowly, and says with affection, 'Frederich has a skill for rhythm and not much else.'

'Then why did Herr Metz give the letter to him?'

'He would not give it to me,' says Eren. Nothing in his voice invites pity. 'I can be trusted with baeckeoffe , not confidences. If you would like me to read it, I will not tell Frederich, nor anyone else what is in it.'

She looks down at the parchment again, and places it onto the table between them.

'Perhaps it is not proper?'

Lisbet bites the soft insides of her cheeks to keep from laughing. The thought that Henne has written her a love letter hadn't crossed her mind.

'I am sure it is proper. My mother-in-law would have had to read it to me.'

Eren breaks the dark wax seal. There is a mark across it from the ring Henne inherited from his father, and wears on his smallest finger. Eren places the seal's two halves onto the table so it looks whole. She has never met a man as careful as him.

He unfurls the parchment with a cracking sound, and even from where she sits Lisbet can smell it, an animal tang rising in a plume and spreading through the room. She covers the bread as Eren begins to read.

'Lisbet . . .' She trains her gaze onto the covered loaf, cups her hands under her belly. Eren's voice deepens as he reads, a burr she feels as much as hears. 'I hope my letter finds the baby well. I hope Mutter and Agnethe are well also.

'My journey to Heidelberg was without incident, the road recently repaired and with houses spread nearly along the whole length. There is a place of learning here, and I was not the only traveller heading north. I was in the company of traders and clergy, men of God. Also a great number of Moors, but there was no trouble.

'Heidelberg is a bigger city than Strasbourg. But here there is some notoriety for our city. They say there is a dancing plague, and that the whole city is running mad. I hope you are keeping my boy away from it, and are never in the forest.

'Heidelberg has five churches and a university. I have found lodgings in the north beside the horse market, and each day I go to the cleric with my petition. I will be another week at least.

'This is likely to be my only letter, but be assured I will come safe home before my boy is born. Henne.'

Lisbet looks up. 'That is all?'

'That is all.' Eren lays the parchment down.

'Excuse me, I must . . .'

She stands up and pushes out through the door to the yard, Ulf following at her heels. Behind her, Lisbet hears Eren call softly, but she ignores him. Something is hot and sharp in her chest and beneath her eyelids.

What had she been expecting? What was she hoping for? Safety for the bees, at most. Affection for her, at least. All she hears in her ears as she strides past the fluttering quiet of the chickens, and the ceaseless hum of the skeps, is *my boy my boy my boy*.

Has he always said this? My boy? No, not with any of the others. He could not hold love for them, only offers this child such an address because it has stayed longer than them. Lisbet though, she loved them all, they were all hers and are still. She alone prayed constantly for their survival, cried at their leavings, begged Henne for his seed until she felt like a common hure and not half as desired. *My boy*. No, it is her boy, just as the others were, her boys and her girls, her children. She has not bled and degraded herself so many times over for Henne to assert his ownership, not when his devotion has come so little, so late.

She goes into the forest, because Henne has forbidden it. The moonlight is bright as the sun and the shadows are cool. The relief of it is delicious as fresh water poured down her throat.

She takes a sharp turn, away from any familiar path. Ulf hesitates – he was a little ahead and now hears her veering – but of course he follows her, his tail lifting and hitting her skirts as he passes her. *My boy my boy my boy*. Branches snatch at her clothes, twigs slip themselves beneath her soles and trap inside the wood of her clogs, but she pushes on until her heart beats louder than the phrase and she is panting. She is running, she realises now, and she comes to a halt, feeling the baby settle inside her.

She wraps her arms over herself, and bends to whisper an apology. But in the sudden silence, she understands something is changed. Ulf is growling. And ahead, there are voices. A man and a man and two women. Now, in the bright moonlight, she can see them – four of them, their hair a thatch and standing so close together they could be one person.

She stumbles back, and the forest takes her quickly, slipping her from view neat as a coin into a pocket, but the sound she makes in her hurry causes them to turn.

She can smell smoke, the attempt of their fire, not for warmth but for cooking, the smell of something caught and skewered. She sees it through the thicket of their bodies, a hare or a small fox or a large squirrel, its insides by turns black and red and raw and burned. And then a new terror: Ulf, still standing his ground, placing his long, thin body between them and her, all the time growling.

They whisper, and one approaches, arm outstretched to the dog, as though to pet him. But from his belt he is pulling a rusty blade, blunted and stained. Ulf barks once, twice, and Lisbet cringes. The man is drawing closer and she must move, but her feet are sunk into the forest floor, into the dried and dead things laid out there like a carpet, and she will watch these men and women kill Ulf and she will do nothing, and she has a traitor's heart in her chest and she must move, must scream, must fling herself yelling between the stupid, precious dog and these desperate, starving people—

'Lisbet!'

How do they know her name? The terror of it looses her

voice, and she gasps. The man lunges for Ulf but the dog is suddenly alert and quick, streaking past Lisbet, the growl still full in his throat.

'Scheiße,' exclaims the man, and his attention switches to Lisbet, shaken from her hiding place. 'You there—'

He is gesturing with the knife, for her to come closer. The moment she hears footsteps behind her, she loses her mind entire. They have surrounded her, and it will be both her and the dog on the spit, her belly split open and her baby taken.

But then she recognises Eren's voice calling her name. The man curses again, retreats to his companions. They cover over their fire with their bodies, their backs turning to fronts again, and as they begin to talk amongst themselves Lisbet follows the dog, the smell of their meat and smoke obscured by the wilting forest once more.

'Lisbet!'

Eren emerges from the shadows, Ulf running in excited circles around him.

Beside him, Frederich looks asleep on his feet. 'Thank God,' he murmurs, rubbing his arm and shifting the drum's leather strap higher on his slight shoulder, a ring glinting on his little finger. 'Frau Wiler, tonight I thought to have a night off from moonlit wanderings. I'm going to bed. Again.'

Eren is staring squarely at her, the curl of his black hair blueish in the light, and his hand by his side is clenched tight and loosening, as though he is resisting a call to hit something.

'What do you mean by it? Coming to the forest?'

He speaks quietly, and she moves closer, around the trees between them, to hear him better.

'I wanted to walk. The baby was restless.' His silence stretches, grows eyes and glares. She purses her lips. 'I may walk if I wish.'

'Do you not know what happens in these woods?'

She is suddenly afraid again.

'Frau Wiler—'

'Lisbet.'

'Lisbet, please. I am not your master, but please do not come here in the dark, off the path. I have seen people here, when I come late from the city. I must carry a knife.' He shows her the bone handle at his hip. 'And there are stories. What makes some dance makes others dangerous. The empirics talk of hot blood, swollen brains. It is throwing people off balance. They are not the kind you should meet so late and in the night. Even in the sun they are dark sorts.'

'I had to—' She swallows. 'I had to walk.'

'Not alone, then. If you'll allow it, I can walk with you. I can walk before you, or behind, far enough off so you do not have to acknowledge my presence. We do not have to speak. If you must walk at night, I will go with you.'

She holds out her arm. The night has made her judgement slippery as Frederich's and she brushes the coarse cloth of his shirt. It throws off scent like mushrooms brought up fresh from the dirt. 'If you will not be too tired, perhaps.'

His beard twitches, and she smiles in answer. It is improper, impossible, and yet they will do it.

They walk home without another word, and when Lisbet creeps on silent and swollen feet towards Nethe's bed, she finds it empty.

One hundred and sixty-three dancing

The first dance Edith Bucer ever went to was for a boy. Jan Drescher. He had very long, light eyelashes and strong calves, a slow, broad smile. She wore her hair down for the first time since her bloods, tucked wood violets behind her ears and crushed more at her wrists. Her brothers teased and called her hure, but her mutti nodded her permission.

The drums and pipes were loud and living as though they played in a hall, not the open fields. The fire leapt higher than Jan's shoulders, cutting a carpet of dirt clear of the frost. Edith walked a wide circle of the dancers, came to stand close to Jan's group. Jan Drescher handed her a cup of beer, stronger than any she had before. It warmed her more than the fire, and Jan looped a long, muscled arm around her waist and pulled her in too close, span her too fast. She screamed with delight and fear, the whites of his eyes glinting in the firelight. The next dance was the same, and the next. He danced like a man possessed, and he returned again and again to her.

Before they could marry, he chased a promised fortune to the city. She was pregnant and in love and happy to follow him. He set her and the baby up in a room in a house on a narrow street near the gaol. She did not like the smell from the river, the sounds from the sheep slaughter yard, that there were no shutters, that the baby wheezed for breath every morning, but Jan wished to stay. He went dancing without her, she could smell smoke and sweat on him, but he wouldn't let her leave, nor would he spin her, or kiss their child.

One morning the baby's lips are blue, and Jan says it is too late for an empiric. She knows it is true, but still pleads for him to give her the last of his coin. He has none. It is all drunk at the dances. She screams and cries, and carries her baby to the cathedral steps, prays for her tiny soul, a white feather drifting away. Edith's heart breaks with the weight of all her love, and the pain is too great to hold.

When she hears the music she thinks it is angels come to take her child to Heaven. She follows it, and there are women, all together in a cacophonous riot, and she knows they are the same, they are like her. They met a boy at a dance, and wore wood violets in their hair. They loved their children, and their children died, and now they begin at the beginning. She slides in among them, her child clasped to her chest, and starts to dance herself back to before.

Ten

It has the heat of trespass when, the next day, Lisbet waits until Sophey and Nethe are abed, and slips outside with a torch to sweat in the yard until she hears the jangle of Eren's lute strings. In the firelight he looks grey under his black beard, his skin so matted with sweat and dust he could lie down in the dirt and blend with it.

'Forgive me,' he says as he reaches her, and her heart sinks. He will not do it, of course. It is absurd. She is already shrugging as if it is of no consequence when he unloops his instrument from his shoulder and hands it to her. It is lighter than it looks, hollow with air.

'May I have some water, and a bowl?'

He means only to wash, to wash before they walk, and her heart lightens with the relief of it.

'I will go to the well,' she says.

'We can pass it?'

'Of course.'

'Today has been . . . but the well will be welcome.'

She wonders about his day, what he has seen, the scenes in the city. It must be like walking through Hell every day. 'Or the river, further on. There the water is cooler.'

'You should drill your wells deeper, if rivers are more refreshing,' he smiles. 'Would you mind taking that inside? I don't wish to muddy the floor.'

'Of course.' She carries the instrument carefully. The door to her and Henne's room is ajar, and she hesitates at the threshold.

The shutters are closed and clearly have been for days, perhaps since the musicians' arrival a week ago. The air sticks in her throat: unfamiliar sweat, sweet and sharp. The sheets on the bed are unmade. There is dirt on the straw and she knows this must be from Frederich, less careful with his boots.

So there, on the floor, is where Eren lies. There is a jerkin wrapped around the thin pillow, a sheet folded back to air. She rests the lute atop it, then changes her mind and moves it onto the stool where their clothes are heaped, in case Frederich stumbles home.

She waits a moment, in the middle of the room, waits for some feeling to come to her. Guilt, for the excitement of the time alone with Eren. Fear for their discovery. Missing for Henne. This is the room they have shared since they married, where he put their babies inside her. Nothing. She pulls the door shut behind.

Eren takes the torch, though they barely need it. The moon- light is bright as it was the night before, and she tries to push it from her mind, how it picked out the starving group's glinting teeth, the blade, the filthy fingernails as they reached for Ulf. She calls the dog forward, nudges him with her knee, glad of his solid weight at her side. Eren is so quiet, she might be alone with Ulf, and she settles into the safety of their silence.

She does not look back, though she wants to, longs to have his face in her sights beneath the bright moon. She could lead them to the river with her eyes closed, but still at the fork where the path could take them to the dance tree, she hesitates.

'Are you all right?' He stops close behind, and she feels his breath graze the nape of her neck, a brush soft as a bee's wing before he recovers his balance and steps back a pace.

There is no one else at the river, though for the first time Lisbet notices signs there might have been — a fresh-turned patch of earth and blunt white stalks broken clean as bones where mushrooms have been pulled, ash at the centre of the clearing. She shrinks back, and Eren passes her, goes with Ulf to the burnt wood and hovers his hand over it.

'Cold,' he says, and her hands unclench.

He moves forward on his haunches and ducks his head to the river, washing away the dust with an audible sigh, a visible slump of his shoulders. He wipes his hands over his hair and it runs down his back in long streaks. She turns away and watches the forest as Ulf lies down panting at her feet.

'Better,' says Eren, sitting cross-legged. His usual colour is restored, his skin gleaming and beard dripping. 'The river in the city is clogged. You can smell it for miles. Sometimes . . .' He trails off, and she guesses the reason for his hesitation.

'I don't mind,' she says. 'I want to know.'

He nods. 'Sometimes the fathers or sons of the afflicted hold the dancers down in it, but they only flail harder to be free.'

Lisbet's gravity shifts. The river smell grows, and the past rises to meet her: she feels soft skin beneath her child's fingers, clammy and cool. 'Tell me something else.'

Eren strokes Ulf down the length of his narrow back, sprinkling water on the dog's head. Ulf places his head on his paws and twitches his eyebrows at him with utter devotion.

'Else?'

She feels foolish almost instantly, but Eren does not roll his eyes, or fall silent like Henne would. Instead he stops stroking Ulf, and rests back on his hands. 'Why don't you tell me something?'

'I have nothing but what others tell me.'

'That is not true,' he says. 'Tell me of your life here, your life before.'

Fields, she thinks, *brothers, and a sick mother. Restlessness. Want.*

'Life here is much changed lately,' she says. 'For years it was the same, Heinrich and Sophey and me and the bees. Agnethe is only recently returned.'

'From where?'

'The mountains.'

'I noticed her hair, of course. But that is something of her. What of you?'

Lisbet feels like a child caught out at simple addition. One added to one, and the answer a blank. What has she to tell?

'What about the bees?' he prompts. 'They are fascinating creatures. How do you care for them?'

She seizes upon his suggestion with gratitude. He listens with the same expression he'd had while she darned his shirt, his eyes hooded. But this time it is not silent music he hears, but her, and she pours her learning about the bees into him. How they lead others to flowers by dancing, how the king never leaves the hive unless it is damaged, how honey tastes different hive to hive and comb to comb, how they can swarm thick as mist and kill a man. How she no longer needs gloves to tend them, how the poison troubles her only a little. How she knows how to breathe, now, how to make her heart slow and her movements as though through water, and so can calm them by the rhythms of her body.

'You speak as though you love them,' he says, but his voice is serious, no hint of jest, and she breathes *yes*, yes that is it exactly.

'I am the same with my lute, though it does not live,' he says. 'It lives when I hold it, and so I become fully alive too. There are not words closer for it than this.'

Lisbet leans back against the boulder, cupping her belly. 'How did you come to play?'

'My father,' he says, pulling his knees up to his chest like a boy. 'That is how he paid our way, in the beginning. We came from Constantinople when I was a boy. I barely remember it, but for the music. That, my father brought with us.'

'You have brothers?'

'Sisters. Five living. All married and elsewhere. One went back, but the others are here.'

'In Strasbourg?'

'We are not welcome in Strasbourg. Other places it is not so bad.'

'And your wife?'

He looks at his hands, spreads them wide, his fingers slender as vines. On an exhale he closes them and says, 'Dead.'

'I am sorry.' She waits, thinking he might elaborate, but the silence grows into something gritty and she breaks it. 'Do you play it for the dancers? The music of your father?'

'Never,' he says. 'It is not the sort of music they want. Arabism is a crime in Strasbourg.'

'Why do you stay?'

'Why should I not?' There is anger there, flared like a caught flame, and then it is gone again.

'I did not mean—'

He shrugs. 'Where would I go? I have lived in Alsace since I could speak. It is not easy here, but it would not be easy there. I know only a few words.'

'*Elinize saglik*,' she says, uncertainly.

'You remember that?'

'Badly.'

133

'No,' he says. 'Though I likely say it wrong. When we came here, my parents taught me to speak your dialect, sent me to study letters. My mutter said it was a waste for a musician. Her father was an empiric.'

'Why did they come?'

'For better,' he says. 'Isn't that why anyone goes anywhere? Isn't that why your husband is gone to Heidelberg?'

'Not me,' she says. 'I came here because of Henne.'

She realises too late it sounds as though she means her marriage was not for the good, but the traitorous thought is out and she lets it hang. She has never been anywhere someone has not bid her go.

'From where?'

'South. My father farmed.'

'And your mother?'

'Dead,' she says, and feels a deserter. But Eren has startled her with his questioning, his seeming genuine interest in her answers. She squirms under his attention, and deflects it.

'Have you travelled outside Alsace?'

'Yes,' he says. 'Frederich and I were in France before this summons.'

She wrinkles her nose at his mention of the drummer, and Eren chuckles, a soft sound. 'You have him wrong.'

'He seems . . .' She searches the trees for the word. 'Coarse.'

'He is soft as fruit inside. He has had hard times. We take care of each other. We are all each other have, now.'

'He is not married?'

Eren laughs softly. 'No.'

'He is handsome enough.'

'He has not the temperament.'

'There are many sorts of women,' she says. 'I'm sure one could suit him.'

'If you are thinking to set him with your sister—'

Now it is Lisbet's turn to laugh. 'It could be a good match.'

'Are you?'

'I am already married,' she taps her belly, smiling.

'A good match with your Heinrich.'

Lisbet chews her cheek. She does not know how to answer, has never talked of such things even with Ida.

Eren shakes his head briefly. 'I'm sorry, Frederich must be making his mark. I am not usually so direct, but . . .'

He trails his fingers in the water, and Lisbet understands. She feels it too, the safety of their exchange. It was the same with Ida when they had first met at church, both their faces pale with the morning sickness of their first children: the recognition of kin. It makes her bold.

'Were you? With your wife?'

He rolls his head on his shoulders, a fluid movement that Lisbet could not replicate without cricks and clicks. 'We were. Young, married before our parents willed it. But we knew each other, from the moment of meeting. It was simple, to love her. She died with our first child.'

Lisbet places a protective palm over her belly and the baby shifts, presses on her, and she realises he has not mentioned her condition once, though it is all people have lately seemed to see of her. But he never looks at her stomach, or asks after the baby. He talks to her of her, and of him, and it is bewildering.

'Have I upset you?'

'No. It's all right. What was her name?'

'Aysel.'

'It's lovely.'

'It means moonbeam, the light that comes from the moon.'

A lump rises in Lisbet's throat. A dead wife, a dead babe, a common enough story. Is this why he is so kind to her? Of course. It is nothing at all to do with her, Lisbet. She could be any woman with a baby inside her.

She dips her hands in the river. The water sluices over her wrists, calming her hot blood.

And then, laughter. Not hers, not Eren's, but familiar enough to make her catch and hold her breath. She straightens, checking Eren is in sight, and sees he has extinguished the torch, and his hand is already on the handle of his knife. Ulf stands, barking, but it is not his guard-dog's growl. He is up and running before Lisbet can whistle him off.

The laughter stops, and Nethe's cry of surprise reaches them.

'Ulf? Down.'

It is not because it is Nethe that Lisbet motions for Eren to hide. It is not that which makes her crouch back into the undergrowth, grateful for her dark scarf. It is because of who follows Nethe out from the trees, with Ulf trotting obediently by her heels. It is because it is Ida.

Lisbet feels like a child playing at hide-and-go-seek. She has the same sour taste in her mouth, the same fear of discovery as Ida and Nethe break onto the bank in their long skirts, Ulf sniffing about them.

'Hello?' says Ida uncertainly. They look about them, but her hiding place holds. Lisbet cannot see Eren at all, only darkness between the trees.

'Must have run off,' shrugs Nethe. 'Ulf, home.'

She whistles thinly after the command, as Lisbet taught her, and it sends Ulf bolting for the farm, the promise of a bone to gnaw in his hopeful bound.

'Quickly,' says Nethe, pulling on Ida's hand. 'It's faster this way.'

Nethe tucks her skirts up into her undergarments, and to her shock Lisbet sees Ida do the same, and follow Nethe across the river, clambering onto the opposite bank and out of sight.

Eren emerges from the trees like an apparition. The knife

is still in his hand, and its glint catches Lisbet across the eyes. She stands blinking after her friend and her sister-in-law, barely hearing Eren.

'Who was your sister with?'

But Lisbet is already lifting up her own skirts, careless of Eren, of her bare legs streaked with dust and sweat, of the slick river stones as she stumbles across the slow river and after Ida and Nethe.

'Frau Wiler?' he murmurs, but Lisbet is all dog, sniffing after the women. They are heading west, parallel to the church, moving towards the main road to the city. It is foolishness to stumble after them through dangerous woods with a musician trailing her, but she must see, must know that she really has witnessed them together, laughing, holding hands like the old friends they once were.

Eren catches her up. 'Frau Wiler,' he says again. 'Where are you going?'

'To the city.'

'Now? On foot?'

She sees no reason to answer his questions, letting her pace be the reply. Her head spins like she is drunk, but it makes her feel light and swift, and she is covering ground easily. The trees start to thin and the sounds of the road reach them, drums and pipes and shouts. The night is alive with it, like a feast day, or the dances in her father's fields.

Lisbet arrives blinking into a chaos of fire and people, so many people, walking and laughing and smoking and singing, the sparse part of the wood where it meets the road full as though it is a port or some other place of arrival, and she steps from the calm sea of the forest into this new crush of humanity.

She does not turn to check Eren is still with her: she knows he will be close at hand, and the thought emboldens her despite the sight's strangeness, the smell of roasting meat and the dust thrown up everywhere from the sun-baked road, the people all around her.

She scans their faces as she makes for the city bounds, but there is no Ida, no Nethe, no Mathias or Plater – no one she knows. She is as much a stranger here as any. No one is watching her, no one even notices her, and she feels a thrill of anonymity rush through her. She is nothing to these travellers, drawn by the dancers.

'Frau Wiler,' says Eren, breaking her thoughts apart. 'It is too loud, the hour too late—'

She is buffeted into earshot of a preacher, calling down damnation on all of their heads.

'. . . and He shall bring such a reckoning as to turn your blood boiling in your veins, and arrow His vengeance to knock your soul rightly to Hell . . .'

The crowd he has amassed is jeering at his warnings, and though they are true, though they are all damned and God will not spare any of them and least of all her, Lisbet finds she cannot care right this moment. She needs to find Nethe and Ida, needs to drag them clear of this melee, this dark and ghoulish carnival. Eren reaches out again to her, and as though time has narrowed to a point, she sees his slim fingers, and his beseeching face, and then the globule of spit, thick and yellow as a bee, arrives firelit and shining and lands on his bearded cheek. A moment after follows a blow, ill-judged and glancing. She reels as though it is she who is struck, but Eren is so impassive it can only be from a lifetime of practice.

The assailant stumbles past, spewing obscenities, and his fellows laugh. Lisbet opens her mouth, but Eren shakes his head, and she contents herself with knocking hard against the man, sending him sprawling into the dust.

He is up in a moment, and it is not Lisbet he rounds on,

but Eren. He shoves the musician hard, knocking him against one of his companions, who shoulders him back. The colours have become red and hellish, her body thick and swollen with heat and the blood of her and the baby both.

'Stop,' says Lisbet weakly, but of course no one hears her. Eren is allowing himself to be buffeted among the drunks, keeping his balance like they are spinning him in a jig.

'Stop,' she says again, and when she plants herself among them, they do. The men move off, and Lisbet's heart flutters in relief. She looks at Eren, and he is looking back with undisguised anger.

'I'm sorry,' she says, uselessly.

He shakes his head once, a sharp and cutting gesture. 'I would rather you spared me your defence, Frau Wiler.'

'Lisbet,' she says weakly, but she has snapped it now, the fragile rapport they had been building. She staggers a little and feels Eren grasp her beneath the armpit. Shame prickles in her chest: she knows she is damp with sweat, that even now those slim fingers will feel it and he will be disgusted.

A warning is shouted from behind and the crowd parts to allow an open-topped cart access along the overcrowded road. She has forgotten Ida and Nethe, forgotten herself.

'Will we go back?' asks Eren.

Lisbet straightens her spine though it costs her, and she is brought tall as he. His lashes are long as Ida's, and brush his cheek where it is bare above his beard, apple-smooth as worn wood.

'I'm fine.'

Her armpit is tender where he steadied her. She feels her pulse throb there, the flush grows up her throat. Henne used to like it, blotches like stepping stones skipping up her neck when they were in bed. He'd press his lips each to each, close his mouth over her earlobe and bite.

She turns away. 'If you are tired, you can go. I must find my friend.'

'Your sister?'

'Ida!' she snaps. 'She is with Nethe.'

She is being a fool, and rude with it, but shame has mingled with her fear and she will not have come all this way and inflicted this on him for nothing.

He sighs, and she knows he is tired of her. She wishes he would go, wishes to be left in this faceless expanse of people and capture some of the recklessness she felt only minutes before. But he does not leave her. Instead, as the cart passes, its bed stacked with sacks and people, he lifts her, so deftly she could be a child, onto it and jumps up alongside, sitting on the edge with his feet almost in her lap.

The man overseeing the cart and its contents holds out his palm, and Eren reaches in his pocket for coin, but Lisbet finds a dusty block of honeycomb stuck to the inner of her apron. The man accepts it with gleaming eyes. Lisbet covers her belly and allows herself to be lulled, rocked by the motion of the cart as it passes over the rutted road. She tilts her head back, sees the sky immense and thickly starred overhead, and closer by Eren's jaw, the underside of his throat, his pulse flickering like some strange current in the black of his beard. She stares until they merge, the night and Eren, and she could not know where one ended and the other began.

She looks away only when the city walls loom, and she hears the drumming.

A hush seems to crush down on everything, so that all there is is that particular sound, rhythmic and somehow indecent. Lisbet knows instinctively that it is not made by a drummer's hand. Even if there were a thousand Frederichs they would not sound like this.

'Are you sure?' asks Eren, and when she hesitates he shakes his head again. 'We can go back.'

But she has come this far, has put him in danger, has followed Ida and Nethe into this spectacle and now she must find them. She slides from the cart, landing awkwardly, and turns towards the sound.

'I want to see.'

The cart has brought them before the horse market, and the high walls seem to thrum. Lisbet can feel it through her feet, in her pelvis. The entrance is thronged but she knows that if she is to find Ida and Nethe, this is where they will be. The whole night, the whole world seems angled towards the guild's entrance, towards that earth-bound and unearthly sound.

Eren takes the lead this time, forcing a path inside, and Lisbet keeps close behind, the dry straw cracking under her feet. The stage is high and wide, leaving only a thin rim of space for the observers to stand and jeer and shout and pray. And atop it are the dancers.

At least a hundred women, crammed onto the canvas-covered wood, their feet beating a firm tattoo so loud and ceaseless it is like a storm gathering itself. They spin and whirl and leap, and every one of them is sweating, shining, radiant.

Eren motions for Lisbet to stay where she is, nooked into the stalls where the brood mares are normally quartered, and indicates he will search the crowd. She nods, barely able to rip her gaze from the dancers. This is different from last time, from the old women spun by the strong men. There are no men at all on the stage, no musicians even, for where would there be room with so many women dancing? Lisbet realises that all she can hear are women's voices, raised and whooping, like she has come across a crush of sprites or witches. She has never heard or seen women in such abundant numbers. Their clothes slip from their shoulders, but there is not the lewdness of last time. Here in the dark, lit by torches and with the scent of horse and sweat all about, they seem heavenly, divine, licked in the gold slick of the fire.

Two dancers part, and at the centre of the stage, Lisbet glimpses a woman spinning another, their hands close about each other's waists. Her breath spikes.

It is Nethe and Ida. Lisbet grips the wood of the stall, digging her nails in until they splinter. The dancers close in a surge, swallowing the women once more, and Lisbet climbs onto the stall door, her belly resting atop the gate. From here she can just see Nethe's short hair, her head tossed back in a shout of delight, head and shoulders taller than the others.

'No sign—' starts Eren, appearing at her side, but she hushes him with a gesture, and points. Again the dancers part, and again her friend and her sister-in-law materialise, marked apart by their connectedness. It is clear they are in no mania, no grip of divine abandon. They look as they are, two women wildly spinning, locked in each other's embrace.

There is a commotion at the entrance. Men crowd into the already airless vault of the guild, brandishing long hooks. The Twenty-One's strong men. And there at their head, inevitable as a nightmare, is copper-haired Plater, the hook swinging from one rough hand. A fist grasps inside Lisbet's throat, and squeezes. If he sees Ida . . .

Lisbet ducks her head, and throws herself towards the stage. There is no gilded allure over the room now, only the reek of shit and sweat from exhausted women, and her sister-in-law and best friend mad or stupid or both, making a mockery of the whole sorry sight. Eren is too slow to follow Lisbet, who hears his cry as though she is underwater. She pushes ahead of the wave of men, and mounts the wooden steps. They creak and sway with the motion of the dancers, as though she has stepped from safe harbour onto the deck of a ship.

Finding her footing, she stumbles on, into the centre of the dancers. Here, the sounds around them are diminished, and a sort of breathing hush composes itself into a rhythm, as though she is back inside her mother, listening to a heartbeat that may as well be a god's for all she knows or cares. How her baby must feel at this moment, no need of knowledge beyond her own body. It is comforting in a way, and dazzling, and as she brushes past the women, she understands suddenly that this is no mania. There is something soaring, hopeful: an abandonment. Perhaps it is transcendence.

A cry rises from the steps, and through the pulsing bodies Lisbet sees the men mount the stage, hooks already jabbing and prodding. Plater is stooped, his full force behind a jab, and as he bends Lisbet sees a boy at his hip, the hook higher than his head. It is Daniel, the Lehmanns' boy, and his face wears a light so bright it terrifies her.

She forces herself forward, until she stands beside Nethe and Ida. The women are so intent on one another they have not noticed the men, or the increasing shouts, or even Lisbet herself until she takes hold of Nethe's shoulder and yanks hard.

Nethe breaks free, and blinks at Lisbet as though she has woken her from a dream. Her face is flushed and slick, her eyes heavy-lidded, and through the cloth of her dress Lisbet feels her shoulder move into taut rigidity, her breath breaking from pants to gasps.

Lisbet, she mouths, and beside her Ida, regaining her balance from the broken spin of Nethe's embrace, matches her astonishment, her growing alarm. Lisbet feels a righteous anger break apart inside her, and she shakes Ida.

'Look,' shouts Lisbet, gesturing. 'Your husband.'

Nethe swears, fear making her eyes blank as Ida's become bright and panicked. Nethe takes Lisbet's wrist in one sweaty palm, and Ida's in her other, and drags them both towards the back of the guild.

There are no steps at this edge, but Nethe gathers her skirts and leaps down into the crowd easy as a cat. The watchers press back from her as though she is diseased, jeering as she reaches up and takes Ida by the waist, as she had only moments before as they span, and lifts her like a girl. The two women look at each other, and unease roils in Lisbet's stomach.

'Lisbet!' It is Eren, beside Nethe, reaching up for her, and without thinking she throws herself forwards, her belly brushing his chest as he catches and lowers her carefully to the ground. The four of them make a chain of hands, as though they had planned it, as though they were children playing and any moment will burst into song.

Eren's hand in hers is calloused and dry, Nethe's mannish and strong, both sliding through Lisbet's sweating fingers so she must redouble her grip on them. Is it her imagining that Eren squeezes back?

As they break out of the guild, Lisbet turns to where Plater and his men and his boy and their hooks weave glinting as needles, darting through the dancers. Daniel spins and laughs as though the hook is a partner, and as he does his eyes seem to snag on Lisbet's. She ducks her head and shudders, taking gasping breaths of the stolid night air as Eren drags them clear of the guild, away and away until the drumming of a dozen dozen feet is swallowed by the carnival of the streets.

Eleven

When they are finally on the main road, Eren looses Lisbet's hand. She grasps after the empty air a moment before dropping Nethe's, and rounding on the women.

'What in the Devil's name were you doing?' she hisses. A stitch has risen in her side, and it darns in time with her breath. Nethe stands with her head bowed, like a chastised child, but Ida steps forward, red blooms in her cheeks.

'Not here, Bet,' she says. 'My father is trading. We must go further off.'

'Then you are all the more foolish—'

'Not here,' Ida repeats. 'Please.'

'Come,' says Eren softly, and it is for him that Lisbet allows herself to be drawn further up the road, her whole body aching, until they are at last able to step into the shadows of the trees where an hour before they broke into the mayhem of the night hawkers. In mute agreement their strange assembly draws away, until the forest has swallowed them and the sounds of the road whole.

Lisbet collapses onto a felled trunk, split to its rotted pulp by a long-ago storm. It is rough and soft, and she scrapes her nail into the mushrooms growing along its length, their earthy scent growing into her nostrils, subsuming sweat and candles and sour breath.

'Are you all right, Bet?'

The trunk bends, sinks beneath Ida's weight. Lisbet can tell Ida's face from her tone: hesitant, her plump lip caught between her crooked front teeth. She can tell, too, that Ida has been drinking, something sharp and strong.

Lisbet cannot bring herself to look at her friend – she will strike her, or else burst into tears, and she doesn't want to do either. She can feel their combined attention on her, and she wonders how she looks to them, hunched over her belly, her whole body heaving.

She concentrates on her breathing, on slowing its pace, deepening its reach so it can stretch to the baby and her own heart both, soothe them. When at last her pulse has stopped racing, and the baby has pressed itself visibly against her skirts, she collects herself enough to look up.

Ida is blur-eyed from drink. Lisbet searches her friend's face. The woman she thought she knew so well is, she now realises, a stranger. All this time Ida has kept these dangerous night-time jaunts from Lisbet, and more besides. The betrayal rises sharp in her throat. Ida looks at her fearfully, sorrowfully, and it makes Lisbet feel powerful. She stares back.

'Well?'

'We were friends, you know it.'

'But no longer,' says Lisbet, searching Ida's face for the lie she is certain will come. 'You told me you cared nothing for her.'

'I wish that were true.'

'We prayed for it to be,' says Nethe, a little too loud, and Ida's face crumples further.

'Why?' says Lisbet. 'What happened between you?'

'Must we do this before the Turk?' says Nethe, and Lisbet

glares up at her. Nethe glares back, and though she wears it better than slight Ida, Lisbet notices a haziness to her gaze too. Both drunk, then.

'He is likely a kinder witness than me at this moment,' Lisbet says coldly.

Laughter erupts from the trees: a man and a woman, searching for somewhere to tup. Lisbet pushes herself from the trunk with immense effort, trying to keep some sort of dignity as her belly overbalances her and the laughter turns to rhythmic pants, the slap of flesh on flesh.

Eren motions for them to move further off, towards the river. To Lisbet's astonishment, as they go Ida lets out a quiet giggle, which she stifles with her palm. Nethe echoes it as the moans rise faintly from the shadows.

'Ida,' hisses Lisbet, 'Agnethe. Stop.'

But both women are laughing openly now, and holding each other about the waists, and though they are out of earshot of the couple Lisbet feels furious, embarrassment flooding her body.

'You are children,' she snaps.

'It is all right, Lisbet,' says Eren, but even his low tone cannot comfort her. She increases her pace, her neck burning, holding her skirts to ford the river, and still on she plunges. She wants to be away and rid of them, her questions and their company both.

Lisbet hears the women's laughter, and Eren's calls, and knows she is worrying him with her pace, but she doesn't care. She all but runs across the boggy ground, hearing Ida's shrieks as the mud sucks her toes, hearing Nethe's voice join Eren's in shouting her name. But she won't stop, won't slow enough for them to catch up, slipping between the silent trees until she reaches her brambles and wrenches them aside, hauling them over behind.

She collapses at the trunk of the dance tree, pressing her palms to her eyes so hard she sees stars. Her body and mind are a confusion of colour and heat, and between her legs there is a throb that matches the couple's cries, the beat of women's feet on wood.

'Lisbet?'

It is Nethe's voice, sober now, and close. Lisbet opens her eyes. She had forgotten, in her fury, that Nethe knows this place, knows how to get through the brambles, and now her sister-in-law stands looking at her, Ida swaying beside and looking up at the ribbons, mouth agape, and behind is Eren, scanning the token-strewn ground.

'Get out,' says Lisbet, but her voice is small, and serves only to make Nethe step closer.

'You shouldn't run,' says Nethe. 'Not so close to your time.'

'You should not give me cause to,' spits Lisbet. 'Behaving like a hure, an imbecile. You and Ida both.'

'And you?' says Nethe hotly. 'Out at night with a Turk? What cause have you for that?'

'I am asking the questions!' shouts Lisbet. She sounds petulant, but cannot control it. Why has she brought them here, to the one place she and her children can be safe and alone?

Ida drops to her knees and shuffles forward so Lisbet can again smell the drink on her breath. 'Where are we, Bet?'

Lisbet feel tears coming. She is so tired, so hot, so heavy. She wants Ida to hold her.

'It's her tree,' says Nethe, and her voice has lost some of its scathe. 'For her—'

'No,' says Lisbet. 'How dare you.'

'You're the one who led us here,' says Nethe mulishly.

'Did I ask you to follow?'

'For what?' says Ida. 'Your tree? What's that?'

She points at the platform, and Lisbet snipes, 'I don't reckon your husband would be happy you knowing.'

'Since when have you cared what my husband thinks,' says Ida, sounding suddenly solemn. 'Since when have you thought I care.'

Lisbet takes a breath. It shudders through her ribs, catching in the back of her throat. 'It's a dance tree. A pagan place.'

'What are those?'

'Ribbons. I put them there. For . . . for my losses.'

'For your babies?'

Lisbet looks up to the strips of fabric, to the sky shredded and star-strewn through the branches, and nods. Ida's hand snakes back into hers. It has none of its usual coolness. It is sticky like a fevered child's.

'Forgive us, Lisbet,' says Ida. 'Don't be angry.'

Lisbet has not the energy to maintain her fury. She breathes out in a great rush, and squeezes her friend's hand.

'Why were you there?' asks Lisbet. 'With her. Why did you dance?'

Ida drops her pointed chin. 'To disappear.'

Lisbet snorts. 'You think that was disappearing? Making a spectacle of yourselves?'

'We were but two of many,' says Ida.

'You are the council man's wife. She is the penitent. You think yourselves anonymous?'

'My husband was meant to be elsewhere,' says Ida. 'I thought I knew his appointments, his movements.'

'As well as he knows yours. Let me be clear with you,' says Lisbet. 'It was obvious to all that you were fakes. I could see it, and Eren, and Plater if he'd spied you. For all I know he did. Any fool could. You were two drunk women, spinning as though it were a dance, not a plague. It was idiocy at best, and blasphemy at worst.'

'We do not need your judgement,' says Nethe.

'It seems your own is at fault,' says Lisbet. 'And why together? I thought your friendship broken. I saw you fighting, after almsgiving.'

'It is long enough past,' says Nethe, carefully. 'And the dancers . . . they offer a chance.'

'A chance at what?'

'A new beginning, a salvation of sorts.'

Lisbet tilts her head back against the trunk, so Nethe cannot see the understanding in her eyes. 'But you are playing at it. It is not a game.'

'It's true,' says Eren, and all of the women turn their heads to where he stands, still at the edge of the clearing among the brambles. Lisbet had all but forgotten he was there. 'Some of the women dance till they die, or until their feet swell with blood, or—'

He glances at Lisbet, who feels herself flicker, and grips tighter to Ida's hand. She tries to anchor herself tighter to the present.

'I am sorry,' says Eren. 'I only meant to impress upon you the danger of what you are doing, Fräulein Wiler.'

Nethe sniffs at his address. 'I need no Turk's counsel.'

'Perhaps,' says Eren. 'But take a musician's, who has seen the truth of this mania. Who has seen the counterfeiters hauled out, their feet burned with hot coals to punish them. There is talk of drowning them, if their numbers increase.'

'I know something of punishment,' says Nethe.

'Plater was there,' adds Lisbet, the man's name as sour as the bile in her throat. 'If he had seen you, what then? Henne's journey to Heidelberg would be for naught. They would brand you, and seize the bees. You know they wait only for the slightest of excuses.'

Nethe is wilting. It is a visible change, her shoulders

slumping. 'We only wished to have somewhere safe, some-where we could be lost.'

'That crowd is no such place,' says Eren, gentler than she deserves.

'But why must you hide it?' says Lisbet. 'Surely Henne would be glad of your friendship.'

'It is Henne who forbade it,' says Nethe.

'I cannot believe it,' says Lisbet. 'He cultivated ours.' She squeezes Ida's hand, but Ida pulls from her grip, and scoops her thin arms around her legs. Her eyes are full of tears.

'I should not have allowed it,' she says. 'I see the cruelty now, Agnethe. But it was all I had, to be close. You see that?'

'See what?' says Lisbet. 'You are speaking in riddles.' She rounds on Agnethe. 'The both of you. Tell me what is between you. Tell me why you were sent away.'

But Ida goes quiet and Nethe is vanishing again, turning solid and immutable. Lisbet feels a fury so large it turns her cold. She grips at the earth, trying to ground herself.

'You speak of salvation, of blessings. You spent seven years in silence and now you caterwaul in the midst of a mania. Do you hear yourself, Nethe? Because as someone who does, who listens, I can tell you you are a fool.'

Nethe remains impassive, and Ida makes a small noise in her throat.

'Tell me why you were dancing. Tell me why you were sent away.'

Another silence, into which Lisbet irrupts.

'Tell me! Why will you not? Why am I being kept outside it all, always tested and found wanting?'

Lisbet catches up a clod of dirt and throws it full at Nethe. Too slow she registers the weight, the hard centre of the pebble she selected for its band of quartz. It strikes Nethe hard above her eye. Ida scrambles to her feet, rushes to stem the trickle of blood running from Nethe's eyebrow. She must reach up, almost on her toes. She presses her sleeve to the cut.

Nethe barely reacted to the blow, but now she takes Ida's other hand, the one not pressed to her brow, and makes a cup of it. She rests her cheek against the open palm, and raises her eyes to meet Lisbet's. It is a movement practised and simple as a kiss.

For a moment, Lisbet does not understand. But then she sees Ida's expression as she looks at Nethe, lit with such love it feels indecent to witness. It is the same beam she had dancing, but Lisbet mistook it for wildness, for delirium. And it is, of a sort, for what that look means is impossible.

Lisbet feels as though she is falling. She places both her hands firmly by her sides, tucks her head between her knees.

In the dark cave of her skirts, Lisbet sorts shadows, chasing them through fog. The token of hair, soft and blonde and secret. A sin so grave as to be banished. The glances, the strange energy between them, until that day Nethe accompanied Ida to the slums. Nethe's night-time absences. Lisbet chews her tongue. There is the shock of the sin of course, black and swallowing, but also a great sort of sadness, that Ida never told her.

She looks up.

'You are damned,' says Lisbet softly, though she wants to scream. *You lied. You lied.* 'The Devil can take you.'

The noise that comes from Ida's throat is airless, strangled. A whimper.

'Don't,' says Nethe.

'This is why they kept you apart,' says Lisbet, her hand on her belly. Let them think she is pious, that she is powerful. Not a scared woman, alone and abandoned in her confusion. 'You are sinners of the worst kind. Unclean, foul, unnatural sodomites.'

Ida flinches, but Nethe returns her glare. 'Those are Mutti's words. Plater's words.'

'They are God's,' says Lisbet, bristling.

'They are not yours,' says Nethe. Blood is dripping from her brow but she does not wipe it away. 'You do not believe it, truly. This place proves it.' She gestures at the tree, the ribbons.

'It is not the same,' says Lisbet, with a wild burst of fear. 'It is a sin, of the worst kind.'

'You do not think we know that?' says Nethe, and she breaks from the hold of her stillness and laughs, a hysterical sound, more fury than mirth. 'By the Church's measure, we are all lost. Me and Ida, you and your babies—'

'Nethe!' cries Ida, but Nethe rushes on.

'Why do you think those women dance? Because there is no earthly way to be saved. You and Mutter have told me enough times – Strasbourg is sliding Hellwards. And we women, we bear the brunt. We are bred or banished, and always, *always* damned. Prayers cannot help us, the priests will not help us. Your babies were never blessed, so they were damned. It is not right, that is the unnatural act, not this.' She thumps her chest, where her heart is. 'Is this not why you come to your doom tree? To reach at a place where you can be comforted, where you can find some semblance of peace? Because you have none, do you, Lisbet?'

Lisbet cannot deny it. Though her pulse gallops at the deceit, at what she is learning, still she feels the effect of the tree upon her blood, cooling, calming as a mother's touch.

'And nor do I,' says Nethe, breathing so hard spit flecks her lips. 'I did not find it in church as a child, nor at my chores. I did not find it searching my soul in silence at that abbey, beating my back until I bled. Not in the cathedral where my penance was meant to be at an end. I prayed harder than ever, there, to find it – the settling of my heart. Peace. Safety. But it is nowhere, except with this woman.'

'Nethe,' says Ida desperately. 'Please, it is too much.'

'She wants to know, so let her know,' says Nethe, pacing like a caged bear. 'We have loved each other since childhood. It is no simple lust, no strangeness. It is a love as deep and natural as the roots we walk on. We planned our lives around it, this love. Planned for Ida to marry Henne, for me to marry Alef Plater and all of us to live together.'

'You could not have thought that would work? To live your whole lives deceitful?'

'It was better than living without each other,' says Ida in a small voice. 'I did not love Henne, Bet. You shouldn't be jealous.'

Lisbet snorts, because she is not jealous. She is simply adrift, aghast that they thought such foolishness any sort of life.

'But Plater discovered us,' says Nethe. 'Seven years ago, here in the forest. He and Henne found us.'

'Henne?' Lisbet steadies herself. 'He knows?'

'He knows, and he watched as Alef beat me,' says Nethe, and now there is not simple passion in her voice. There is also astonishment, that her brother could have acted so. The sadness. 'He let him beat me almost to death. He watched—'

'No,' says Ida. 'She does not need to know all.'

'She does,' says Nethe. 'Let her know what she married.'

The women stare each other out, and Lisbet can feel Nethe relenting. But she doesn't want to be spared. 'I want to know.'

Nethe takes a deep breath. 'Henne watched. He didn't make any move to stop him, not even when Alef knocked me unconscious. Perhaps he stopped Alef doing worse, but I will not absolve him of his inaction. And then he let Alef give me a choice. Alef said I could marry him, or be sent to the mountains. He was early in the employ of the Twenty-One, then, already their power was hardening his heart.'

'He gave me a choice, too,' says Ida, her voice very small. 'The same banishment, to a different abbey, after Nethe chose to leave. This is what we fought about, Bet. I chose the coward's way. I chose to stay.'

'I was wrong to call you a coward,' says Nethe thickly. 'You are the bravest of us all, to bear such a marriage.' She turns her attention to Lisbet. 'Plater took what I loved most and bound it to him. He knew that would hurt worse than any blow, any banishment. And Ida stayed for her father, I see that now. Plater would have let Mathias fall to the mercy of the Twenty-One and their taxes. Ida took a loveless, brutal marriage for her father.'

'It was not all loveless,' says Ida. 'Not with my children born safe. Not with you as my friend, Bet.'

Lisbet feels herself sinking further away from reality, into the shadows, into the pit of what she's discovered. Ida was married as punishment. Every child, penance. And Lisbet thought her so blessed.

Nethe's face shines with defiance. She seems to have forgotten Eren stands at the clearing's edge, seems to have forgotten every word she says damns her deeper. 'And every moment of those years I have spent trying to slough her from my skin, unmake myself so I can forget all the parts she helped build. Bled myself to rid her, like a sickness. Believed that it is a sin, to love her. I thought I had managed. But from the moment of my return I have felt her goodness in everything, from the bread of my first meal to her attentions at church. I could not forget her any more than I can forget myself, Lisbet. And so, I stopped trying.'

She looks taller than ever, seeming to spread out over the clearing like another tree, rooted just as strong. 'If that makes us sinners, so be it. But I think you know there is more in this world than simple sin. That is why you came here, to this pagan place, a place the Church would condemn, and made it holy. I think that is why you walk with a Turk, a sign and symptom of Christendom's worst enemy.'

At this, Lisbet glances to Eren, crouching in the shadows. His gaze is downcast, and he is so still he might have become stone himself.

Nethe stops pacing. Her chest heaves. 'I think you understand.'

'It is impossible,' croaks Lisbet. 'You must not do this.'

'We are chaste,' says Ida, in a small voice. Lisbet snorts mirthlessly. 'Believe me. I know the risk we take by even being seen together, but our love is chaste, Bet. It is the best we can do. I cannot be without her.'

She begins to cry openly, and Lisbet's already fading resolve vanishes. 'Don't cry,' she says. 'Oh, Ida, why did you not tell me?'

'For all the reasons you fear. If Alef were to find out . . .' She shudders. 'I did not want you to join us in the lie.'

'But if you are truly chaste, then it is friendship. They cannot damn you for that.'

'Of course they can,' says Ida. 'Alef will never believe it. He will wring my neck, and the law will allow it. Not that he will let anyone know he is a cuckold.'

It is Lisbet's turn to shiver. She knows Plater would not hesitate to do violence to any of them. The true darkness of his punishment for Ida comes to her: his possession of her is torture. He sent the woman he wished to marry into silence, kept the woman she loved in a sort of purgatory.

Lisbet rubs her friend's arm. 'What should your children think, if you were exposed?'

'She is Ida, too,' says Nethe. 'Not only a wife, not only a mother.'

'I am not saying—' Lisbet drives her palms into her temples.

'This is all in circles. All I am saying is this cannot continue. The dancing, for all to see.'

'I know,' says Ida, in a tiny voice. 'We know. We have nowhere else to go.'

The words rise before Lisbet can swallow them down.

'Here,' says Lisbet. 'If it is true you are chaste, and only friends.'

Blinking away her tears, Ida nods. 'It is, Lisbet. I swear it.'

'Then we can meet here, together.'

Astonished silence greets her words. Lisbet herself cannot believe she has spoken them.

'You are sure?' Nethe's voice is hoarse with excitement.

Slowly, Lisbet nods. 'There must be one place safe for you. I would not have you discovered. And it is a dance tree, after all.'

Nethe whoops, and Ida's face comes alight with joy.

'But you must not touch anything, and cover over the path with brambles. And you must not tell a soul.'

She looks at Nethe as she says this, and knows she understands her to mean about Eren, as well as the tree. Nethe nods, and holds out her scarred hand to help Lisbet to her feet.

Nethe places into her hand the pebble, and Lisbet drops it gently back beneath the ribbons. She watches them sway in a slight breeze, the sightless stars beyond. They are bound up in each other's secrets now, bonded tight as roots to earth.

Two hundred and twenty-nine dancing

Dorit is a life-long penitent. As a girl, her mother and father bred atonement into her and her siblings. The ones that survived are shut up in monasteries and a nunnery now, but Dorit has a higher purpose. She cannot bolt herself behind high walls, enclose herself in prayers. It is her calling to follow disaster like a bloodhound, offering up her mind and body in hope of salvation.

To this end, she took the road to Strasbourg. Times are desperate there as in many a city, and worse than in most. Since the comet damned the century, Strasbourg has become infamous, beset by devils. Dorit packs her sharpest shears, collects the ash from her night-time fires. She blunts her teeth on sticks, eats only raw mushrooms and grass. Her belly swells and she does not wash, and she arrives to the city stinking, triumphant.

She is not the first to have struck upon the idea. The road is thronged with men and women, their backs rent by whips, heads shaved, ash smeared over their faces, their breasts, and all of them rosaried and praying. She will have to reach further than her usual penances. She sells her final teeth and has them pulled without a sip of spirits. She refuses the gauze and bleeds openly, letting the thirsty dirt drink it in. With the coin she goes to a tavern and pays three women to leave. They shrug and say they wish to see the dancers anyway.

Dorit follows them. They are hures, it is clear from their dress and their manner, the easy way they throw their bodies through the streets. Dorit has never had such ease. Her body is the site of punishment for all her earthly sins, and all others' besides. She is proud of her suffering but, watching these women, something in her pangs.

They go to the horse market, but there is not a horse in sight. Instead, a stage that the women mount, beginning to weave through the others that dance there. But it is clear that while they are fakes, most are not. She recognises the glaze, the true apartness a trance can bring. It is a place she has reached only twice, through extreme pain, and the patch where she flensed the skin from her calf itches in the precious memory.

Dorit forces herself among them. It is clearly their first time in the grip of divinity for many. They will wear themselves out fast as a candle in a draught. Even as she watches, a woman collapses, convulsing once, twice, eyes rolled back, white as peeled eggs. Her exhale is long, and when she is trodden on, again and again, she does not flinch. Dead, then.

It is a while before anyone but Dorit notices, and then the dancer is borne aloft over the crowd, limp wrists like wrung-necked doves. She will be taken to a paupers' pit.

Dorit smiles, her gums bare and tender, and begins to spin. There are martyrs to be made, here. She will show them how it's done. She will teach them how to atone.

Twelve

'Up so early?'

Without her starched white headscarf Sophey looks shrunken and frail, like a baby without its swaddling. A teething baby, thinks Lisbet, not wholly unkindly, as she watches Sophey hobble into the kitchen, cradling her cheek. Her jaw is swollen around a sore tooth, the skin flushed. Her hair sticks in thin strands to her forehead, fluffy as a chick's behind her ears. Her pale scalp shows through, and Lisbet thinks of what Eren had told her of the theories in town, of hot blood and enlarged brains, wonders if her mother-in-law's is pushing at her skull.

The skin around Lisbet's own eyes is tight and bee's-wing thin. She has not slept, though her whole body ached with tiredness. The baby kicked and kicked, shuddering her ribcage until she could do nothing but rise and tend the bees, hoping their hums would soothe the child, soothe her own racing mind.

'What is wrong with you?' Sophey's black eyes bore into Lisbet's belly. 'Is it Henne's boy?'

Lisbet shakes her head and pushes her hair back. Sophey narrows her eyes. 'Your hands are filthy.'

Lisbet clutches them in her lap. Though she has scrubbed

and scrubbed, her fingernails are still rimed in muck from the forest floor, from where she flung dirt at Nethe. Looking back those hours have a dreamlike unreality, but there, under her fingernails, is proof.

On their walk home, Eren trailing at a distance behind, and Nethe focused on her feet with the deliberate steps of the drunkard, Lisbet had asked Nethe if she understood, truly, what she was risking, if Plater discovered them.

Nethe came up short, and her gaze was so like Henne's, so completely serious, Lisbet shuddered.

'Dismemberments,' she said. 'Drowning.' Then turned her head back to the path ahead, and kept walking.

Now, Lisbet looks across the table at her mother-in-law, who after all these years spent side by side is so distant from her. They still know so little of each other.

'You look a wreck.'

Lisbet meets her gaze unblinkingly. Her eyes burn with exhaustion. Sophey sucks on her tooth, and spits blood out to the yard, picking up her scarf and beginning to tie it with swift, practised movements. With it on, she is herself again, unassailable.

'There is fresh water?' says Sophey. 'And you have seen to the bees?'

Lisbet nods, her head heavy on her neck, her tongue stirring dryly in her mouth.

'To bed then,' says Sophey briskly. Lisbet blinks at her, amazed. 'You are no good like this. Mute and dead-eyed besides. Back to bed, and wake my daughter.'

Lisbet rises meekly, her knees clicking.

'It will be easier,' says Sophey. 'When Henne is back.'

Finally, Lisbet clears her throat. 'Yes.'

Sophey has mistaken her silence for missing, her dull countenance for lovesickness. But after what she learnt last night at the dance tree, Lisbet would gladly never see Henne ever again. How could he watch his own sister beaten and banished, Ida be married under duress, and not protect them? Lisbet eyes Sophey, and wonders if and what she knows. Her evident dislike of Ida, her need to keep her away from her daughter – could Lisbet ask?

Sophey pulls a face in cruel imitation of Lisbet's probing stare. 'Are you going?'

No, Lisbet decides. She could not.

Nethe is spread across the bed, her mouth wide open, just like Henne's when he sleeps.

'Nethe,' says Lisbet, and when she does not stir, she places her hand on Nethe's shoulder and squeezes. 'Agnethe.'

Nethe smiles lightly, and tilts her cheek down so it rests on Lisbet's hand. Lisbet withdraws sharply, and Nethe opens her eyes.

'Nethe, your mother needs you.'

Nethe groans: a waft of sour beer reaches Lisbet. 'I am tired.'

'Not as tired as I,' says Lisbet. 'She wants you up.'

'Can she not make do with you? Tell her I've a headache.'

'I'll wager you do,' says Lisbet. 'I am ordered back to bed.'

'You meant it, didn't you?' says Nethe, unmoving.

'Meant what?'

'The dance tree,' says Nethe. 'We really can go?'

Lisbet does not want to have said it, doesn't want any of last night to have happened.

'Tonight?' asks Nethe.

'If I cannot sleep, nothing will be possible.'

'I can find it without you,' says Nethe.

'And I can wake Sophey.'

Nethe glares at her, but it is without her usual intensity. The last of the beer still blurs her eyes. 'You will not.'

'No,' admits Lisbet. 'But if you don't let me sleep now, Sophey will find her daughter murdered and her daughter-in-law on the gibbet.'

Nethe laughs. 'Black, Lisbet.'

'As pitch.'

•

Lisbet wakes with confusion. Her sleep was dreamless but for the fact she was at sea, on a boat that lifted and fell on rolling waves. Her thighs are sticky and in the dark, shuttered room she cannot see why. She fumbles with her shift, hauling up her skirts and rubbing her hands across her legs. She brings her hand up to her nose, already knowing her fingers are bloody, anticipating the stink of iron coating her palm – but no. She licks her forefinger. Salt. It is sweat, only.

She lies back on the pallet, her heart slowing by increments, and places her hand on her belly. *Still there, still here. My boy.*

She levers herself upright. The room is unbearably hot. Her hair is stuck in stringy ropes down her back, on her forehead. No doubt she stinks as badly as Nethe did. Did Sophey smell the drink on her daughter? Lisbet used to think her mother-in-law all seeing, all knowing, but now she realises she is only a woman, suffering often, and as scared as any of them of the damnation her cherished Geiler bestowed on them all, and especially upon Agnethe.

She listens, but can hear nothing. Not the musicians' snores, nor Sophey's clattering. Her eyelids start to close. She could sleep more, sleep again. She should, if their visit tonight is insisted upon by Nethe.

Lisbet is beginning to drift when a cry rises from an indeterminate distance. She pushes herself up again, listening. Another cry, of anger or alarm, and then, belatedly, the dogs begin to bark. Lisbet forces herself to her feet.

The yard is dusk-darkened. She has slept the whole day. Lisbet scatters chickens as she hurries towards the commotion, her body not yet awake enough to entrust itself with a run. Her belly always feels heavier after sleep, and she is gasping by the time she reaches the skep yard. What she sees is enough to stop her breath entirely.

It makes no sense to begin with. The dogs are running in crazed loops around the fence that borders the skeps. Sophey is standing at the boundary of the forest, waving her rake and yelling. From the trees Lisbet can hear but not see Nethe, bellowing as though on a hunt. And between them, between Lisbet and Sophey, and Sophey and Nethe, the air is smudged, made thick with bees.

Lisbet's ribs grow sharp, slicing with each breath. It is because the pain is so intense that she knows she is not dreaming. She gathers herself, holding her upper arms and squeezing, pushing away the panic buzzing around her body.

'Stop shouting,' she calls, making her voice melodic, as though singing a nursery rhyme. 'Stop shouting, Sophey, Nethe. Stop shouting.'

Sophey cannot hear her. Lisbet checks the sky. The bees are floating over everything, making the heat visible, waving on the stifling air. But they are not one body. She can see the deepening sky through them, see wisps of cloud, see that there is no moon, no stars yet. They are not a swarm. But whatever has unsettled her sister- and mother-in-law has unsettled the bees, and the threat is only growing with their shrieking.

First she must deal with the dogs. They are the most like to be targeted. She whistles them over. Ulf obeys, and Fluh follows when she sees Ulf sitting at Lisbet's feet. She lifts the smaller dog, who snaps and yaps, and leads Ulf to the kitchen, throwing Fluh inside after Ulf and closing the door.

Lisbet eyes the pressing shed. She could fetch her robes, her wicker mask, the net. But more immediately, she must stop the noise, soothe the air so the bees start to calm.

'Frau Wiler?' Lisbet turns her head. Frederich is there, his mouth agape, the drum at his hip. He is raw-eyed, just returned from the city.

'Don't speak,' hums Lisbet. The drum has given her an idea. 'Where is Eren?'

'I believe in bed—'

Lisbet shushes him. 'Fetch him,' she says again, in that same mellifluous voice, thrilled at the thought they lay with only a wall between them and no soul else in the house. 'And his lute.'

Frederich nods his understanding, and runs toward the house, his drum banging at his hip. Lisbet winces, but the bees are still a floating tide, not a cloud. In the forest, Nethe has stopped shouting, or has moved out of earshot. Lisbet walks closer to Sophey.

'Stop shouting,' she says as she walks, over and over until at last Sophey turns to her, her swollen cheek a livid red, her face bright with fury.

'A thief!' she says. 'Look!'

'Stop shouting,' says Lisbet again, and raises her hands slowly overhead. Sophey falls silent and her face blanches. She lowers her rake.

'What do we do,' mouths Sophey. Lisbet moves her hands down to her sides.

'Stay there.'

She walks as slowly as she can towards the house. As she goes, she sees what Sophey was pointing at. The upturned cones of two skeps flung atop one another, and beside them: nothing resembling a hive. Only debris. She forces herself to look away, to move past the mess and towards where Eren now stands with his lute, Frederich beside him.

She gestures to him, to play. He raises his eyebrows. *Are you sure?*

Slow, she mouths. *Gentle.*

He lifts the instrument to the centre of himself, to the place she carries her child, and cradles it. He begins to play.

The loveliness of it catches Lisbet in the chest. It is nothing she has ever heard before, and entirely familiar, like something someone sang to her in sleep. She eyes the bees, and by some miracle they are still not swarming though two colonies among them have had their homes ripped apart. With Eren playing to them, she trusts the situation enough to leave.

In the hot, cramped well of the shed, she breathes more deeply. The smell of wax coats her nostrils, cosseting and clean. She takes the veil and the robes, the net, keeping her movements slow though there is no one to see her, trying to make her heartbeat match the rhythm of Eren's music, so when she approaches the bees they will see her as nothing but an extension of it, a soothing lull made flesh.

She dabs two stripes of honey from the ruined hives onto her wrists. They are older hives, colonies Henne's father culti-vated. Their honey is pale gold and smells of the forest. She takes one of the bees' shallow bowls and fills it with tallow, dropping in a cube of beeswax to mellow the smell. She lights the wick with the wall flint, and when she comes outside she strips rosemary from the shrub outside, and scatters it over the fire so the whole thing begins to shed scented smoke.

Sophey walks carefully to join her, and takes the bowl in her stiff fingers as though this is a dance they have rehearsed, both moving in time with Eren's tune. The old woman straightens, and without fear leads Lisbet through the heart of the skep yard, as if they are a procession at High Mass, scattering incense through a cathedral.

The bees, already lulled by the music, stumble lower in the

sky, falling over them like a net even as Lisbet raises hers, and begins to work. There is a slight hesitation in Eren's playing, his fingers stumbling as the women enter the bees, but he soon finds his place again.

Lisbet sorts among them, gently guiding them towards their sections of the yard, towards their hives. From the corner of her eye, she sees a figure emerge from the forest, but Nethe has the good sense to remain where she is, and not ask questions.

It takes an age, but Lisbet is revived from her sleep, and she works as though she had practised for just this moment her whole life, a life that until now had been full of ruin and curses and blood and now is nothing but music and beauty and bees, her mother-in-law processing before her, anointing her path with smoke. She feels some of the power a priest must, giving each animal their place, clearing them of their panic, their confusion. Giving them peace. The unhomed bees gust and plume, making a column above the destroyed hives.

'What now,' murmurs Sophey, barely moving her lips. Lisbet knows there is nothing to do for them. They have no spare skeps, no hives readymade, and even if they did the bees would not take to them so soon. Lisbet places the net aside, and lowers herself carefully to her knees beside the first hive. She sorts among the ruins, the honeycomb bleeding over her hands, the perfect halls and chambers shattered, until finally she finds him. The king bee, large nearly as her thumb, his wings broken and stuck to the remains of his cavity. From him, all else grew. Without him, the bees are lost. She crushes him with her fingernails, as quick a mercy as she can bestow.

It is useless to cry, but she feels the sharp prickle of tears as she turns to the other hive. This king is harder to find, and she scans the bees overhead, searching for his mass among his subjects. There is no sign.

'Lisbet—' starts Sophey, but Lisbet shakes her head.

She lifts the hive to search its underside, finds the perfect shapes of their combs, rakes through the fine webs of paper, so intricate no man could make it, until, finally, trapped behind a crumpled shell of wax, she finds him.

The king rises from the remains of his hive, buzzing enormously. He sways, bumbles against Lisbet's cheek. She feels the graze of his wing, light as broken cobwebs, and then he lifts higher and is encased inside his colony. The bees rise with him as though he is an anchor made air, as though their tethers are suddenly cut, and they follow him into the forest.

Thirteen

They sit, the five of them, around the scrubbed table in a stunned silence. Frederich is looking at Lisbet with an expression that is almost reverential, Nethe breathes audibly, and Eren has his slender fingers outstretched on the wood. Sophey has given Lisbet the good chair, the one that stands steady on four even legs, a respect Sophey usually reserves for her son alone.

Lisbet can barely keep silent, let alone still. Her leg jigs, her skin tingles. She feels flooded with blood and breath, triumphant.

'Astonishing,' says Frederich at last. 'Extraordinary. Are you a hexe, Frau Wiler?'

'Fred,' hisses Eren. 'Do not be foolish.'

Lisbet glances at him, seated between Nethe and the drummer. She imagines she feels the same energy glowing off him, the same glory. The lute lies mute on the table, posed between the cups of dark beer Sophey has poured for all of them. She even smiled when she offered Eren his, didn't flinch when their hands brushed. Only Nethe's is untouched, her face paling at the smell.

'What happened,' says Lisbet at last. 'Who did this?'

'A boy,' says Sophey. 'Nethe saw him.'

Nethe nods. 'He was stealing the combs.'

'Badly,' says Sophey. 'He left as much as he took, and ruined more besides.'

'A boy?' A crack of alarm shakes Lisbet's voice. 'What did he look like?'

Nethe shrugs. 'A boy. Dark hair, skinny. They all look the same at that age.'

'Dark hair,' repeats Lisbet. 'How tall? This?'

'About that.'

'Blue eyes? Set far apart? Sallow-skinned?'

'I told you,' says Nethe impatiently. 'Could have been any number of children. He had a mouth on him though. Seemed to think he had a right to be there.'

Lisbet falls back in her chair. A fear is gnawing at her, a suspicion.

'What is it?' says Sophey, eyeing her beadily. 'What do you know?'

'Nothing,' says Lisbet, a little too quickly. It is the truth, but she suspects.

'One of your alms brats?' presses Sophey, and Lisbet flinches because she has struck so near the mark.

She remembers the boy at Plater's side, wielding a hook, the boy who saw her at the guild with Eren. Who maybe saw Ida and Nethe dancing.

Daniel Lehmann.

His family is certainly desperate enough. And what Nethe says, about believing he had a right to take the combs – could he have thought to hold what he saw over them in exchange for silence? She hopes not, for Nethe has already broken any such accord before it was begun.

'There are a great number of needy,' she says, with as much authority as she can summon. 'The Twenty-One has driven half the city onto the streets since the dancing plague began.'

'It is true,' says Eren, but Sophey doesn't look at him. Her newfound tolerance for the Turk clearly does not extend so far. 'All the taverns have been closed, and the boarding houses.'

'Nearly all,' smirks Frederich, and Eren makes a convulsive gesture that is unmistakeably a kick under the table, aimed at his companion's shin.

Sophey cradles her cheek. It seems to be growing more swollen by the minute. 'We will need protection,' she says after a moment. 'More than those useless dogs. They only began barking when you shouted, Nethe.'

'Protection?' says Nethe. 'Of what sort?'

'Men,' she says, and Frederich puffs out his chest. 'Strong men.' Frederich wilts.

'Surely you know that means Plater's men?' says Lisbet, unable to keep the disgust out of her voice. 'He controls all the brutes in the city.'

'Whatever we must do,' shrugs Sophey. 'We cannot have another theft.'

'Plater seeks to aid such theft,' says Lisbet hotly. 'Was that not the purpose of his letter? What should Henne think—'

'He should thank you for showing respect to his mother,' says Sophey, all warm feeling forgotten. 'I'm to the empiric tomorrow as it is, to have this tooth pulled. I'll speak with Plater then.'

She pushes herself forcefully to her feet, and stomps from the room.

Frederich blows air noisily between his lips. 'Drummers are strong, you know.'

'This is no time for jest, Frederich,' snaps Eren.

'No,' yawns Frederich. 'But it is time for bed. I have had quite the day.'

'None of us needs to hear about it,' says Eren. He is watching Lisbet; she feels his attention like a brand.

'Charming,' says Frederich lightly. 'Good night, fair ladies, mistress of the bees.' He makes a mock bow to Lisbet before turning to Eren. 'Go safe, friend. The city is a sorrier spectacle still. I do not envy you the night stretch.'

He goes whistling through the house, closing the door a little too loudly. Lisbet has always marvelled at this habit in men, from her brothers to Henne. How they move through the world so loudly, so unashamedly, without thought for who hears them, or if they disturb others. Not Eren though. He seems to share her quality, the quality most women possess, to sit so still you could forget he was there.

Lisbet looks from him to Nethe, and finds her sister-in-law staring at her.

'Now?'

Lisbet sighs. Their illicit meet. The bees had driven it from her mind. 'So soon?'

'I told Ida after dusk, to meet us at the river. She'll be waiting.'

Lisbet shakes her head. It is so unlike her picture of Ida, to think of her friend leaving her children sleeping, to come through the dark forest to meet a woman Lisbet thought she despised. But then, she has learned much about Ida that was unknown before.

'It's safe. Mutti is taking poppy for her tooth,' says Nethe, rising and running her hand through her short hair. 'She will be asleep already.'

'Are you tired, Frau Wiler?' says Eren, gently.

She understands he means to advocate for her, but the truth is the question irritates her. Had he not seen what she did, what she is capable of? Perhaps Frederich is right – perhaps it is a sort of witchcraft, a white gift, the one good she has to give the world. *Mistress of the bees.*

And part of her wants to go to the tree, to see her babies'

ribbons and tell them what their mother managed, how she conjured the bees, composed them to her rhythm as easy as Eren played his lute. How many times has she gone there weeping? Wouldn't it be good, to carry her victory to them?

'No,' she says. 'I'll come, Nethe.'

Nethe gives a low cheer, and gathers up the rest of the flask of beer, the last of the bread, wrapping it all in a sack as they had done for Henne before his journey to Heidelberg.

'Won't Sophey notice those gone?'

'We can blame the drummer,' says Nethe.

'It's the least he deserves,' says Eren, amused. Lisbet returns his smile despite herself.

'Shall I accompany you?' he asks. 'I am not needed in town for a few hours. I may not be a strong man, but I have my knife.'

'Your knife does not interest me,' says Nethe, in higher spirits by the moment. 'But bring your lute, and you can play something more suited to women than bees.'

'Nethe,' says Lisbet warningly. 'You forget yourself.'

'That,' says Nethe, her eyes blazing, 'is precisely the point.'

•

Lisbet has not forgotten the first time she went through the dark to the dance tree with a baby in her belly. How she felt its strings coming loose, its delicate assemblance scattering, but she lets herself not dwell on it, not draw a line from that, to this. Tonight, she decides, she will forget all her sadnesses, all her trespasses, even as she steals through the forest on a sinner's errand. Nethe's giddiness is infectious, she feels it filling her own blood.

Eren's lute strings jangle as he walks with it strung across his back like a bow. She senses him keeping close behind, but

173

not so close she can hear anything but the discordant chiming. They go without a light, with a flint and a bundle of candles Nethe insisted Sophey wouldn't miss, scenting their way through the hushed forest. They should be afraid, and maybe that is the edge of what she feels under her delight, her elation, but it makes those all the more delicious.

Ida is already at the river, a small, slight figure wreathed in the glow from her torch. Though Nethe runs towards her it is Lisbet Ida embraces first, tightly and for longer than usual, and Lisbet understands and accepts it as an apology.

Lisbet leads the way through the trees. She can hear Nethe telling Ida about the theft, about Lisbet's mastery of the bees, and revels in Ida's exclamations.

She feels untouchable, forged by the feel of the bees all around her, the king cracking beneath her fingers. Her worries about Daniel Lehmann and Plater are forgotten. The brambles part, the light from Ida's torch washes over the clearing, and there is her dance tree, and her babies' ribbons, and she feels at peace.

Nethe whoops and breaks away from Ida, spinning with her arms outstretched, as though she is drunk again.

'Can we go up there?' she asks, pointing at the platform. Lisbet nods, eyeing Nethe's feet, coming perilously close to disarraying the carefully laid tokens.

'It's steady enough,' she says.

'Are you all right climbing?' asks Eren. He has come to stand at her shoulder. She imagines she can feel the heat from his body. In answer, she leads the way to the ladder, haphazard but strong, and begins to climb. In truth, she has never attempted it so large, never in such darkness. But her glee carries her, and with her breath coming sharply she clambers across the platform to wave down at him, laughing at his astonished face.

Nethe and Ida follow close behind, and Eren comes carefully after, until they sit cross-legged across from each other, as they had with Sophey and Frederich at the table, in a disbelieving silence. Then Ida starts to laugh; Nethe follows suit, and pulls the flask of beer from her sack, her queasiness seemingly forgotten.

'You really made this?' asks Nethe, wiping her mouth and passing the flask to Ida.

Lisbet nods. 'The planks and rope and all came from one of the houses deeper in.' Eren is frowning, and Lisbet elaborates. 'There are abandoned places, houses from the pagans and rebels and others besides.'

'These woods have a history of secrets,' says Nethe, now placing the candles about the platform.

He shakes his head. 'I can hardly believe you built it.'

'Repaired it only,' Lisbet says, and accepts the beer because there is nothing else to do with her hands. 'Dance trees were common even when my parents were children. This was disarranged but the supports were firm. It was simple, only five planks rested across the boughs, some nails.' She laughs at the unflattering astonishment on his face. 'I was young once, and smooth-bellied, and strong.'

'She was ever strong,' says Ida, reaching for the flask again. Lisbet passes it on without drinking. 'When Henne brought her I thought her a slip, a sheaf of barley easily shaken, easily snapped. But she has not so much as bent, even after all that has come her way.'

To her dismay, Lisbet feels something swell in her throat. Ida is wrong, though. She has bent, she has broken, many times over. She looks away, at the ribbons hanging limp in the trees.

Ida slides her slim hand into hers. 'You are a marvel, Bet. Agnethe told me how you managed the bees.'

'And about the thief?'

'Of course,' says Ida, her forehead crumpling. 'It is sad there are many so in need, so wretched.'

Lisbet takes a breath. She wants to tell Ida of her suspicions, her fear that it was Daniel, that even now he'll be taking his message to Plater, bringing ruin down on them all. But then Ida turns away, reaching for the beer again.

'I am surprised you came,' says Nethe, eyeing Eren. 'Is it usual for a Turk to keep the company of sodomites?'

'Nethe,' says Lisbet warningly.

'Perhaps not,' says Eren lightly. 'But it is somewhat common for a musician.'

Lisbet smiles despite herself. She has never known a man with such good humour. Henne finds nothing funny, has inherited his mother's disposition for forbidding looks over mirth. And his cruelty, to betray Nethe – where did that come from?

'I knew it,' says Nethe. 'The drummer?'

Eren ducks his head, smoothing the strings of the lute. Lisbet feels her belly flip.

'Frederich? He is . . .' She feels naive as a newborn. All around her, lives unlike anything she knew existed, a secret language.

'He loves a guard,' says Eren. 'At the gaol.'

Lisbet's cheeks flush, and she hates it, hates her naivety.

'Ha!' says Nethe. 'See, we are all about if only you know where to look. In the Twenty-One's employ, no less. Even at the abbey, I wondered about some of the sisters. But of course,' she says, reaching out as if to soothe Ida, 'I had no interest.'

'Nethe,' says Ida quietly. 'Please.'

'So proper, our Ida. I think we are ready for a dance,' says Nethe, clapping her hands. 'Play us a tune.'

'Nethe,' snaps Lisbet.

'My apologies,' says Nethe, standing and bowing like a man. Ida giggles and Lisbet looks at her, astonished. What is inside these women? They have gone daft in each other's company. 'Please, good Turk, play us some music.'

Lisbet looks in apology to Eren, but he only lifts his lute. This time he plays something brisk and bracing, a jaunt with none of the intricacy of earlier. But it has Nethe pulling Ida to her feet, and soon the two women are hooting and stamping, testing Lisbet's confidence in her work as the platform judders and rocks. They have not paused to light the candles, and the women are all glinting eyes and teeth.

Feeling out of place, Lisbet pulls herself back to give them more room, leaning against the trunk. Nethe again takes on the attitude of a man, swinging Ida wildly about beneath the canopy. This has always been a quiet place to Lisbet, akin to the church Nethe first recognised it as. But the music has filled it to the rafters, catching in the branches and shimmering the leaves, and it makes utter sense to her now why the pagans chose to have their halls so.

Eren runs straight into another tune, and the women dance and dance, tucking up their skirts to let their bare feet and calves show, until Ida begs Eren for something slower. He begins to play a threshing song, its melody familiar and even, and Ida reaches out a hand to Lisbet, gasping.

'Come, you are not so old.'

Lisbet rolls her eyes and takes it, but Nethe must offer hers too before they are able to haul her to her feet. The three women whirl in the dance tree, hand in hand, a ring outside which Eren sits, anticipating and orchestrating their pace. Lisbet closes her eyes and lets Ida and Nethe guide her, her head spinning until she knows she will fall, fall and hurt herself and the baby both, fall from the tree if she does not stop spinning, does not open her eyes. But still she lets herself be led, around and around, until the music stops.

The women don't break apart, but look at each other until

Ida pulls them to her. Lisbet feels arms go about her, her belly clamped between them, hard as a pit. Lisbet feels Ida's soft cheek against her own as she in turn encases them both with her arms, all of them swaying together, their hearts pounding against each other's. Lisbet feels she could stay forever here, breathing with these women, held in the moment where she understands nothing and everything that is between them.

But then Ida looses them, and Lisbet collapses sideways against Nethe, solid and strong as her brother, who laughs and helps lower her once more to the platform.

'No need for drink with a move like that,' says Nethe, as Ida drops to her knees, panting.

'I need water,' she says. 'It is too hot.'

'It is hot every night and every day,' says Nethe, swigging again from the flask. 'Water will not touch the sides.'

'Still,' says Ida. 'I must go to the river.'

Nethe rolls her eyes, and hauls Ida once more to her feet. 'You were ever a whelp.'

'Take the flask,' says Lisbet. 'I would be grateful of some water too.'

'You are not coming?' asks Ida, looking from Lisbet to Eren. Lisbet feels her face flush.

'I shall sit further off,' says Eren, 'and not move until your return.'

Still Ida hesitates, and Lisbet knows how it looks. Eren is not only a man: he is a Turk, a stranger, a travelling musician. He is every bad thing in every bad tale they were ever told. But thirst wins out and Ida allows herself to be led away by Nethe, the flask in her hand.

Lisbet has been alone with Eren before, but it is different tonight, in this place she never thought to share with a soul. Her boldness vanishes, and she keeps her eyes trained on the sky, held up by the cross-hatched branches. Eren seems content in their silence, and picks up his lute again.

This time he plays something lovely and low, more mournful than what he lulled the bees with. It is a keen with the edges smoothed, an unmistakeable lament. Lisbet closes her eyes again, and leans back against the trunk.

She lets herself drift, lets her thoughts wander, and it makes her remember. She remembers the first child she carried, and the second. They come to her, each of her children, spooling from the music like spirits: bodies of light, souls of gold. She has always thought it was not true, what Pater Hansen preached in church, that any child not anointed by his hand before death is damned. But here, she feels it too, knows it cannot be so. They are each of them remembered, each of them counted. They are all of them saved.

When Eren stops playing, she makes herself look at him. He is looking back. He knows what she feels, and it is a sensation of such power, it takes her breath. She bends towards him like a reed to water, eyes already closing, lips parted.

'Lisbet . . .'

Instead of his lips on hers, a hand on her shoulder. Instead of an embrace, gentle pressure pushing her away. Heat floods her cheeks. She cannot look him in the eye.

She stumbles to her feet. 'I have to – I must . . .'

She ignores his soft call and descends the ladder, belly bumping the rungs, and when she hears him begin to play again she knows he is not following. She calls herself every bad name she can think of, embarrassment and shame thumping in her head like a drum.

She tells herself it was a moment of madness, though she knows it is a lie. If he had kissed her back – she shakes her head to rid it of the thought. Of course he would not. She is married, and old, and has another man's child inside her.

Lisbet's mouth is parched, her body aching. She will meet Nethe and Ida at the river, walk off her strangeness, the feeling flooding her bones. If he can pretend it did not happen, so can she.

She moves through the forest, eyes adjusted to the dark, collecting her wandering thoughts, her heart, bundling them tight up inside her again, containing them. They rise against their restraints like gleaming fish in a net, and she pushes them back down.

As she nears the river, she sees small circles of light, hears murmurs, short laughs. There are people grouped at intervals through the trees, and she tries to pass unseen, remembering the hungry man with his rusted knife. Her pace slows: she becomes more careful with where she steps, her heartbeat quickening. But the groups seem to be of a different sort. The Twenty-One's decrees have driven even families into the trees, and they are as cautious as she: she sees children's faces illuminated by the firelight, piles of clothing upon which babies sleep with their small mouths pursed.

She hugs the shadows, choosing thicker undergrowth where the families have not ventured. Here the ground is once again boggy, and the bank riddled with washed-up branches. She is so set on her task of becoming invisible that she does not recognise the sounds for what they are, thinks them an owl calling, a fox barking far away. But as she reaches a bank Lisbet has used before for bathing, enclosed by bracken, sheltered and perfect for passing through unnoticed, what she sees is impossible, unmistakeable.

Ida is sitting on a large, rotted trunk, where Lisbet sometimes dries her clothes. She'd found a deer drowned and washed up here once, its small brown body soft and swollen. The sight of the deer comes to her now, in the obscene glint of Ida's tongue between her teeth, the way her head lolls against her shoulder. Her pale limbs are parted, and she is open from arms to mouth, her face washed in an expression of such abandon Lisbet feels ashamed to witness it even before she sees Nethe on her knees before her, her golden head between Ida's legs.

If Lisbet were in any doubt about what she sees, a moment later Ida moans again, a keening, animal sound, and reaches down to Nethe and grasps her by the back of the neck, yanks her forcefully up, bending down to meet her mouth with hers, and they are kissing then, Nethe's knees in the mud, Ida's legs wrapped around Nethe's waist, pale switches binding the cloth of her skirts, her arms digging into her back.

Lisbet should tell them she is there. She should yell, or shout, beat them for their sin, for their foolishness. But she cannot speak, can't do anything but stumble clumsily backwards into the shadows, her heart thumping. Then, suddenly, she sees something move behind the women.

Someone else is watching them. A crouched figure, its face swollen and monstrous, its fingers webbed and closed around a pitchfork. Beside it, a larger form looms from the dark. They could have stepped straight from the walls of the cathedral. The Devil and his accomplice, come for their souls.

'Ida!' she shouts. 'Agnethe!'

But it is too late. Even as the women break apart, the figures rush into the mud. Not the Devil and a demon, but as dangerous. Lisbet knows them the moment they reach Ida and Nethe. Daniel, his cheeks red raw and weeping from bee stings, his skinny fingers made fat by poison. And behind him, unblemished but more grotesque, is Plater. His face is gleaming, triumphant as he grasps Ida by the hair, and pulls her from the trunk.

'Hure,' he shouts. 'Sodomite. Heretic.'

Nethe roars and raises her fist to strike Plater, but Ida yells.

'Go, Nethe, please!'

'Bitch,' snarls Plater, face to face with Agnethe. Hatred mingles with want on his twisted features. 'I should have beaten you to death.'

'It's the closest you ever got to me, Alef.' Nethe matches his height and his fury. 'Let her go. She doesn't want you, any more than I do.'

'Agnethe,' moans Ida. 'Go.'

'Quickly, boy,' says Plater, his hand snarled in Ida's hair. 'Gut her.'

Daniel has his hook in his hand, the same one he used to part the dancers on the guild stage. His eyes swivel in his poor, swollen face, and Lisbet sees his hesitation. Surely he will not? He is not so quickly made a monster – it takes manhood to do that. His pause at last calls her to action. She hurries forward and places herself between Nethe and Daniel.

'Do it!' shrieks Plater.

'Daniel,' she says. 'Don't. You cannot take it back.'

His breathing is laboured – he must have swallowed a bee, its stings lodged in his throat. She hears his wheeze and wants to gather him in her arms.

'Now, boy!' orders Plater. But Daniel's wheezing becomes more pronounced. His bloated eyelids droop, and Lisbet steps closer to him, knocking the hook aside.

'It's all right, Daniel,' she says, in the same tone she used to calm the bees after he ruined their hives. For a moment, she thinks he will let her hold him, but Plater roars and takes a step forward. Ida shrieks as he drags her, and this makes Daniel raise his hook as though he is a puppet on a string. Lisbet turns and shoves Nethe away with all her might.

'Go,' she hisses, chest heaving. 'Go!'

Nethe's face is stretched in a silent scream. She looks more rageful, more hopeless than any being Lisbet has ever seen.

'I'll take care of her,' says Lisbet. 'Go, or it is all for nothing.'

Force then, a shunt of wind as Plater shoulders past Lisbet, and she overbalances, falls against the trunk. He grabs Daniel's hook, and Ida calls at Nethe to run once more.

Panting, wretched-faced, Nethe picks up her skirts. Without a backwards glance, she flees into the trees.

Ida is still caught, her hands gripping her husband's wrist, the sort of surrender in her body that shows this is not the first time he has treated her so roughly. Lisbet kneels over her friend, trying to free her. Ida is whimpering.

'She finds leaving you so easy,' needles Plater, but his voice shakes. 'You dog. You hure.'

'Please, leave her alone!'

'This is none of your business, Frau Wiler,' spits Plater. 'How does it feel, Ida? To see her abandon you once more to your fate?'

'Release her!' says Lisbet, trying to muster some of the naked rage she saw on Nethe's face.

'Bet,' says Ida in a tiny voice. 'The baby.'

'Yes,' says Plater. 'We would not want another failure, would we?'

She hates him, with a heat so enormous and swallowing she could be tied to a stake and feeling flames lick her cheeks. Wildly, she thinks of snatching Daniel's hook from his hand, plunging it deep into Plater's gut and twisting and twisting.

There is murmuring from the surrounding trees, and Lisbet looks up. From the shadows step people: women and children, older men supported by found and fallen sticks. The families driven from the city. They are formless in the dark, their faces carved by the same hunger, eyes huge and unfamiliar. Except – there.

Eren. Lisbet could cry with relief, to see him. He moves as though to push through the crowd towards her, but she shakes her head ever so slightly. *No.*

Their presence has a new effect on Plater. He hauls Ida to standing, and transfers his grip to her upper arm.

'Where are you taking her?' says Lisbet, emboldened by the watchers.

'That does not concern you,' he says.

'If you mean to murder her,' she says, lifting her voice. 'We are all witnesses.'

'I am the council's man. This is a matter for our court.'

'What did she do?' calls a watcher.

'She was falsely dancing,' says Plater. 'She will be punished alongside the other blasphemers.'

'He's lying!' shouts Lisbet. 'She did nothing wrong.'

'If you mean to perjure yourself,' says Plater, but Lisbet doesn't care. She would say anything, do anything to mend this.

'I can swear it on my child's life—'

'And what does that count for?' sneers Plater.

The breath leaves her.

'Frau Wiler?' Daniel's voice is needle-thin. He holds out his hand beseechingly. 'Shall I walk you home?'

'Do not come near me,' she spits. 'I regret every moment of kindness I gave you. The Devil can take you.'

Plater is pulling Ida away, not in the direction of the mill, but to the city. Lisbet starts after them, but Ida looks back over her shoulder.

'Home, Bet,' she says. 'Please.'

Inside, the baby is still. After a stretch of countless time, when the watchers have left and she feels alone, she hears Eren's voice, feels his hesitant touch on her shoulder, the same pressure he used to push her away.

But now, she turns to him and collapses into his arms, and he lets her. She burrows deep inside his tunic, howling until her throat is sore. It is so dark, her eyes pressed tight shut, it's like being beside the river again when she pulled Mutti from it, her pockets full of stones. Holding her mutti, beloved and mad and drowned in her arms. She feels the same disintegration, the same certainty of ruin.

She was so naive, to think they could have their peace. To think any of them could be saved. The world is ending, she thinks, and she can do nothing but watch its crumbling.

Three hundred and fifteen dancing

She came only to gawp. Trude reminds herself of this as she stands beside the stage, but since she spied the woman with the loose black hair, her resolution is fading.

She has seen manias before, of course. The priest, Mutti, her brothers – they had different names for what her father was, but all were clear that it was not something he had. It was not like a pox, or a split-open skull. It was what he was.

Maniac was one word, the worst word. Trude knew the story of Greiger, who in the grip of St Anthony's fire felt brands burning his skin until he tried to flay it from him, and in the cities there were always a great number of maniacs who flew into sorrow or rages so consuming they seemed more animal than human.

Papa's mania was not like that. It was not loud, nor for the most part terrifying. It was a quiet emptiness, like an abandoned nest, or else he was a bird tipped from its roost and left dying, twitching on the ground. He felt pain, like Greiger did, and sorrow and rage like those pitifuls in the city, but all of it was borne quiet. His limbs were heavy with it: his legs dragged and his arms were weak so Trude must turn and wash him.

He and Mutti never lay together after Trude, and he had a cot beside the fire while Trude slept with Mutti.

By the end there was no cure but vinegar, and poppy, and prayers. Before, when there was hope for change, it was relics, heated in the fire and pressed to his temples and ankles. Trude made an amulet of faeces and hare fur and placed it under his pillow until it fell apart with flies. Mutti even took them to see the comet, lifted from the ground and placed on an altar at Eninsheim. It was the size of two men's fists bunched together. The size of Papa's hands, joined in prayer. The journey was long, and they could not go again, but when they returned home Trude bunched both her fists together and placed them in Papa's hands, so he could remember the comet sent from God.

Trude loved no one so much as she loved Papa. She didn't say this to Mutti, or her brothers, because they seemed to hate him. She didn't even say it to Papa aloud, but she hopes he knew.

Since he died she has been lost. But there is a woman dancing, up there on the stage, who has Papa's grey eyes, and Trude cannot keep herself from her. She walks to stand by her side, and tries to place her fists in her palm, but the woman is elsewhere. She is not her Papa, of course not. And there is not the same pain in her face: her grey eyes are elated. All these women: they bare their teeth in joy, not sorrow. How would it feel, Trude thinks, to loose her sadness and turn it to light?

Trude tells her Papa she loves him, out loud. She joins the dance.

Fourteen

Thick-tongued, Lisbet wakes. She reaches out, but of course Nethe is not beside her. The memory of the night before crashes over her, and it is all she can do not to let herself sink again. The baby kicks once, twice. She must drink, must feed them something.

The skin of her face feels stretched. She can hear two people speaking, a man and a woman. It is Sophey, but not Eren. Not Henne. And not, thanks be to God, Plater. She hears children laughing. Lisbet forces herself to the door, and opens it, her hands feeling like a thing apart, appendages tied to her at the wrists.

Sophey and Mathias sit at the table. Their knotted hands are bound around one another's, and both their faces are shining with tears. Mathias has a bundle of cloth on his lap.

Sophey looks up at her. Her cheek is so swollen around her rotting tooth it looks full of wadding. Beyond them the door stands open. Ulf is collapsed at the threshold, and Lisbet sees children chasing Fluh. It is copper-haired Ilse, and her brothers. On Mathias' lap, Ida's youngest boy Rolf stirs. Outside the children laugh and clap as Fluh runs about in the brightness beyond, after a fly or a bee. She can only have slept a few hours. *Good.* She needs time on her side.

'Lisbet,' croaks Sophey. Her voice is muffled by the swelling of her bad tooth, thick as Lisbet's tongue feels. 'Can it really be true?'

Lisbet pours herself a small cup of beer. She must concentrate on the actions so as not to knock the cup over, not to grip it too hard or too loose. She drinks deeply, the tepid liquid unsticking her tongue from her gums.

'Mathias says they have Ida in the gaol. Agnethe is a fugitive, hiding in the forest like a rebel.' Sophey lets out a hollow laugh, and blood sprays out of her mouth, onto her spotlessly kept table. She doesn't move to wipe it away, and Mathias' eyes are so hollow and far-off Lisbet suspects he does not notice the blood flecking their joined hands. 'The Turk says he found you walking as though enchanted in the woods.'

'Eren?' says Lisbet, and Sophey looks at her sharply.

'The Turk, as I say.'

'Where is he?'

'He and the drummer both are in the city. He says he saw Ida arrested. Is any of this true?'

'Yes,' says Lisbet. 'Plater took her.'

'Did you see them together? Agnethe and Ida?'

Lisbet hesitates, her addled mind too slow to build upon the careful foundation Eren left her. Mathias lets go of Sophey's hand and throws himself face down. The baby squalls and Lisbet hurries forward to rescue him, easing him out from between Mathias' shuddering body and the hard edge of the table.

'Mein Gott, mein Gott,' cries Mathias. 'They are doomed. They are damned.'

Rolf's pink eyelids crack open and she shushes him, rocking him side to side as she has seen Ida do. His cheeks huff and he blows out a sweet mouthful of air, before his lids close again. Her breasts ache. She feels his body relax, and her own tenses in response.

'No,' she says. 'We can go to the gaol. They must be overrun with false dancers, with pickpockets and others. They will be glad to be rid of her. They do not know she is—'

She doesn't have the words for what Ida is. She does not want to use Plater's, flung at her in the clearing. A mother, Nethe's lover, the best friend Lisbet could ever know.

'Why she is really there,' she finishes. 'We can pay them. You can pay them. We must get her home.'

She looks down at Rolf, asleep and heavy in her arms. She will not see him unmothered.

'You think you can free her?' says Sophey, her voice equal parts sneer and sob. 'They will not listen to you, not over Plater. He testifies against his own wife. What do you think your voice can count for?'

'Then we sit here and cry, do we?' snarls Lisbet, startling Rolf. He begins to cry immediately. 'We let him visit his punishment on them, like last time?'

'You know?' says Sophey.

'No thanks to you,' says Lisbet.

'Then you know they are sinners,' she says. Mathias moans, his head still cradled in his arms. 'We must let the courts decide—'

'The courts are men like Plater,' says Lisbet, over the din of Rolf. Ilse comes shyly to the door. Her face is exactly Ida's, and it makes Lisbet's teeth ache. She holds the baby out to her, and the girl takes her brother in plump, practised arms.

'There's milk,' points Lisbet. 'And honey. Go through there to feed him.'

Ilse hurries away, her copper head bent obediently, Rolf nearly as long as her body.

'He will do it,' she says. 'He will leave his own children motherless, because she disobeyed him. Not God. Him. Plater acts as if he and God were one and the same.'

'Blasphemy,' snaps Sophey, crossing herself.

'Blasphemy yes!' shouts Lisbet. 'But he is no servant of God. He serves only himself.'

'All the more reason our going will do nothing.'

'Then try, at least. If you will not, I'll go alone.'

Lisbet turns her back, and pushes out past Ulf. The dog rises to follow her and she tells him no. The boys don't break their playing to watch her. They are in their own world, Fluh racing among them. She ignores the sight of children at last making dust in their yard.

Mathias' cart and horse is tied next to the pressing shed. It is sleeker than theirs, better kept, and in the bed are sacks upon sacks of flour fresh-milled. A plan is forming in Lisbet's mind. She will go to the gaol, offer up all of Mathias' flour, all of their wax. She will offer anything, if they will only give her back Ida.

A tug on her sleeve. Vinegar and rot.

'It will not work.' Sophey's voice is all sadness. Lisbet's annoyance fades as she looks the old woman in the face. The cloth pressing her sore tooth ludicrously encircles her face.

'I must try.'

Sophey sighs, and hauls herself up before the reins. 'Mathias will watch the children. You untie the horse. My fingers cannot manage the knots.'

•

The approach to the city is nightmarish even in full daylight. They reach a blockage, a place where the number of carts and people back up and halt. Lisbet leans carefully out, and spies Hilde Lehmann darting through the turmoil, her face dirtied with ashes and palm outstretched. Hilde sees her and weaves toward her.

'Any coin?'

'None,' says Sophey, but Lisbet searches her pockets.

'Where is Daniel?' she asks.

'Not home since last night,' says Hilde, and points to the snarl of people ahead. 'My mother is dancing.'

Lisbet stands in the stationary cart and sees a woman stained in dust jigging up ahead. It is Frau Lehmann, and her husband is beside her weeping enormously loud, though in the bright, early morning sunlight Lisbet can see no tears on his cheeks as he holds out his hands to passing gawkers.

Hilde ignores her. 'Are the musicians still at your house? If they are, we could cut them in, if they could play while she dances.'

Lisbet waves her away sharply. 'Tell your mother to stop. If the Church finds her falsifying—'

'Daniel works for the Church now,' says Hilde primly. 'He hooks the dancers.'

'I—' Lisbet stops herself from saying *I know*.

'Have you coin?'

'Only a little.' Lisbet gives a meagre piece, and Hilde snatches it before running to the next cart. They inch forwards, past Frau Lehmann, who now affects a lewd shake that makes the onlookers jeer. Lisbet looks away queasily.

They approach the horse guild, Sophey whipping the reins and pulling the mule around the line of bystanders, taking them in a long loop to the gaol. As they pass the open doors Lisbet sees the women wheeling inside. There is none of the calm she felt the other night: in daylight they look gaunt and haggard, lifting their feet like mules on their way to the knacker's yard.

Sophey's cheeks are sucked between her teeth: from the

motion of her jaw beneath her swaddling cloth Lisbet knows she is chewing on them, pausing only to spit blood in the dirt. Lisbet thinks she had the measure of her mother-in-law wrong all along. She was not indifferent, only terrified. She is terrified still, and yet here she is beside Lisbet, passing through this tumult.

The gaol is built along the outskirts, siding the river, so they follow the road that hugs the city walls. At each turn comes the sound of musicians playing, occasionally broken by the bells ringing for blessings. Lisbet wonders how anyone sleeps. The baby stirs, and she imagines it raising its arms in answer, knowing music in the way all people seem to from birth and before. They reach the tanners' guild, similarly thronged. There is a stage at the mouth of the guild, and Lisbet spies Frederich, feet planted wide, striking his drum. The commotion is extraordinary: it batters at her ears and shakes the baby with its beat. It is the first time she has seen him since learning what he is, but she feels nothing but glad of the sight. With a gasp, she hauls on Sophey's arm to stop.

'Wait. One moment.'

She climbs down from the cart before it is fully halted. If Sophey calls after her, Lisbet doesn't hear it as she makes a fence of her elbows to protect her belly, and pushes toward the stage. The tide of people carries her, and she must side-step to release herself from them, crouching under the stage itself.

The smell is new wood and piss. She looks directly up, and mud from a stamping foot crumbles over her face. She edges out in front of the stage, clinging to the wooden strut like it is a raft.

Frederich's face is grim, and he keeps his eyes trained at the sky as he slams his palm against the stretched skin.

'Frederich,' shouts Lisbet. 'Frederich!'

He is made deaf by his own drumbeats. She strains to reach his boot, and hits his ankle as hard as she can. He steps back and looks down, eyes widening when he spots her.

'Frau Wiler!' He squats so their faces are level. 'What are you doing here?'

'You must come with us,' she says, 'to the gaol.'

He frowns. 'Why?'

'I know you have a lover,' she says, and Frederich's face closes over. He makes as though to stand.

'No!' cries Lisbet, yanking him down with such force he falls to his knees, his drum clattering. 'I don't care. I only want to see my friend.'

'Frau Plater,' he says seriously, in a voice that tells her Eren has informed him of the whole sorry business. She is glad: she does not think she could recount it without weeping.

'He will not be able to help,' says Frederich. 'He is a guard, only.'

'Please,' says Lisbet. 'Please come with me. If it were you—'

Frederich shoots her a warning look.

'I do not threaten you,' Lisbet hurries on. 'I only mean wouldn't you at least want someone to try?'

Frederich's jaw works. He glances at the surrounding musicians, stamping and playing as before them in the tanners' guild women dance themselves to death. 'It will not make a difference.'

'Please.'

He sighs and unloops his drum, hands it to one of the fiddlers. The man places his instrument down and ducks his head through the strap of the drum. No questions, no hesitation, he begins to play it. Frederich wrinkles his nose.

'No mind for a rhythm,' he says as he jumps down from the stage, and Lisbet leads him to where Sophey sits in the cart. A queue has built up behind her, other cart drivers throwing insults, but she sits there stolidly, the crowd moving around her like a river about a rock.

'Nice hat, Frau Wiler,' says Frederich, eyeing her swaddling as he climbs atop the sacks of flour. Lisbet hauls herself back up beside Sophey, who leans in and hisses.

'The drummer?'

'Quickly,' says Lisbet. Sophey clucks her tongue, at the horse and Lisbet both.

The gaol's stone rises sheer from the Rhine, only a marshy bank beside it, leading to a wooden platform where boats dock and people are drowned in the brown water. Upriver, the sheep slaughter yard spills guts and blood into the river, the banks discoloured. As they cross the bridge Lisbet sees white hands fluttering from the tiny, barred windows set in the rock, like flags of surrender.

There is a line of people outside the main gate in varying states of distress. One woman, naked-headed in the sun, howls and rends her clothes. Beside her, two thin children shake, moving from bare foot to bare foot, clutching her skirts. The cobbles here are well maintained, and hold heat ferociously as coals. After she dismounts the cart Lisbet searches her pockets, but they are empty, the last of her coin given to Hilde. Frederich approaches her.

'That's Peter,' he says, indicating the head of the line. Lisbet cranes her neck and sees a guard standing there, blocking the main doors. 'He doesn't like me, but he'll let us in if we give him something. What do you have?'

'Flour,' says Lisbet, indicating the cart. 'And plenty of honey at the farm.'

'He prefers beer,' says Frederich, 'but let me see what I can do. What is her full name?'

'Ida Ilse Plater,' says Lisbet, trying to block out the sound of the wailing woman, the sight of her clearly starving children. 'She was arrested—'

'This morning, yes.'

Frederich strolls to the guard, forcing through the throng with that easy way he has, like he has every right to be there though it is clear others have waited for hours on the baking street. Sophey nudges her hard in the ribs.

'Does he know him?'

'Yes.'

'Been here before has he?'

'It is not what you presume,' she says. *It is worse*, she thinks.

Sophey sniffs, and eyes the woman with the two shivering children. She steps forward, unlooping from about her cheeks the swaddling cloth. Lisbet sees her wince as the comforting pressure is removed from her face, but Sophey rips the cloth into four neat strips.

Astonished, Lisbet watches as Sophey Wiler kneels on the blistering cobbles before the two children – girls or boys it is impossible to say. She indicates for them to rest their filthy hands on her shoulders so she can lift their feet, one by one, to bind them. Their mother does not notice, but the children's faces loosen from anguish into relief as the cloth forms a shield between their feet and the burning cobbles. Sophey heaves herself up, and returns to Lisbet's side.

Lisbet must try not to stare at her, focusing instead on the guard and Frederich, now gesticulating at the cart.

'That was kind,' she tells the air.

Sophey grunts. 'I know you think me ice, Lisbet. But I am flesh and blood same as you. And I love my daughter. And I love the woman she loves. Do not look at me like that, like you expect me to be a monster. I hate their sin, I hate that we are here. But for Ida, for Nethe – I have always held nothing but love, and hurt that it was not enough. That they were so foolish to continue.'

Lisbet is saved from replying by Frederich, who gestures them forward. Sophey rolls her shoulders back and pulls Lisbet through the crowd after her.

'Two sacks of flour,' he says. 'It'll get Lisbet in, and then you'll have to find Karl on your own.'

'Karl?' says Lisbet, at the same time as Sophey says, 'Two?'

'If it is two sacks,' continues Sophey, addressing the guard directly. Her swollen cheek shines, pitted with pox scars. 'Then it will be two of us going in.'

Peter sighs. He is short and broad, like Eren, but his face is beet red from the heat. 'That was not the agreement.'

'Is there any official agreement for such an arrangement?' says Sophey, fixing him with her familiar black-eyed glare.

Peter shifts foot to foot. He is hot, and bored, and Lisbet knows he will give in even before he says, 'Fine.'

'Good,' says Sophey. She turns to Frederich, who despite the seriousness of their mission has not lost his air of faint amusement. 'Who is Karl?'

'He is blond, has a beard,' says Frederich. 'Tall as me and with brown eyes. Give him this.' He slides his signet ring from his middle finger. 'He will know it's mine. He'll help you as best he can.'

'Thank you,' says Lisbet, taking the ring and clasping the drummer's hands, and repeating herself, for there is nothing else she can say. 'Thank you.'

Frederich shrugs, and takes a pipe from his pocket. 'I cannot promise anything. I'll watch the cart at least.'

Peter knocks three times on the heavy wooden door. A small window at head height swings open, and Peter has a muttered discussion with the guard inside. It opens without so much as a creak onto a dirt courtyard. Lisbet's stomach drops, but Sophey grips her hand, and leads her without hesitation through the gaol's outer door.

Fifteen

Frederich's ring is hot in Lisbet's hand, and Sophey's palm matches it in her other. They have never held hands before, and Lisbet is surprised by how easy it is, like holding Mutti's. She looks around, at the high walls segmenting the blazing sky into a square cut from blue cloth. Ida is here, somewhere. From the barred windows hang hands, shirts, underthings, and for a moment Lisbet's vision flickers, and she is back at the dance tree, ribbons swaying, the sky sliced apart by branches. There is the same sense of having crossed a threshold into another world entirely. But this one has an altogether different feel: utter isolation, complete dejection.

'Is that him?'

Lisbet follows Sophey's finger and sees that there, at a second door, stands a man matching Frederich's description, alongside another guard who sits at a broad table with a ledger before him, and leans back in his chair as an elderly man supports himself upon the wood and makes beseeching gestures.

'I believe so.'

Sophey squares her shoulders and approaches. 'Karl?'

The standing guard squints down at her. He is narrow-faced

as a ferret, with ruddy cheeks. Lisbet thinks of him lying with Frederich, with his head tipped back as Ida's had been. Why does he stand here, before the gaol gates, while Ida stands behind? Even in sin, men have the upper hand.

Lisbet holds out her palm, showing the ring. The seated guard tries to see, but before he can Karl closes his gloved hand over hers, bunching it into a fist. His eyes are suddenly wide and afraid. He grips Lisbet's wrist tighter and pulls her away from the table, towards the barred door.

'Who sent you?'

'Frederich,' she whispers back, aware of the other guard ignoring the elderly man in order to try to hear.

'I do not know him.'

'Of course you do,' says Sophey, and Lisbet startles. She has not explained the plan to Sophey and yet she already seems to have the measure of it. Her mother-in-law is a trove of surprises today. 'And you need not fear us. He sends us with a favour.'

Karl's eyes flick between them. He still suspects a trap. 'Who are you?'

'Frau Wiler, who he rooms with.' Sophey purses her lips. 'When he rooms at all.'

'We are here for Ida Plater,' says Lisbet. 'She is my friend. We wish to see her.'

'Plater . . .' Karl's face is grave. 'The council man's wife?'

'The same,' says Lisbet hungrily. 'Please, where is she?'

'Still here,' he says cautiously. He still holds Lisbet's fist, and now he looks down and gently unfurls her hand.

'Yes, we know she is here,' says Sophey impatiently.

Karl's gaze is trained on the ring. 'But not for much longer.'

Lisbet's stomach flips. 'She is to be released?'

The guard shifts. 'No.' He hesitates, looking at Lisbet's belly. 'I do not know if—'

'She can hear whatever it is you must say,' says Sophey. 'Speak it.'

Karl looks Lisbet full in the eyes then. His are brown, as Frederich said, and kind, and sad.

'She is sentenced.'

'Already?' says Sophey, and her voice shakes. 'How?'

'There are many fast judgements now,' says Karl, not taking his eyes from Lisbet's face. 'The dancing plague has brought many falsifiers and strangers to the city. They pass out sentences by the score, because there is not room in the gaol for them all.'

'Where do they move them, then?' says Sophey.

Karl chews on air. 'I am sorry. The penalty is set. She is to be drowned. Today.'

It is all Lisbet can do to keep herself steady. She must pale, because Karl holds her under her arm, and Sophey grasps her waist. But Lisbet is done with swooning, done with being thought weak. She pushes them away.

'I want to see her.'

'It is impossible—'

Lisbet holds up the ring. 'It is all impossible. It is impossible that Ida is sentenced to drown for the same sin you also carry.'

Karl gapes at her. 'She is a false dancer.'

'She loves a woman.'

Karl blanches, hushes her, but she will not be silent.

'She is in there still, and you have keys. So this thing, it is possible. And you will give me this one thing, though it is all wrong and rotted. You will take me to my friend.'

They look at each other a long moment. He is afraid: Lisbet sees it in his flaring nostrils, the colour high in his cheeks. But he takes Frederich's ring, and slips it onto his finger. 'Come with me.'

•

They step into the darkened passage and turn from the wooden steps leading up into one of the towers, taking instead those leading down. Lisbet holds the courage she forced into herself outside, takes it like a bit between her teeth. She must be strong, when she sees Ida. She must not show her terror.

Karl had offered his companion some excuse to sate him, and the guard replied lewdly, eyeing Lisbet. No doubt he thinks Lisbet holds some power over Karl, has his bastard in her belly.

They reach an underground passage lit with tallow lamps. The stench of them lingers over other, worse smells as they pass barred doors concealing cells that sound crammed full. Snatches of song and shouting rise, becoming muffled as soon as they are past the narrow slats. Karl takes a lamp from a bracket as they come to yet another set of steps, these ones stone and carved into the bedrock of the river itself. Lisbet imagines the water rushing past, held back only by the walls, imagines the foul brown Rhine entering her nose, her throat.

No.

They reach a floor of packed earth. It's cooler here, and quiet, and there is no light save the flicker from Karl's torch. The smell is different, too. Gone is piss and sweat, and instead the murky scent of stagnant water. Something scuttles just beyond the reach of the torch.

'She is kept apart,' Karl says, 'at Plater's order.'

'He treats his own wife like vermin,' spits Sophey.

'It is better perhaps,' he says. 'Quieter, and she shares with no one. We are overrun as you saw. This used to be a store.' He halts before another wooden door, short and broad, the size of a barrel. 'Here.'

'Open it then,' says Sophey.

'I cannot,' he says, indicating the lock, large and rusted. 'Only Plater has the key.'

'Why didn't you say so?'

'You cannot expect to break her from her confinement?' says Karl. 'You asked only to see her.'

'And we cannot.' Sophey gestures at the door. Karl holds the lamp closer to it, to its base. There is a gap there, a clear handspan, where the cellar has flooded and water rotted the wood away.

Lisbet lowers herself to the ground. It is cooler than anything she has felt against her skin for months. She rests her cheek against the dirt, and the river smell fills her nostrils. She can see nothing, but then Karl sets the torch down against the wall, and its light slithers beneath the door.

Lisbet can see straw, the scurrying of rats fleeing. And then, a foot, bare and filthy.

'Ida?'

A gasp from the darkness, and suddenly there she is, crawling forward as though from the mouth of a cave.

'Lisbet? Is it really you?' Ida's hair is loose, and her forehead bruised from where her husband dragged her. 'I thought I heard your voice, and thought I was asleep and dreaming. Oh, Bet!' She reaches her hand out and Lisbet shoves her own under the door, sleeve catching on the decaying wood.

They clutch each other, and Ida comes as close to the door as she can, mirroring Lisbet's pose so they lie face to face. Ida's breath is rank, and huge hollows are pressed under her eyes. But she wears no manacles, and aside from the bruise seems unharmed.

'How did you get in?' Fear clouds her eyes. 'Does my husband know you are here?'

'No,' says Lisbet, to soothe her, though in truth she had not given a single thought to Plater's whereabouts. 'We're safe.'

Ida sobs out a laugh.

'You know what I mean,' says Lisbet. 'We won't be disturbed.'

'Oh, Bet.' Ida searches Lisbet's face, moves closer so their noses are almost touching. 'I am glad you're here. Where are the children?'

'With Mathias, at our farm,' she says.

'They are fine,' adds Sophey briskly. 'Your Ilse takes great care over Rolf.'

'Is that you, Sophey?'

'Of course.'

'Thank you for coming.'

'Of course.' Sophey's voice is hoarse.

'Ilse is like a tiny mother.' Ida is crying, but she is smiling too. 'She will be able to help you, when your child comes.'

'Hush,' says Lisbet. 'You will help me.'

'Do you not know? That I am to be—'

'Please.' Tears close up Lisbet's throat, and she swallows them down. 'We will find a way through this.'

Ida's laugh is soft, and so cherished Lisbet could howl and claw at her clothes like the woman outside the gates. 'Listen to me. You must keep yourself safe. You should not be down here, lying in the dirt.'

'There is nowhere else I would be.'

Ida squeezes her hand tighter, and Lisbet closes her eyes. They could be on the dance tree platform at night, safe and held within its branches. They lie in silence, breathing in time. Then Ida speaks.

'Make sure my father does not come to see.' Lisbet goes to interrupt, but Ida fixes her with a stern glare. 'Not my father, not my children. Not you.'

'I am going nowhere,' she says, but Ida continues as though she has not spoken.

'Nethe is still not found?'

'No.'

'Then she is safe,' says Ida. 'If she is safe, it is not for naught.'

'They cannot do this.' At last, Lisbet's voice breaks. 'I will not let them.'

'I'm not frightened,' says Ida.

'There must be something we can do.'

'You know there is not. All I can do is go bravely. All you can do is go on. You go on, and you must be happy, Bet. If you can live and happily, you have beaten them.' She gives another high, short laugh. Lisbet knows she is lying. She is deathly afraid. 'I have never met a more unhappy man than my husband. He and I loved the same woman, and only one of us was loved in return. He has never been anything to anyone. He has never been anything at all and that is what makes him cruel. Because then at least he has cruelty as his kin. I had three years of joy, and it is more than most get. It will have to be enough.' She grips her hand so tight it hurts, but Lisbet would not draw away for anything. 'You can have the rest of your life, you and your child. Bring him safe into the world.'

'I will,' says Lisbet, crying in earnest now. For the first time, she believes it, all of it. That her child will be born safe, that Ida will be drowned. That the worst and the best of her life is to come.

'Frau Wiler,' says Karl, gently. 'The time draws near. There is only one passage, and we will be caught.'

'No,' says Lisbet, panic fluttering in her chest. 'This is not right, it is not just!'

Karl's own voice is thick with emotion. He reaches into his pocket and pulls out a small cloth pouch. 'Look, I have poppy. It is enough for . . .' He cannot bring himself to say it, but they all know. He weighs it in his hand. Enough for death. He places the pouch beneath the door, between them. 'Take it all. It will help the pain.'

'Thank you,' says Ida softly. 'Now go.'

'I will not.'

'You will,' says Ida. She reaches through the gap and clasps Lisbet's tear-stained cheeks. 'You will go, and you will live, Bet. For the both of us.'

She pulls away then, takes the pouch of poppy and folds back into the shadows, as though she was never there at all.

Lisbet calls after her, but between them Sophey and Karl are hauling her to her feet. She is in the reeds of her childhood river again, her brothers peeling her fingers from cold flesh, and now as then she does not struggle, only feels a tearing, a rending of the material of her soul, as she leaves part of herself behind.

Sixteen

Lisbet has seen an execution before, the hanging of a rebel. The man had entered a church and stabbed a priest, shouting Joss Fritz's name, damning their emperor to Hell. He repeated his sermon on the gibbet, the crowd roaring. Lisbet had shut her eyes at the moment he was hung, buried her face in her father's side.

She has seen a drowned woman before. Her mother had been in the water a day by the time she found her, her skin green and eyes empty. Lisbet had not been able to look in them, could only wrap her body around Mutti's. But she is determined to watch this, to be as brave as Ida.

She stands next to Frederich and Sophey on the bank facing the gaol. The stink of the river wafts between them and the platform where Ida will be drowned. It's accessed from a scrubby, underdeveloped stretch of bank beside the gaol and overlooked by a bridge, nearby rickety buildings subsiding like herons wading out to forage.

There is even a stage set up here behind them, with about fifty women dancing and bordered by a low fence like livestock. The crowd is muted and the musicians play lazily, but it does not affect the ardour of the dancers. The spectacle is no less powerful for its familiarity: Lisbet cannot help but turn and gawp.

The whole stage is crafted of wood as in the horse guild – she can see the struts emerging and spiking the dirt – covered over with cloth of some kind, wrinkling and billowing. The stage is raised so high, Lisbet can see only heads and shoulders, sometimes an arm thrown up.

Even as she watches there is a tussle as two of the dancers tangle together, their fingers flung out and dragging through knotted hair. One of the caught dancers moans: she is a woman in a stained grey tunic, spittle collecting at the corners of her mouth. There is blood too, in the folds of her cheeks, and her whole head is beetroot with the sun. And then a hook parts her from the other dancer, and her greying hair is ripped from her head and falls in a tuft, more blood springing up on the mottled skin of her scalp.

Lisbet reels: the hair is caught on the wheel of another hand and flung to the knot of onlookers. One raises it as a trophy. Sophey grips her arm too tight.

'Here they come.'

There are nine of them on the opposite bank, flanked by guards. Nine women, tied to one another at the waists, processing, faces downturned, from the gaol gates. Their crimes are read by a guard as the crowd begins to gather, the Twenty-One keen to set an example. Three hures, two thieves, four falsifiers. They are close enough for Lisbet to see Ida's golden hair. She is third from the back, only one of a number. Behind the procession walks Plater. Lisbet is glad to see he looks wretched, his face gaunt. Let him regret what he has begun. Let him carry the weight of this until it crushes him to pieces.

The women are ordered to stop and turn. Lisbet looks at each of them, determined to remember their faces. The musicians continue to play, the dancers continue to dance. All goes on, even as the women begin to be nudged forward by the guards.

A sense of unreality grips Lisbet and squeezes. This cannot be, it cannot. But there she is, the friend who Lisbet laughed and shared secrets with, who gave her bread and kindness easily and without limit, and love so pure it shone through her. It cannot end here, in that filthy river, where desperate mothers drown their babies to better feed others. Sophey takes her hand.

For a moment, Lisbet thinks she means to comfort her. But then she yanks her hard, and Lisbet looks to see Sophey is not watching the tied women at all, but the stage behind. Horror is etched in every line and pockmark of her swollen face.

Lisbet follows her gaze, and sees a familiar figure hauling themselves up onto the stage.

It is Nethe, cheeks scratched, dress torn, face furious and wild. She stands at the front, legs parted as though to take root. Before Lisbet can process it, any of it, Nethe opens her mouth, and screams.

It could be *Ida*. It could be *no*. Lisbet cannot make out the word – all there is is the enormous power, the volume of the shout, a sound hauled up from some black, bottomless place. It cuts through the drumming feet, and causes the musicians to down their instruments and stare.

Someone laughs uncertainly, and then Nethe screams again. It catches the bound women, snares Plater around the neck and jerks their attention up. Lisbet sees his snarl, his motion at the nearest guard who peels away and makes hurriedly for the bridge. She sees Ida, her mouth opening in shock, in despair.

Plater orders the guards to push the women forward. Again,

Nethe makes that inhuman, guttural sound. She stamps her feet on the stage, bends double with the effort.

'Mein Gott,' says Frederich.

The guards look uncertain, frightened – none of them move. Another scream, and this time it has an echo, and another. Around Nethe, the women are bunching closer, still spinning and thumping their feet. The hair on Lisbet's arms rises.

The guard Plater sent for Nethe has reached the stage, but he makes no attempt to arrest her. From her radiates an energy vivid and sharp as lightning: Lisbet's teeth ache with it. The next time Nethe opens her mouth, it is as if she has a hundred voices caught in her throat, flying out like locusts. All the women on the stage scream as one and many, the power of it physical, visceral. They seem possessed, full of righteous, riotous fury.

The crowd around them shifts uneasily, and some of the men begin to shout, calling some of the condemned prisoners by name.

'Beatrix!' 'Claire!' 'Helene!' Beside her, Sophey calls, 'Ida!'

There is a commotion on the bridge, a surge as some of the watchers break away from the bank. Lisbet sees them: dark clothes, intent faces, as though they are merely waiting for a signal. Some of them dart through the crowd and across the river, towards the bound women.

Plater is shouting now too: Lisbet can see the ropy tendons of his neck knotting tight. But he is drowned out by the dancing women's screams, their cries like a call and answer. The guards at the water's edge back away as the bank is stormed by a group of men. Lisbet sees the glint of a knife.

'Rebels?' shouts Frederich, but Lisbet cannot be sure. They seem like avenging angels, mercenaries. The men shoal about the women, pulling them clear. The guards dissipate, repelled by the hysteria. Lisbet holds tight to Frederich, to Sophey, as they are buffeted closer to the river. She keeps her eyes fixed on Ida's bright hair as she is hauled in by the mob, reclaimed.

'They are freeing them!' Frederich's eyes burn with a dark delight. 'They have them, look, Frau Wiler!'

As if Lisbet could look away. She watches agape as the women are held aloft, their faces dazed, limbs dangling as though they were already drowned, and borne over the bridge like effigies. She loses sight of Ida, of her blonde head.

'Where is she?' Lisbet cries, her voice lost to the racket. She spins around, searching, and then sees the women being lifted onto the dancers' stage. The crowd lets out a collective cheer, a bray of triumph, as one of the men goes between them with a knife, slicing the ropes that bind them together.

Ida is set down beside Nethe. The rope trails from her waist, cut in half. Nethe has stopped screaming, but she is among the dancers, and her feet are stamping. *It is too late*, thinks Lisbet. Nethe is already elsewhere, unaware that Ida is beside her.

'Careful!' warns Frederich, as the mob surges around the stage, lifting Lisbet almost off her feet, carrying them to where the musicians sit, silent and uncertain. Someone sets up a chant at them, and they pick up their instruments, and begin to play. All around them, the crowd break into maniacal dancing, buoyed by their act of disobedience. The atmosphere is fevered, dangerous, exhilarating. Lisbet looks up at Ida and Nethe, high on the stage above.

Ida's pupils are huge and black, dilated with poppy. She is looking around herself, dazed. But then she looks at Nethe, dancing beside her, and a dreamy smile plays on her lips. She takes her lover's hand, and joins her in her trance.

Men and women alike flood the stage, and Lisbet again loses sight of them, but then they are there as they were that night in the guild, spinning and spinning as though they are alone in the whole world. Dread grips Lisbet.

When she was a girl she rode a horse astride. It was only a knackered old mare, its knees thick as ship knots with inflammation, its coat scabbed and worn thin as old cloth. She loved it and rode whenever Mutti slept and it could be spared from the fields. Loosed from a harness, it ran like a colt. One day, it jumped a hedge and left her behind it: as she fell, she felt exactly this sensation, the air made rapid and cool. The certainty of hurt. Despite the din, all Lisbet can hear is a whining sound, like flies around rotted meat.

'Fakery!' bellows Plater. Lisbet sees he has climbed up on the musicians' stage, and is brandishing his hook at the dancing women. The crowd boo and spit, and he ducks to avoid a thrown patten. He cannot reach them, dare not descend the platform. 'Deceptors!'

But Lisbet knows that Ida and Nethe are no fakes. They shimmer with something otherworldly, something divine. They move like they are made of feathers, each of their fingers lifting light on nonexistent currents, their faces smooth. Their eyes are soft closed as in sleep, lids pearly pink and glistening with sweat or tears or holy water. Only their feet make them less than angels, crashing up and down as they wheel and loop, dive. Their bodies a murmuration, perfectly in time, moving with a singular clarity.

Lisbet draws up short of the stage, the crush thickest here, people squabbling to grasp the dancers' feet, some holding up vials to catch their sweat and blood. Lisbet doesn't want to touch Nethe or Ida, who are now within reach, doesn't want to interrupt the perfect pendulum of them. She wants to sink to her knees and watch until they have danced the platform clean, their minds empty, their bodies into flight.

Peace, Nethe had said. *I want only peace.* There, amidst the chaos with Ida at her side, she seems to have found it.

But now Sophey is pushing roughly past. 'Nethe,' she moans. 'Ida. Agnethe, no.'

She mounts the stairs, pushing through the dancers, and wrenches Nethe's arm down from where it flutters skywards. Nethe's eyelids shift: it is exactly as though she is asleep, being roused before she is ready. But she doesn't stop dancing. She buffets away from her mother, but Sophey has her hands outstretched, arms flapping as though to shoo the chickens into their coop, and both of them are moving close, too close, to the edge, and the men with their sticks.

'Careful,' cries Lisbet, uselessly. The crowd jeers as one as Nethe slips off the edge, Ida following close behind. Nethe's eyes snap open. Her whole body changes, her dance no longer lingering and light, but heavy and fast, until she is slapping her body, her joints making cracking sounds like twigs. Beside her, Ida begins to fit too, eyes rolling back in her skull. Frederich grasps for her, and Lisbet snatches at her legs.

'Help us,' calls Lisbet, and Sophey comes forward, pressing down Nethe's shoulders.

Lisbet moves closer to Ida, and remembers dimly something about tongues, about how you must stop them from rolling back and choking, but she can no more reach into Ida's mouth than stop her from bucking.

She lies bodily across her, her stomach feeling too soft to bear her weight, wonders if babies can be crushed inside. She hears a clicking sound, a grinding. Lisbet concentrates on being a mercy. She is a rock, a boulder, heavy and ancient and still.

'Ida,' she murmurs, as Ida's hand escapes and flails. 'Ida, hush.'

But Ida is moaning, crying now, and her breath is stale and reeking of poppy. Ida's eyes are stretched wide, and all the calm, the placidity with which she went to face her death, is gone.

'Put her back,' says a watching woman. 'She must dance.'

'We will not,' shouts Sophey, her voice hoarse with fear.

The guards are coming now, Plater screaming orders to take charge of the situation once more. He is searching the crowd, has not seen them.

'They must be on the stage, or at the shrine,' says the woman. 'They will take them else.'

'The shrine then,' says Frederich, and he scoops up Nethe with great effort. Sophey and Lisbet follow after with Ida, whose legs hop and drag by turns.

They reach the cart and lower the women onto the remaining sacks of flour, swaddling them like wax and tying them gently with ropes. They are still moving in the limited way they can, rhythmically, to the inescapable sound of drums. It is indecent, and Lisbet's own cheeks colour as Nethe tips back her head and moans as though in ecstasy, the sound she drew from Ida the night before.

'And mine!' A man is behind them, holding a bucking girl younger than Nethe, little more than a child. A woman dithers at his shoulder, a mirror of the girl with worry lines furrowed deep into her forehead, a badger stripe of grey at her temple.

'We can pay,' she says. 'Please.'

Sophey is nodding even before this offer, dull-eyed and motioning for them to place their girl beside Nethe. Frederich and the girl's father tie the writhing bodies gently, the man weeping. Lisbet looks away.

'Will you be safe?' says Sophey, as the parents climb up beside her. 'Will you tell Mathias?'

'Poppy.' Lisbet can barely speak. Can Sophey understand her? Her head is full of the rush of water, or wind, full of everything and nothing at all. Surely she sleeps? Surely it is all of it a dream?

'I will ensure she is, Frau Wiler,' says Frederich, and Sophey waits no longer. She jolts the reins, without a further word of farewell to either of them. In the bed of the cart, Nethe and Ida still sway beside the child. Lisbet and Frederich stand watching until they are a toy, a speck, and round the corner and gone.

Seventeen

Frederich leads Lisbet from the crowd, which is approaching a riot as the guards break their way onto the stage, and takes her directly through a narrow gate in the city walls. They are at the opposite end of the city now, far from anything she recognises, but Frederich seems to know exactly where they are. She barely notices him disappear and re-emerge with a flagon of beer, and a man with a cart besides.

She drinks deeply, then he helps hoist her into the cart. She watches the sky as they ride, seemingly for hours, around the boundary of the walls, until finally she spies the trees beginning to crowd them, the forest on the approach to home.

As they go, she combs the strands of her memories, all of them edged with disbelief, frantic. She has again that feeling of floating, of detaching from her body and hovering above. Ida tied by the waist, eyes black with poppy. Nethe, screaming with the voice of a hundred dancers. The crowd overriding it all, overtaking Plater and his guards. Sophey's face as she turned the horse for the shrine, her daughter and her daughter's lover thrashing in the bed. All she has to hold is this: Ida is not drowned. Ida still lives.

Lisbet's mind wanders on, to follow the cart bearing Nethe

and Ida away. St Vitus' shrine is two days' ride, through thick forest that rises fast into mountainside. The road will be thronged with desperate families taking their daughters and wives and mothers to the spring, to wash them in the holy water and release them from their abandonment.

But why would they wish to return? To come back to this earth-bound, sun-baked place, this interminable summer where every priest preaches their damnation, where their husbands drag them by the hair and they must drown their children to save them from starvation?

'Frau Wiler? You are home.'

Frederich sounds soft, unlike himself. The cart has stopped, and he helps her down, dismissing the driver with a word of thanks. Lisbet wonders dimly if the man is another of Frederich's lovers, if every face she sees holds some dark secret frowned upon by the Church. Her own heart has trespassed, that night with Eren in the dance tree. They are all of them doomed.

'Lisbet?' She blinks. Mathias is there in the yard, is watching her with rheumy eyes, his granddaughter clutching his shirt. 'What happened?'

Frederich overtakes her, greets the miller warmly. 'Please, sir, I will explain.'

Mathias nods, and pushes Ilse gently forwards. 'Take her in, kleiner leibling.'

Ilse's hand is soft as her mother's, and only slightly smaller. Lisbet follows the girl obedient as a child, and allows herself to be settled at the table, given bread and milk. Ilse watches her with large eyes.

'Where are your brothers?' asks Lisbet.

'Asleep,' Ilse says.

'Are you not tired?' The girl hesitates. 'Go. It is all right. You can sleep now.'

'Where is Mutti?'

Lisbet's tongue stirs dryly in her mouth. 'She is safe. Sleep. It's late.'

Obediently, Ilse leaves for Nethe's room. As she pushes open the door, Lisbet catches a glimpse of the boys curled up in bed, the infant on his swaddling board on the floor. Ilse gets to her knees beside him, and adjusts his blankets. The door swings shut.

After a long while, Mathias and Frederich come inside. Mathias' face is wet with tears, and wordlessly he grasps Lisbet's hands.

'It will be all right,' she says, wanting to believe it. Mathias pats her, trembling.

'Thank you,' he says. 'For going to her.'

'I love her,' she says.

'And she loves you.' He swallows. 'May we stay here? I cannot take them back there. Not if he—'

His voice cracks with anger, with fear.

Lisbet doesn't need to ask who Mathias means. 'Of course.'

'Will he go after her?'

'He didn't see us,' says Lisbet. This alone is comfort to her. 'There was so much happening. Sophey took them away unnoticed.'

Mathias takes a shaky breath. 'I don't know what will happen when—'

'Don't dwell on tomorrow. There is nothing to do but wait.'

Mathias stifles a yawn. 'I can sleep on the floor with the baby.'

'Don't be absurd,' she tells him. 'Take Sophey's bed. Through there.'

'Bless you.' Mathias looks wrung out, grey with exhaustion. He heaves his body upright, and leaves. Frederich collapses beside Lisbet.

'Can I get you anything?' she asks.

Frederich laughs hollowly, and starts to sob. She doesn't know what to do, as the drummer buries his head into his hands, his shoulders heaving. Lisbet reaches out to him, patting his arm.

'I am sorry,' he says thickly. 'Only, it is easy to forget. How much we are hated, how little others understand.' He looks up at her. 'But you do, don't you?'

'I am not—' Lisbet is flustered, scattered. 'I am not like you.'

Frederich's face hardens. 'That is not what I meant.' He takes a breath. 'I meant you know what it is to love without hope of safety. Your babies . . .'

Lisbet's throat closes, voice coming out strangled. 'How do you know?'

'You must not think he betrayed your confidences,' mumbles Frederich. 'But Eren said you had lost children. I made some careless joke, and he was only putting me right. He said you knew bravery. It takes courage, to love beyond what others deem the right boundaries. We are alike in this.'

'Yes.' Lisbet reaches out and squeezes his hand. 'We are.'

'Frederich?'

He is there. Lisbet could weep at the sight of him. Eren, standing in the doorway, backed by fast-fading light. Frederich rises, and goes to his friend. Eren embraces him like a brother, and hushes him, frowning at Lisbet. She shakes her head in response. She doesn't know how to begin to explain.

'Outside,' she says at last. 'Ida's children are sleeping.'

•

They sit in the dusk, Ulf and Fluh trotting over to sit beside Eren while Frederich and Lisbet parcel out the events of the day, passing the story between them like a hot coal, neither willing to speak more than a few sentences of the

218

horror, the strangeness. When they are done, they sit in silence a long while. Lisbet watches Eren's shape in the growing dark. She wants to lean against him, feel his precise frame measured out against hers, stretch herself bodily as a canvas across it.

'I'm sorry,' he says, his voice a comforting burr. 'If I had known—'

'What could you have done? We did all we could.'

'Of course,' he soothes. 'I only mean . . . I wish I could do something.'

Lisbet nods. The sky over their heads is the same darkening blue as the bruise on Ida's forehead, as Nethe's eyes. She wants them home. But what awaits them? Plater, his fury stronger than ever. She would not be surprised if he meets them at the shrine and drowns them in it.

'And this makes sense of the news I was given today,' says Eren, and his voice becomes graver still.

'Please,' groans Lisbet. 'No more news. My mind is full.'

'The Twenty-One have a new approach to the plague.' She hears him swallow. 'They no longer require our services. In fact, we are blamed for the worsening of the mania.'

'What do you mean?' says Lisbet, her voice traitorously high.

'I heard about the ruckus at the gaol. I didn't know the circumstances, of course. But it seems some of the men involved were rebels, returning to the city under the guise of musicians. At least that is the story being put about.'

'I thought the quality of playing was poor,' says Frederich, a half-hearted attempt at mirth.

'So what will they do?' whispers Lisbet.

'We are banished,' Eren says, simply. 'Every musician must leave the city and its surrounds, tonight.'

Lisbet's stomach plummets. 'No,' she says. 'You cannot go.'

'We must,' says Eren. He will not meet her eye. 'It is not a request.'

Frederich sucks air through his teeth. He looks down at his finger, the pale skin where his band once lay. 'Tonight?'

'Do not risk it,' says Eren. 'Guards are already stationed at each gate. They are beating those musicians that will not leave.'

Frederich nods and sighs. 'Very well.' He looks at Lisbet. 'Your mother-in-law will be glad, Frau Wiler. I do not think she ever liked us.'

Lisbet is worried if she so much as breathes she will speak her mind. *You can stay. Please, don't leave me.*

'We'll collect our things,' says Eren, 'unless we will disturb the miller?'

She shakes her head. What will she do, with him gone?

'You will be safe,' says Eren. 'The miller will stay with you.'

'And you?' asks Lisbet. She rakes her eyes hungrily over his jaw, his nose, his lips, trying to hold his features in her mind, as though she hopes to draw him. 'Where will you go?'

She wants him to say, *nowhere*. She wants him to say, *I won't go.*

'You mustn't worry, Frau Wiler.'

'Lisbet.'

'Lisbet.'

His voice has a new clarity to it, clear as cool water. She waits outside while he and Frederich collect their things. She doesn't want to watch the evidence of them leaving.

Frederich is done quickly and emerges to embrace her briefly. 'Be well, Frau Wiler. I hope all is remedied soon.'

He pulls his pipe from his pocket, steps further off to tamp it full. Eren is slower. He comes out with the bundle he arrived with. His shoulders are hunched, and she feels certain he does not want to go any more than she wants him to. They are both of them weary. They could lie down in the shade of the skeps and let the bees lull them to sleep, she thinks. She could rise without waking him and collect the comb, go to him with honey on her lips—

'Thank you for your kindness, Frau Wiler. I wish Fräulein Wiler and Frau Plater a full and fast recovery, that they come to themselves again soon.'

He bends to Ulf, to Fluh, and they come, butting their noses against his hand.

This may be the last time, she thinks, the last time she sees him, speaks with him.

'Take care of yourself,' he says. 'Keep to your yard. You know the forest is not safe.'

'I will go where I like.' Anger now, hot as sun on her neck. He is not her husband, her master. If he leaves her now, he is not even her friend. Eren looks at her then, his black eyebrow arched to a perfect degree. She wants to trace it with her fingertip, to draw a line from it to his earlobe, to his pulse working the thin skin beneath his beard. She wants to look, and look, and look so well she could know him forever, for this last look to be enough to keep him with her all her days. She turns away.

'Goodbye, Frau Wiler.'

Lisbet goes inside and closes the door before he can turn his back: plunging herself into the airless room, she drags breath into her body in great, heaving gasps. So, she tells herself, it is done. He is gone. It is done.

She goes to the dirty sheets on her and Henne's bed and sleeps heavily, as though crushed under the boulder she made of herself to weight Ida. When she wakes it is in complete confusion, her tongue furred. It is dark and she does not know if it is the middle of the night or before dawn or in between.

She lies a long time, curled around her stomach, and only when the baby forces her to the pisspot does she rise. If it were not for the baby, she would never rouse herself again. *My boy*. All she does now, is for him.

A long time ago, after the ninth baby was lost, she thought she should go to the empiric for something to keep her barren. She thought to let Henne leave her, and she join an order of nuns, or to go home and live as a spinster among her brothers, or else to run into the forest and see how long she could live among the trees and rebels. She dropped the thoughts soon enough, but they linger as words that cannot be unsaid, like a declaration of love or hate.

More than anything, she needs a child with an ache so base and animal she has never tried to understand it. She has passed through every phase of want. Through the hatred that comes with desire so strong you could blunt your teeth on it, the closest to true hunger she's ever known. Times when she would pluck her heart from her chest and fill their tiny, limp bodies with its beat, a cavity for her love. She understands why pelicans peck their own breasts for blood, why cuckoos cast out eggs. She would do violence for this child. For any of her children. A mother so many times over she cannot count it on her fingers alone. This child must stay, she prays for it until her knees chafe and blister, just as she had prayed for her mother. And see how that ended.

Henne thinks it pathetic, but hasn't he bred this need in her? Isn't it his seed he plants but she cannot grow? *What has become of you, Lisbet*, he asked her once, as she lay with her legs open, begging him. But it is the wrong question. She has not yet become. And what wouldn't she give?

It is a similar urgency she feels for the bees, the desire to understand them, to own something that can't be owned. It is even – she allows herself to give full attention to the thought in this murky, indeterminate time – how she feels for Eren. And they all leave.

She will cleanse the house of any trace of him. She moves quietly, so as not to disturb Ida's father, Ida's children, and starts in the kitchen, rubbing the table with tallow and water and wax, and sweeping out the old, crinkled rushes the musicians stood upon, and covering over the scuff marks from the benches with new straw. She dusts up flour, setting the chair and benches into their usual places, dragging the table to the centre from where they'd allowed it to abut the wall. No more sliding past each other, no more not touching and wanting to touch.

She sweeps the corridor next. Outside the dogs are whining for their breakfast, but she cannot open the door, because while she does not he might still be outside. To open it and find him not there would be impossible.

By this time the atmosphere in the house is awful, full of her sweat, and she knows she must air it but first she needs to reclaim her and her husband's room fully. She nudges it open with her foot, stands in the doorway. There are boot marks to be polished out of the walls, a stray blond hair on the sheets of the bed. She stops herself from getting down on her hands and knees and feeling the floor for Eren's black hair. She must not be wanton. *Up*, she tells herself, *up and finish*.

She sweeps the floor and finds a snapped string from his lute, laid flush against the wall, so perfectly hidden it could be that he left it there for her to find. She loops it around and around her finger, watching the skin turn from red to white, to paler white, bone yellow.

Only when she can bite the tip and feel nothing does she release it, allowing the pain to rush back. She throws the string on the fire and at last, as Ida's baby starts to cry, throws wide the door.

Eighteen

Once the baby, dogs and chickens are fed, she goes to the bees.

She decides to make it holy. Now Eren is gone she is determined all her thoughts of him will be too, all the unclean grime swept out of her, made pure again for Henne's return.

The sacred animals are at work. Henne told her how they are the only animal come unchanged from Eden, how Eve and Adam before their sin would have seen such creatures and tasted honey from their hives. She imagines herself a saint, then, to match them. Saints must suffer, and hasn't she?

Taking the stick of ash and rosemary, she begins to smoke the apiary, walking the length of the skep yard until the whole world hums. She clears the damaged hives, rights the skeps. Her fingers cramp with care. She works slowly on each of the hives in turn, attending to it as a single rosary bead, turning the combs over in her hand, the wax bucket settled on the soil at her feet, touching each hive's honey to her lips, soft as a prayer. With each exhale, she breathes out thoughts of Eren, casts them aside.

Her thoughts turn to Henne. Her husband has changed shape to her in his absence, in her fresh and terrible knowledge. He flickers at the edges, his passive solidity grown jagged.

Must she love him, when he returns from his mission in Heidelberg? If they lose the bees, and she is left to be only his wife – she stops herself. This will not be the last time she tends them. For all his sins, his cruelties, Henne loves the bees too. Loves the child inside her. If she is to be a good mother, she must be a good wife. If Ida could, to such a man as Plater, Lisbet can go through the motions, at least.

She turns her back on the trees as she works, humming tunelessly to calm her nerves. She collects the darkest honey in a separate jar. She will make mead, she will brew it herself and make it the finest drink Henne has ever tasted.

The honey is amber, sap-gold, and though she pulls her mind again and again away from him, she thinks of Eren, his eyes turning amber in the sunlight. The wax is soft and giving under her touch, still warm from where it has been plucked from the hive's heart, and the bees brush over her wrists soft as kisses. Her vision blurs. She wants to hike up her skirts and run, keep running until she catches Eren on the road or in the forest, to tap him on the shoulder and then—

What? She has imagination enough for it, especially after sighting Nethe and Ida by the tree trunk. She straightens, turns to the tree line quickly, as if to catch someone staring at her. If anyone were to approach, she could rouse the bees, have them swarm and sting to death any attacker. *Mistress of the bees.*

'Frau Wiler?'

Lisbet forgets all her comforting thoughts, and screams. She drops her bucket, and a figure starts towards her out of the trees, dark pinned against dark.

'Sorry, I—'

She is slow to recover herself. Her heart is galloping, driving hard hooves into her chest. The figure has resolved itself into someone much smaller and slighter than she. A boy.

'Frau Wiler,' he says again. 'It's me, Daniel Lehmann.'

'I know it's you, Daniel,' she snaps. 'What are you doing here?'

She reaches awkwardly down, tilting the bucket to stop the honey on its slow encroachment towards the ground, then straightens and looks full at him. His left eye is swollen shut, his neck splotched with poison. He is wearing the clothes he wore as he stood with Plater: she can see his cuffs are stained with blood. It turns her stomach.

'I have a message.'

'From who?'

'Plater.'

'What does he want now?'

'Your husband has been refused.'

'Refused.' Dully, she registers him scratching his eye and she catches his wrist.

'In Heidelberg.'

Her blood roars. *No.* She forces herself to stand steady, to show no weakness to this child, but beneath her the ground feels soft and swallowing. *No.*

'The debt must be paid in wax,' says Daniel, pulling free of her grip. 'Or the hives will be taken. It will be collected in two days.'

There is no way she can match the debt in wax. This is a false offer of salvation. She would have to strip every hive. It is the work of a week, and several men. It is impossible. But she will not cry in front of this whelp.

Coldly, she says, 'Anything more?'

Daniel looks dartingly at her. 'I did not want to lead him to them.' He scuffs his foot. 'He made me.'

'My friend was to be drowned,' says Lisbet, allowing her terror to morph into anger, fly upon the boy. 'He ordered you to murder my sister.'

'They should not have been dancing.'

Lisbet wonders if he did not understand what he saw at the river. 'Your mother does.'

He nods at the ground. 'Not on the stages. They are sanctified.'

'And our hives?' Lisbet gestures at the newly righted skeps. 'They are nothing to you?'

'I only meant to take a little,' says Daniel. He scratches his neck: she sees fluid leak from the stings.

'You are lucky,' says Lisbet, her anger weakening. 'They could have killed you. Or else Nethe would have, had she caught you.'

'Where are they now?'

Lisbet laughs hollowly. 'To tell you would be to pour it straight into the ear of Plater. We are not friends, Daniel.'

His face crumples, and he scratches his stings again. She looks the boy up and down. She should hate him, but she feels only an enormous pity. Ulf sniffs gently at the boy while Fluh runs in a loop, snarling and barking until Lisbet throws her shoe at her, and the dog settles down to chew at it instead.

'Are you hungry?'

•

The kitchen is sweltering. She had left the door open and the sun is angled squarely through the doorframe, heating the rushes into warmth beyond bearing. Ilse and her brothers sit around the table uncertainly, eyeing the last of the bread.

'Did you sleep?'

The girl nods. Alef yawns widely.

'We have company. It is too hot in there,' says Lisbet. 'Come into the shade, here.'

All she can think to do, with the world shattering to pieces around her, is be a good host. They arrange themselves around the log pile, the place Lisbet had sat with Ida and felt the fine grain of Mathias' flour. Before Henne's journey and Nethe's return, before women danced themselves to death in the city streets. A lifetime ago.

Alef and Martin ask Daniel what is wrong with his face, and take great delight in counting the sores. Lisbet brings the bread and some raw honey, milk for the infant. She takes Rolf from his sister and dips a clean cloth into the cup, drips it into his pink little mouth. He sucks hungrily, mewls for more. The warm weight of him makes her breasts ache. Among it all, can it really be her own baby still lives, still grows inside her? An everyday miracle, at last bestowed on her in the midst of this, the most cursed of times?

She looks around her, at Ida's beautiful children, at Daniel, filthy and sore and thin. Five children, like she'd always imagined. Children filling their yard, fighting over crusts and chasing the chickens, as a baby sleeps in her arms. She swallows down tears.

Alef reaches for the last of the honey, and Lisbet shakes her head.

'That's not for eating. It's for Daniel's stings,' she says. She frees an arm from under Rolf, and dips her finger into the honey, motions for Daniel to tilt his head toward her. He does so, and she dabs it onto the worst of the stings. 'You must not scratch,' she says. 'It spreads the poison.'

He is in a far sorrier state than she realised, his wrist bones poking out like robin's eggs from his blueish skin, his swollen eye radiating heat. When she finishes his neck she pours some raw honey into her cup, and dissolves it in the water before pouring it over his eye. He licks his cheek where it runs down his face.

'Thank you,' he says, and then, through a mouthful of crumbs, 'My sister is dancing now.'

'In earnest?'

He nods.

'I wish I had known,' she replies, then stops herself. She had been about to say there was space enough in the cart. But she cannot trust Daniel with this information.

'They will lead them all from the city soon, when St Vitus' effigy is ready.'

'What effigy?'

He smiles, smug with knowledge, and takes another bite of bread. 'The Twenty-One have ordered an effigy built from wax. Now the musicians are gone, the plague must end. They will take the effigy to the shrine and burn it in his honour.'

So this is what they need their wax for. She looks over his head, at their skeps ranged so neat and peaceful, the bees' hum. And she must plunder them for all they have.

'Who is this?' Mathias stands in the doorway, blinking in the light. He looks very old, every line on his face picked out in shadow, his sparse hair mussed by sleep. Ilse immediately stands and hurries to her grandfather, pulling him outside to give him her seat.

But Daniel, his meal eaten and sores salved, stands without greeting or thanks. He snatches the last of the honey, and takes off at a run.

'No one,' says Lisbet. Beside the feeling of unease, there is sadness. Daniel seems entirely taken in by Plater – if she had the means to remove the boy from his influence, she doubts there would be much left to save. 'Mathias, I need your help.'

'Anything,' he says, his hand resting on Ilse's head.

'There is much work to be done.'

•

It is as though she has stepped through her own shadow, and exists suddenly on the other side of her life. There are children running among the skeps in small, makeshift wicker masks, children at her elbow, learning the bees. So many children, she must kill a chicken to feed them, and shows Ilse how to strip and stuff it with herbs.

This is what they eat, those two days. Mathias keeps the fire hot as he can, while Lisbet and sometimes Ilse work through at the hives, Lisbet doing the skilled work of melting and straining and re-forming the wax into thick cylinders, large as she and Mathias can lift. It is the work of many men, and she revels in it. It keeps her alert and strong, though she is so much on her feet her ankles have swelled thick as her knees, and her back aches perpetually.

Sophey will have reached St Vitus' shrine by now. Lisbet imagines her washing Nethe and Ida's bruised feet, wonders if they danced the whole way there. Soon the effigy will be built, Henne will return, the stages will be dismantled in the streets. She will forget Eren.

The fear, too, will be forgotten. For now, if she sleeps, Ulf sleeps with her, hot and heavy over her ankles. She even lets Fluh lie on the kitchen floor. The dogs stink, the matts of Ulf's fur catching in her fingers as she strokes him, but she doesn't care about that either. It is the only time she feels safe. She dreams in colours vivid as prophecy that Daniel returns with Plater, come to pluck the hives from their places, or take her screaming away.

Mathias and the children show no sign of leaving, even when the wax is bound in place in the cart, lined up in neat cylinders that sweat slightly in the heat. They have wrung the hives dry, the bees are distressed and Lisbet, Ilse and Mathias are exhausted, but it is done. She has met Plater's demand.

Three men arrive to collect it, slinging their careful work

without delicacy atop a pile that must have come from the monastery. It already begins to soften, throwing up an overpowering smell of honey.

'You should cover that,' she tells them, but they laugh.

'All being melted anyway,' says one.

•

They kill another chicken that night, to celebrate their work being done. It is a luxury Sophey will no doubt scold them for, but they need the food, as well as the reward it represents. The kitchen fills with its slow scent, and Ulf twitches his eyebrows so hopefully at the door Lisbet relents and gives him a leg not fully stripped, and a wing to Fluh. The children are exhausted too, but elated. They gabble about the wax press, compare their bee stings and scars from hot wax, and as Lisbet feeds Rolf she feels a sense of such contentment she sighs aloud.

It cannot, does not, last.

The next morning, with the chicken carcass stripped and making stock in the pot, she knows the knock the moment she hears it. The dogs leap to their feet and growl at the sound.

The children and Mathias are still asleep. She resists the urge to bar the bedroom doors, to pick up the knife she used to chop the last of the carrots for the broth. She considers pretending she is still abed too, but then he speaks.

'Frau Wiler, I can see your shadow beneath the door.'

She hovers at the latch. 'The wax is already collected.'

'Open the door.' Plater's voice is pleasant enough. It makes Lisbet's skin crawl.

'For what purpose?'

'I wish to see my children. And do not pretend they are not there. The Lehmann boy saw them.'

Lisbet bristles. 'Where else would they go? They know they

are not safe at home, with the man who would have seen their mother drown.'

'And where is their mother now? Is she there too?' Lisbet knows he doesn't really think so. He would have battered the door down days ago. 'You know I can return with a guard. I could have you arrested for abduction.'

'Is that my father?'

Lisbet jumps. Ilse has moved on catlike feet to stand beside her.

'Ilse.' Plater's voice is silky soft. 'Open this door, will you?'

Ilse looks uncertainly up at Lisbet. 'It is up to you,' she tells the child.

'Open the door, girl,' says Plater.

'You do not have to—'

'Do as I say, Ilse.'

Ilse opens the latch. Plater moves immediately inside, shunting Lisbet back, and lifts his daughter with one arm. He looks haggard, his red hair slick with oil and sweat.

'Where are my boys?'

'Asleep,' says Lisbet. Her fingers twitch. The knife is within reach.

'Wake them.'

'They are tired—'

'Alef! Martin!' Plater kicks aside the bench. Still holding Ilse, he thumps on the doors. Immediately, Rolf begins crying. Lisbet rushes past Plater into Nethe's room. Alef and Martin are tousle-haired, Martin's lip beginning to tremble. She scoops Rolf up from the floor as Plater snaps his fingers at his sons.

'Come on. We are going home.'

Lisbet rocks Rolf side to side. 'They are fine here, they are settled. The least you can do is—'

Plater drops Ilse to the floor and comes very close to Lisbet then. Even Rolf stills as his shadow breaks over them. The

232

clove on Plater's breath does not mask the liquor. He is drunk. His eyes are bloodshot, and she wonders if he has been crying.

'Do not tell me what I may or may not do with my own children, with my own wife. They are here, all of them, by my grace.'

He thumps his chest once, twice.

Mathias crowds into the already full room. 'Alef. I thought it must be you making this racket.'

'Shut up, old man,' sneers Plater.

'I will not,' says Mathias. 'I have held my tongue all these years, watched you portion out punishment to my child as though you yourself are without sin. But you are just a man, Alef Plater. Less than a man. Look how your own children cower from you. All you have over them is fear.'

Mathias places himself between Plater and Lisbet, forcing the man to retreat a few paces. 'Know this: fear is a weak hold. It will not bind. That is what you never understood. You could have given Ida mercy, even love – but all you offered was pain. You failed her, and I will not let you fail her children too.'

'They are my children.'

'Then ask them,' says Mathias. He advances, and Plater steps back again. 'Ask if they wish to go with you.'

'They will come,' says Plater, glancing back to where the children crowd around Lisbet's skirts, at Rolf squalling in her arms. 'Ilse, Alef, Martin. Home, now.'

Martin burrows deeper into Lisbet's skirts. There is no mistaking the expression on Plater's face as his son withdraws from him: it is despair, complete and abject. And then it is masked by his familiar, cold smile.

'What need have I for such sops, such misborns? Stay if you wish, but the mill is no longer yours, Herr Metz. You will never set foot on my property again.'

Mathias' hand starts to tremor, and he places it behind his

back so Plater will not see. Lisbet knows the mill is Mathias' soul, that he hacked it from the forest, built it plank by plank with Ida's mother.

'And I would not rest so easy here,' he says. 'There will be a reckoning, Lisbet Wiler.'

Now Lisbet steps forward, made bold by Mathias, by the children watching her. 'You threaten me in my own home? The debt is paid. I owe nothing.'

Plater growls. 'You think the wax a clearance of all? Debt and stolen honey besides?'

Lisbet grips Rolf tighter. 'It is not stolen.'

'It is as I told your husband. You stand in quicksand. All you have is not yours.'

'You're lying. Daniel said—'

'Is it a lie if I can make it so?' Plater sways. 'You have made a powerful enemy in me. *He who is not with me is against me, he who does not gather with me, scatters.* You have made an enemy of the Twenty-One, of God Himself.'

'You do not speak for Him,' says Lisbet. 'Leave my house.'

'Gladly.'

He leaves the door hanging open. Lisbet watches him go, disappearing unsteadily. She has the sensation of a lamb circled by a wolf, rocks Rolf until he and her heart both quiet. Into the silence, Ilse speaks.

'Thank you, Bet.'

The girl draws close to her side once more. Ida's children circle her with their arms, and hold on with all their might.

Five hundred and eighty-seven dancing

Agnethe remembers the first time they kissed. They were so young it was not even wrong. A chaste touch of lips as they paddled in the river, hands clasped to keep themselves from falling. It had been a kind summer, soft and mellow, and she and Henne and Alef and Ida were allowed from their chores early each evening to run in the forests like Gyptians. It was the last summer it was ever so, for there followed the bad year: ice stones the size of fists pummelling the fields and churning the harvest to mush, the bees dying frozen in their skeps.

But none of that mattered. Because from that moment, with the river running sweet and full over her ankles, and Ida's lips just the same on hers, Agnethe at last felt there was somewhere she belonged. Ida prayed so hard for their sins her knees bruised, but still she came each week to her, to the skep yard or the forest, and they would kiss until their lips were tender as her knees. Agnethe could never bring herself to pray. She could not see what they did as unholy, had never come so close to bliss, to heaven, to an angel as Ida.

It was Ida who touched her first, a clear year after the first kiss, Ida who moved her mouth down over her body by the well, her fingers finding a place Agnethe never knew existed.

She reached right to the core of her, and she did the same for Ida, and though they never named it, it was love.

They would still marry of course, she to Alef and Ida to Henne. They would raise children together as though they were their own, as brothers and sisters. The whole thing was arranged, and it was not until Alef and Henne found them in the forest that she realised it was all built on rot and sin. She saw it in Henne's face, in Alef's raw anger, and if she was in any doubt they taught her. She longed for punishment, for resolution.

The mountains offered plenty of punishment, and no resolution. She could not find peace without Ida near her. Even time did not soothe it. And God saw fit to punish her again, and worse, giving them to each other, and parting them a second time. The sight of Ida tied at the river almost made her lose her mind. She danced because there was no earthly way to stand the pain of it. She danced and all her mind was a cavern, black and empty. Until here, until now.

She wakes between Ida and a stranger. Nethe would think she is dead and travelling some long road to purgatory but for the girl, who flails and moans. But Ida is still, so still. Nethe takes her hands in hers. If she closes her eyes she could imagine they are alone, lying as they used to under the cover of trees. Ida's eyes open, and they are black as pits. But she sees her, Nethe is sure, and so that she can be doubly sure, she kisses each of Ida's fingers, and whispers that she loves her with each one. She does this until the words tangle and lose meaning, and beyond that until Nethe says it only in her head.

And though Ida does not reply, though her breaths are slowing now, her eyes so terribly black, so terribly far away, Nethe knows she hears her, knows her, and knows it to be true.

Nineteen

They spend the days approaching the Feast of St Magdalene
in a state of forced joviality. Lisbet feels as though her whole
life is halted as she waits: for Plater, for Henne, for Sophey
and Ida and Nethe. She carries her belly with the closest thing
she's ever felt to pragmatism, allowing herself now to make
small preparations for the baby's arrival: fetching the stool
from the beekeeping shed to use for birthing, ensuring there
are always cloths kept clean, coin stored aside should an empiric
need to be called. Each act feels like a triumph, a stoking of
a tiny flame in her heart: hope, white hot as the comet in her
father's field.

Ida's children are a welcome distraction, and suddenly it is
a full week since Lisbet has visited her dance tree, and longer
still since she went almsgiving. She knows Ida would wish her
to go, to help those most in need, especially on a feast day,
when all around is excess and incense with no thought for
the unfed.

She tells Mathias of her plan, and he is unhappy. The
encounter with his son-in-law has shaken the very meat of
him, and he sees any breach of the farm's boundary as asking
for trouble.

'Plater never bothers with the almshouses,' says Lisbet. 'You know this as well as me.'

'You will not go to the city?'

Lisbet crosses her fingers behind her back. 'No.'

She feels bad lying to Mathias, but the worry would be more harmful than the lie. She knows she will not be able to resist going to the cathedral, trying to learn news of the shrine, the dancers, the effigy that their bees gave all for.

Mathias sighs. 'I'll stoke the fire.'

They spend the day baking: coarse wide loaves that will fill hungry bellies, sweetened with honey. Ilse has her mother's touch with dough, the muscles in her tiny forearms already strong. Away from their father's influence, the boys have softened even as their sister becomes bolder. They cry for their mother and hang on Lisbet's skirts, and take turns feeding Rolf. It is a lovely balance, to watch them all in these new roles, and Lisbet hopes Ida will soon return to see it.

The morning of the Feast of St Magdalene, Lisbet rises before the sun. She harnesses the long-suffering mule to the cart, and sets out for the slums, bringing Ulf – the dog has become her constant comfort and companion.

The road is quieter than last time she took it, and the trickle of people is all one way, all towards the cathedral for Mass. Lisbet stops at the outskirts and distributes the loaves to lack-lustre thanks. There is no sign of the Lehmanns, their hovel boarded up. She remembers what Daniel said, about Hilde. She wonders if the effigy has yet left the city.

'What do you think, Ulf?'

She eyes the spires. Dust hovers over them, the sunlight licking them to poisonous yellow. Why should she be afraid to approach? She has as much right to be there as any. Plater is only one man in several thousand, and likely kept busy on such an important day.

She places her hand on her stomach. Lately she has been talking to him, her boy, asking him for answers like others pray. And isn't he just as much a miracle as God? The skin between her boy and her fingers feels like the divide between the living and the dead: so fragile, so charged with desire and fear. She should turn the cart around, go back to their farm, continue to wait, for him, for his father, for his aunt and grandmother and Ida.

Restiveness tickles her calves. Before she can think better of it, she flicks the reins, and follows the growing crowds in the direction of the market. The bells are ringing for Mass, running up and down their scales, offering their music in the musicians' absence. She follows them like a master's whistle until the increasing crowds block the cart's way. Tying the mule at a trough, she and Ulf walk the rest of the way to the cathedral.

They reach the square just as the bells stop. She hears their echo, a pressure in her eardrums, as she surveys the astonishing scene. It seems the guilds have been emptied, their dancers disgorged into the square, where it all began with that one woman wheeling alone. Hundreds of women dance in the shadow of the cathedral, the exhaustion lifting from them like smoke. In the aftermath of the bells, there is an unnatural silence, only scuffling feet, occasional moans from the afflicted. She sees men with hooks marking out a boundary between dancers and observers, imagines them herding the entranced women like sheep into the square. She searches their faces, but Plater is not there.

Into the anticipatory hush, the cathedral doors open. Inside blazes with the fire of a hundred candles, and into their extraordinary light step five men, dressed richly as burghers. Lisbet recognises one face, for his portrait was toured around all the churches of Strasbourg after the last Bundsuch, so all could see the man who ordered the rebels to hang: Sebastian Brant, the city's syndic and convener of the Twenty-One. Plater's ultimate master. Severe in black velvet, red slashes of silk at his wrists, he raises his pale hand into the quiet.

'People of Strasbourg, you have not known peace for weeks.'

The word 'peace' strikes Lisbet like a blow. She thinks of Nethe, who never knew peace unless she was with Ida, of her own serenity at the dance tree. Brant is wrong. Many of them have not known peace all their lives.

'We have consulted priests, and physics, doctors and empirics. Our own Emperor has heard our entreaties. Every moment, we have worked to restore order. We banished the musicians—'

With no mention they brought them. Lisbet forces aside the welling image of Eren.

'We have punished the forgerers. The hures and thieves are pushed from the city—'

Into desperation in the forests. Now Lisbet's anger rises anew.

'We have reclaimed the guilds. And now it is time to reclaim our city entirely. This shall be the end to it: all who dance are to be taken to the shrine. The plague ends today, on the Feast of St Magdalene. Now we purge ourselves of this chaos. We have the eyes of God upon us, and we shall show Him Strasbourg is His city, the dearest of them all, the most blessed.'

Lisbet could laugh, but it is swallowed by a roar from the crowd. It is not a sound of simple jubilation, but entangled in fear and relief and horror and awe. For now Brant steps aside, and the effigy is carried out of the cathedral, and into the daylight.

Lisbet smells it before she sees it, cutting even through the reek of sweat and sour breath and human excrement. Beeswax, pure as the highest note in a choir. Standing twice as high as a man, higher than the stages, and reeking-sweet, is the effigy of St Vitus.

The saint's wax double stands in a cauldron, painted with tar to give it the effect of black and tarnished metal. His torso is bare, showing lurid nipples and carved ribs, and though his face might once have been finely carved it is already dripping, melting in the gathering heat, as though the cauldron burns hot and is rending the flesh from his bones. She almost expects to see the clean white of his skeleton emerge.

Lisbet turns away. The usual comfort she takes from the smell of her beeswax is tainted, made vicious by this grotesque purpose. Nausea wells in her gullet as the effigy is lifted on a pyre of crossed wood. It takes six men, three at each side, to lift it, and as it descends the cathedral steps wax drips a path behind. The crowd parts around it like a river around a boulder, rushing in to scrape the scattered wax from the ground with their fingernails. Lisbet is caught in the crush, Ulf barking his dismay, and she grips the fur at his scruff as they are turned about and after the paraded figure.

The dancers are reaching new heights of mania, shrieking and hopping as the effigy approaches. Some tear their clothes, exposing breasts, legs, backs. Lisbet sees guards prodding at the dancers with their hooks, and then sees more men with sticks beating the dancers into a line behind the effigy. Some fall and do not get up, are trodden on again and again.

Lisbet now fights her way backwards, hauling Ulf with her as the afflicted trip like a bewildered flock, snarling and crying.

Lisbet breaks free and looks back. The dancers are ranged behind the effigy, leaping and spinning, herded into a haphazard line that stretches like an awful snake, St Vitus at its head. The whole thing slithers past, hundreds of dancers chased by hundreds of citizens, all so wild-eyed and excitable it is difficult to tell one apart from the other. They will walk all the way to the shrine.

She stands there until the streets are nearly empty. Children comb the ground, where detritus is scattered like the leavings of a wreck. She sees pattens, strips of cloth, scarves: remnants of some enormous celebration, some enormous atrocity. At the base of the stage steps, something glints. She plucks it from the dust. A thin bracelet of gold, still warm from its wearer. Lisbet drops it, fights the urge, sudden and foolish, to weep.

•

She cannot go directly home, cannot take that awful reek to Ida's children. She must wash the city from her. The forest has the same sense of abandonment as the market square: she passes leavings from fires and nestlike structures of filthy blankets, but no sign of the people who surrounded them at the river. At every turn she expects Plater or Daniel or some unknown assailant, but Ulf's hackles do not rise, he does not bark, and she sees no one. Perhaps they are all following the procession, the dancers and the melting figure of the saint.

The smell of the river comes before its sound, a very green scent like scratching moss. She has always feared this smell, and after the encounter with Ida and Nethe and Plater, it is all she can do not to flee in the opposite direction.

Ulf runs ahead as Lisbet approaches the felled trunk.

Ida's face, tipped back. The moan from her pale throat. The shriek as Plater's hand wrapped tighter in her hair. Eren's mouth, his fingers on the lute. Lisbet does not want to think on it, any of it, but the river is running her backwards, through her years, through her losses, to that: the first loss.

The fields around the river near her childhood home gave no

crops and grew full of soft grass. That was where the comet had fallen, allowing the water a new channel. If someone were to walk across the untended fields as you washed, you would not hear the approach. *Not that the Devil walks on loud feet. On silent hooves, he steps towards you.* The Devil lived in the comet-hewn river. That's what they were all told. Her eldest brother Michael saw him, among the jewel-bright eyes of toads. His forked tail twitching between the smooth, unnatural banks. His wide smile among the young, lank-necked reeds. Lisbet turns her head away, toward these trees, this time, this river, but they flicker, fade.

•

They cannot find her mother. That morning Henne had come, asked to marry her. She said no, as she had to three others, because she could not leave her mother. And now her mother is gone.

Her brothers are searching the barns. Her father is searching the town. Lisbet is left the house, though it is clear it is empty. No one in the bed they lie together in, nose to toes. No one in the rafters, or hiding absurdly in the largest pot. She knows there is one place she has not looked. But Mutti will not be there. She hates it just the same as her. They are alike in this, know each other's minds.

And it is because they know each other's minds, that Lisbet knows if her mother did not want her to find her, there is one place she will be.

She goes empty-handed, bare-headed, barefoot. Her feet make no sound in the long grass. The comet tore a full field with its landing, at the moment she tore from her mother. She knows the way as well as she knows her mother's face. Lisbet stands at the bank, at the mouth of Hell. She knows Hell boils, but the river is deceitfully cool. She feels the suck of the earth, the smell like hidden places rising at her.

'Mutti?'

Her voice is reed thin, bending into the black. Somewhere, some tiny slice of light catches and glints. The Devil's mouth, opening. The glass of a water-smoothed piece of quartz. She wants to run screaming. But she steps into the reedbeds at the water's edge.

'Mutti?'

She puts her arms out in front of herself. The Devil brushes her hair from her forehead. The reeds brush her hair from her forehead. She feels among them, sorting their slicing bodies. Her heart is blocking her throat. She can breathe only shallowly, the thick smell of water.

Lisbet moans, grips the trunk where Ida gripped Nethe and kissed her. She has come this far, she must go through. There is another smell. The smell is rosemary and cloves. The smell is the salve she rubs on her mother's feet. The smell is her, and her mother, them together. Lisbet sinks to her knees in the river.

'Mutti?' She whispers it. She crawls, so the reeds no longer brush her head. So all there is is sweetness. It grows as she reaches the edge of the reeds, the place where her brother saw the Devil's tail. But instead, there is a foot, swollen, greenish, cold.

She pulls it, hand over hand, towards her, pulling it from the deeper water. She can hear nothing but her own breath. She closes her eyes, so she doesn't have to see. She noses her way into her mother's shoulder. She runs her hands over her body. Sodden clothes, lumpy with rocks. There, the smoothly shaven head. Here, the soft hands, so soft they might have no bones in them. Here, her chest, fearsomely still. She kisses her mother lightly on the lips, tastes poppy.

Though there is no one there to hear her, except maybe the Devil among the hanging reeds, Lisbet hums to her mother, and rocks her as though to sleep. It is hours before her brothers think to search the river, minutes before they find them curled together. It takes them only seconds to prise Lisbet's fingers from her mother's waist, and part them forever.

•

The baby kicks. Lisbet is on this bank, by this river. She smells of beeswax, not clove, and her body is too hot. She must cool it, for her boy. She must be brave. Lisbet moves carefully down the gentle slope of the bank, and into the water. It is blessedly cool, and she groans aloud. The silt sinks up between her toes, and reeds twine about her ankles, their loose grip and release seeming conscious, deliberate.

'Mutti?'

But her mother doesn't speak to her, and for the first time Lisbet understands that to be a blessing. She stops when she reaches the smooth stones that line the riverbed proper. She knows even without the measure of the dog that at this point in the river's channel, three more steps would have her waist-high. Ulf splashes past and she clicks at him to move further away, but he brings a length of branch to her, nudging at her with his nose, and he looks so daft she relents and throws it downriver.

When Ulf returns with the stick, she heaves herself back up the bank, smooths a whisper of river weed from her calf where it has weaved amongst the dark down of her legs. Ulf places the stick before her and shakes himself, water flying over her skirts.

'Scheiße, stupid dog.' She kicks the stick away with her bare toes. She sits on the felled trunk and attempts to replace her stinking leggings. They snag and catch at her damp legs. She gives up. There is no one to see her.

Even as she thinks it, she feels eyes upon her. And then a rustling, too gentle to be Ulf. Fear grips her throat. Someone is watching.

Like a child, she wants to squeeze her eyes shut, count to one hundred, make the forest disappear. Still she feels a gaze, so direct it is as though they had a grip of her neck. She could pretend not to know there is someone there, whistle for the dog, start home. Perhaps they mean her no harm. She holds this thought tight to her like a doll, and calls for Ulf. He does not come.

Fresh terror grips her now, and she rises to her feet. There is a cracking sound to her left. Ulf barks twice. Then another crack, and he is silent. Lisbet listens, and calls for the dog. He makes no reply. It has happened, she thinks. He has been taken.

She snatches up the stick he fetched, the bark flaking but the central column weighty, and creeps in the direction Ulf ran. There is just enough sound to follow: rustling, a path being taken through the brittle trees. She stops often to listen, holding her breath, closing her eyes the better to hear. It is like the game she would play with her brothers, a stinking piece of sacking tied about her eyes and them spreading through the wide gullies of the fields, clapping her closer as she nosed towards them in the self-made dark.

She follows the noise to a break in the trees she knows well enough. It is the path leading to the dance tree, and she swallows drily, the faint tang of the river hitting the back of her throat. Perhaps the desperates have found it at last, have made it into a camp. She imagines all her babies' ribbons torn down, the platform filled end to end with bodies. She longs to go for help, but there is no one she can turn to. She is alone utterly. But she cannot abandon Ulf to his fate. If it is not already too late, she will go and bargain with them. They can have all the bread from her table, all the honey she sluiced from the wax.

She takes the path, whistles as high as she can and as often as she dares in the hope Ulf will hear and return to her. Her damp feet scrape inside her shoes, and all the refreshment of the river is forgotten, replaced by the hot flush of her fear. Now she hears a voice, low, and Ulf barks once more.

Lisbet moves faster, careless now of noise, pulling her skirts up high. She smells a fire, smoke not yet visible, but sending its tendrils up her nose, the clean scent of very dry wood. She grips the stick tighter, and a shard splinters, sticks deep into her skin. The bloom of pain sends courage through her blood, and she grits her teeth as she reaches the clearing, presses into the shadows of a young linden, and peers ahead.

A fire burns, recently tended, pale grey smoke rising and a rusty kettle crouched like a toad in the embers, a log dragged beside as a seat. There is no sign of Ulf, nor his abductors.

It is reckless to enter the clearing without knowing their location, but this is what she does. As she breaks her cover, the low voice comes again, and Ulf barks twice.

They are in the tree. Weight shifts above her, the boards straining, and she moves closer to the trunk, seeking out a snicket of emptiness that will allow her to see through the gaps in the slats. There is movement now, and she can hear the clumsy slap and skitter of Ulf's paws as he runs about the platform.

She moves slowly to the ladder, readies her stick, lifting it high. But when the man's voice comes a third time, she knows it. The stick falls from her suddenly weak hands.

Twenty

'Eren?'

The creaking stops, and then Ulf's head emerges from the platform's railings. He barks joyfully, and backs up, scampering headlong, almost falling, down the ladder as Eren leans over, his face split wide open in a smile.

Lisbet returns it, a relief so strong it spreads from her chest and stretches through all her fingers. Ulf has reached her and is licking her fingertips, but she can no more break Eren's gaze than scale the linden's trunk with her bare and swollen hands.

'I'm sorry,' says Eren finally. 'He followed me. I tried to send him back.'

She shakes her head, and laughs, an abrupt chaos of sound that sends a small bird flapping from the trees behind her. Her heart has not yet forgotten the danger, and throttles her throat. She presses her hand to it, tries to force it back down. Colours burst in front of her eyes, pigmented like the stained glass in the cathedral's windows.

'Lisbet?' Impossibly, Eren is beside her. 'I have frightened you.'

'No. Yes. I am glad it is you.' Her voice sounds insubstantial, high and girlish. She sits on the log, to ground herself.

Her vision dances, bathing Eren's brown skin with the gold and glitter of sunlight. She had forgotten the sun could be a soft thing, giving beauty. She presses her hand to her eyes, and withdraws it with a hiss of pain.

'You have a splinter,' says Eren, taking her hand. His are cool and dry, miracles against the throbbing, slick heat of her palm.

She tries to focus on it, his hands on hers, sees the splinter like an extra vein thrust crosswise through the meaty heel of her hand, darker than his skin against hers.

She is no sop but the sight makes her queasy. 'It's deep.'

She scrabbles at the place with her other hand, and he shushes her like a child.

'I will try.'

He pours water from the kettle over his hands, then kneels before her on the crackling ground. She watches the sworl of his crown, a perfect spiral disintegrating into tangles of black curls, the remains of broken leaves where he must have lain on the platform. She remembers how shocking his gesture had been when he'd offered to walk with her. And now here he is on his knees before her, both his slim, cool hands upon her, his eyes intent upon her skin.

He probes the tender places around the splinter, and she chews her tongue as the wood moves. 'Will you have to split the skin?'

'With a needle, perhaps,' he says. 'Shall I fetch one, with your permission?'

But she does not want him to loose her hand, cannot abide the thought of returning to the house. She shakes her head, tightens her grip on his and winces. He returns his attention to her hand, bringing his head so low over it his hair tickles her palm.

His breath is warm, and very close. And then his mouth

is upon her, his beard gently sharp, his lips very soft. Before she can fully understand what is happening, he sucks in his cheeks. She feels the splinter hold its place, and then the release as it works out of her skin. He spits the wood to the ground, and she feels the absence of his mouth like a wound.

He does not look at her as he holds out the kettle for her to pour over her hand, though there is only a little blood, tiny gemlike droplets that she sluices from her skin.

'Thank you,' she says at last, and he still does not look at her, but reaches down to scratch Ulf behind the ears. His hand is trembling, and her own feels unsteady as she lifts it to her face to examine it. Her palm is a little red where his lips gripped it, the tear where the wood entered tiny. It joins the other minute craters of her skin, their new topography carved by her toil. In Eren's fingers, her own seemed bearlike and clumsy, but she is proud of them, looking at the evidence of their usefulness. They suit her.

'Sorry.' His voice is hoarse. 'I didn't think.'

'It is no matter,' she says, watching his slim fingers on Ulf's matted fur, the way he combs the burrs from the dog's pelt, plucking them delicate as lute strings.

'Why are you here?' she asks finally. His face is shadowed, bent to the dog. She wants him to look at her, fix her with his steady, clear gaze, but he seems determined not to. 'Eren?'

'I am staying here,' he says, gesturing to the platform.

'In the forest?'

'It is good enough for the other dissolutes.'

'You are no dissolute,' she says hotly.

'Please, calm. It is not good for you—'

'For me?' It is a shriek, she cannot contain it. Fury burns suddenly through her: for all she has witnessed, all she has borne. For the shame the joy at seeing him had provoked, for how now he will not even look at her. 'Do not act like you care for me. You left me, like everyone else. All care is for what I carry, and there is none, there is no one left for me—'

She heaves, and inside her the baby stirs as though it heard and understood her. Eren is standing too, but the easiness of earlier is gone. He does not touch her, though his arms are held out in readiness in case she falls. She turns away, sucks in air in great, heaving gasps.

'I care, Lisbet,' he says, finally. 'I never left.'

He is closer, so close she could step back and be pressed full against him.

'I watched, after the Twenty-One ordered us gone,' he continues. 'I could have left with Frederich and the others, but I stayed to ensure you were safe. Until your husband or mother-in-law returned home. I saw Mathias and Ida's children were still with you. I promise you, you were not alone a moment.'

She looks back at him, is close enough to count his eyelashes, spot a small scar almost hidden by his beard to the side of his mouth. He let Frederich leave without him, his dearest friend. He stayed, for her.

'Forgive me,' he says. 'I did not wish to alarm you. I only wanted you to be safe. So that if you were in danger, you would have help nearby.'

'I can help myself,' she says, weakly.

'I know it, Lisbet.'

Kiss me, she thinks. *Put your lips on mine*. But instead he steps back, and she wipes the last of her tears from her face. 'Do you wish me to walk you home?'

'No,' she says, too suddenly, with too much force.

'You can go alone, I know.'

'No,' she says again, more steadily. 'I'll stay a while, if I may. Ulf has already made himself comfortable.'

They look at the dog, lying on his side with his tongue lolling, softly snoring. Eren snorts. 'If you wish.'

•

It is simple as breath, to stay. They sit together by the dying fire and talk. There is plenty to speak of: more on Frederich, more on Nethe and Ida, more on the monstrous parade of the wax saint that will be the saving of them all. They circle the natural question to ask, of what he will do and where he will go next. Lisbet does not want to know. Surely he will not stay here, where people shrink away or strike him. Perhaps he will wait long enough for Henne to return, and then be gone, and she will never see him again. She holds this thought like a cloud at the corner of her mind's scudding sky.

'You think it will be over?' she asks.

'It must,' says Eren. 'Manias are like boils – they must be lanced and poulticed, the poison squeezed out, but then they are in the past.'

'I know something of manias,' she says, soft. 'And it is true they pass. But sometimes they take people with them when they go.'

'You have knowledge first-hand?'

She opens her mouth, already full of Mutti, of her swollen feet. How Lisbet soothed her with her hands when in her heart she prayed for her to die, to be released from her agony. But what if he recoils from her? What if he, a man who can tolerate a sodomite as a best friend, who is himself a sin in the eyes of the Church, judges she alone is worthy of his disgust, his condemnation?

'My mother . . .' she starts. 'She lost her mind. She died, just before I married Henne.'

Because she wanted to escape, and marrying Henne offered that. A vice tightens around her heart and squeezes. The awful fact of her fault. The awful fact of her.

'That's a terrible loss to bear.'

Everything about him suggests a safe haven to share in, and everything in her wants to tell him. But these are the darkest things, the deepest places. She recoils, diverts.

'What about your mother?'

He tells her, about how she could read three written languages, and about his sister, who died when she was five from fever. She had a braid thick as a rope, eyes like his. His father who walked with a limp from a war he never talked about. She asks again about him, as a child, and he gives her more about his sisters who survived, more about his mother who sang, his father who played, how for a while they trained a bear cub to dance with him so they would raise more money, but the bear pined for its mother and died.

He tells her they travelled always, from town to city and village, how he travels still, with only the shirt on his back, his father's lute and his mother's kettle. How he has been as far as Copenhagen and Greece, how no two months hold the same qualities. How he learned to play music by watching his father's fingers. How they could not afford another instrument so until he was ten he practised on a plank of wood that he scratched lines into and hummed so he could hear the music. Lisbet holds out the stick that splintered in her palm to him, and he takes it, laughing.

'Like this,' he says, and holds it as he had the lute on the stage before the dancers. He hums, the tune fast and playful, and she jiggles her knees and claps along.

When he is done he throws the stick and Ulf goes haring after it as Eren bows and Lisbet cheers. She fills giddy with the absurdity of the day, which is fast now dropping into night.

'And you,' he says, flopping down at her feet. 'What of you?'

'There is no story.'

'There is always a story.'

Lisbet feels her joy leave her, feels the crush of everything press upon her. She wants to be rid of it, and perhaps this is the only way, this the only place, he the only person it is possible to share it with. A confession.

'You think me prying,' says Eren. 'I'm sorry.'

'There's no need for apology,' she says.

'You don't have to tell me anything.'

'I do. I want . . . I need . . .'

He waits, and she tries to sort her thoughts, comb through them like wool carded.

'You don't have to—'

'Please,' she says. 'Do not speak.'

She finds her place, the start of it all. The start of her.

'My childhood was full of havocs. The night I was born, a comet fell in my father's easterly field, burnt up a year's corn and rendered the place barren ever after. I expect you have heard of the comet – it fell in Eninsheim.'

She sees his nod of recognition in her periphery, keeps her eyes set ahead, on a whorl in the dance tree's trunk.

'Geiler preached it was an omen. God damning us all. He seemed to damn my family especially. Aside from the lost field, there followed harvests felled by hail, or else storms. Rain that fell like tides or else not at all. Flood and drought, in endless cycle. As I grew, so did the misfortune. Revolts that took our best farmhands, almost took my brothers. Rebels hung like old sheets from every wall, failed flags of surrender. And when I turned twelve, my mother started to run mad.' She swallows. She cannot tell him how intimately the two were linked, how her bloods began and Mutti's mind disintegrated.

'You say mania is like a boil, but hers was beneath the skin, in the blood of her. Her feet swelled so she could barely walk, and the empiric cut off all her hair.' Tears prickle her eyes at the memory of this particular cruelty. 'She had beautiful hair,' she says impotently.

She does not tell him of the other remedies. The empiric Pater brought was young, unproven, his face still smooth but for whiskers beneath his jawline. He barely touched Mutti before selling them a tincture of mustard.

'The womb floats,' he told Pater. 'Nooses up around the neck, bunches over the heart and lodges beneath the throat. Children fill it, weight it, return it right, but when childbearing is past we rely on mustard forced into the gullet to scare it away, or else sweets placed at the lips of the legs.' Lisbet imagined the womb a hungry infant crawling towards the promise of delight. The mustard made Mutti's throat blister. They had no money for sweets.

'But still, her mind shattered. Some days she knew me, and there was still such love. But more and more, she did not. Her hands would flutter, her mouth would foam. Towards the end, she could not speak.'

Her black feet and her gaping mouth, her bad days and her worse ones. Endless, endless devotion. The language they alone spoke, how Lisbet was her only comfort, how she brought Mutti poppy when she asked for it.

'One day, she went to the river – no.' Lisbet catches herself. If this is to be a confession, let her tell the whole truth. 'One night, I went to a dance. There, I met Henne. Heinrich, my . . .' She doesn't want to say husband. She doesn't want to align herself to another man in front of Eren, no matter how foolish that is, when she has Henne's baby inside her, the evidence of their trying fluttering over their heads. 'And he asked to marry me. But marrying meant coming here, leaving Mutti, so I said no.' Her voice breaks. Eren's eyes are so kind she wishes he would close them. She does not deserve kindness.

'But Mutti guessed why. She took poppy. She went to the river, the river the comet had created through our easterly field. She filled her skirts with stones.'

Eren's hand is shockingly warm on hers, and dry. Not cool any longer, not clammy. Alive, and tender. She tells him how Mutti loved her, despite it all, and that is why Lisbet has kept living, has borne her dead babies without complaint, because she deserves it. She deserves it all.

Here, Eren holds up his hand, to stop her. He has listened with his body completely still, as though he barely breathed. But now he looks full at her, his slender brown fingers inches from her lips, his eyes fixed on hers.

'We have known each other but a short time, Lisbet, but I feel I know you.'

The relief of hearing it spoken is almost painful. 'I understand.'

'Then you must also understand, that while I am not your father, your brother, your husband, not anything but a friend, I am certain when I say this. You are not the cause of all you have described to me.'

Lisbet laughs hollowly. 'You do not know me well enough—'

'Please,' he says. 'Now may I speak?'

She catches her laughter, swallows it.

'The Church believes in such things as cursed centuries. It believes manias can be cured by effigies, it prays to heal broken bones. It believes lost babies are punishment for sins. But there are other ways, other beliefs. I have encountered many from childhood, growing as I did with a foot in each world. In the land of my father, we have a different prophet.

The medicine there relies on herbs and splints. We write our histories so they cannot be twisted and taken from us, cannot be misread.'

'You are speaking blasphemy,' says Lisbet.

'Another word that is different according to whose mouth it comes from. I prefer to think of it as another way of living the same, good life. I believe you have been misread, Lisbet, since birth. A dozen women lose their lives, or their minds, every day. A hundred children were born the night of the comet. A thousand farmers lost their harvests in the same storms. The rebels fight because they too believe there are different ways to live. That maybe your priests have gone astray. Even your mother-in-law believes so. I have heard her praise Geiler.'

'That is not the same,' says Lisbet. Heat is growing at the base of her neck. 'And there is no misreading Mutti's calamities—'

'My own mother had a fever of the brain that rendered her speechless for a month. My sister died of the same. My wife, my child – these are all calamities, Lisbet. And they are nothing to do with you.'

He might have struck her. She holds her fist to her chest, where she feels the blows of his words land. No one has ever offered her this scope before. No one, not the priests, nor her prayers, have offered her such a gift as to place a different pall over her entire life.

'You think this true?'

'With all my heart, I do. But can you?' He leans into her. 'Can you believe it too?'

She doesn't try to argue. She does not cry blasphemy. She chooses, in this place she herself has appointed as sacred, to nod. 'I do.'

With those words, she feels it, all of it, lift from her shoulders, and travel up through the branches of the dance tree, spinning away through the stifling air. Tears run from her eyes.

'Do you understand me?' he asks, gently. 'You can loose it now, Lisbet. Leave it behind.'

She looks at him. She wipes her cheeks. Smiling, she nods. 'I will.'

His shoulders slump, as though he shares her relief. 'Good then. You must look to the future. What next? When the baby comes?'

'If.' The word is out before she can contain it.

'You should not speak so.'

'Alas I must,' she says. 'Cursed or no, it is a fact. It would not be the first time.'

Eren tilts his head back. His beard is still neatly trimmed, the line of his jaw strong as a furrow in earth, the apple of his throat appearing and disappearing as he swallows. She thinks how she should like to press her lips to his skin where it meets his beard, to feel the rough and soft of him.

'You are very strong, Lisbet.'

She laughs, surprised. 'The opposite, surely, to have failed to keep them.'

'But to mark them, to keep carrying them, to love them.' He nods, breaking his enchantment. 'I love my wife and daughter still, though they died.'

'In birth?'

'Just after. There was some part that didn't come. She died, and then the baby. I would have too, if not for Frederich. He took me along with him, and we have travelled ever since. I think he recognised a fellow lost soul.'

'You parted with him though.'

'I believe we will find each other again. And we will travel on.'

What must it be, to be a man and be able to leave your

grief behind, or else to shrink it small enough to carry about in a pocket, and bear it enough to live a different life? Could she do such a thing? Would she even wish to?

Yes, is the answer, swift as a blink. *Yes, of course.*

'But we mustn't talk further on that,' he says. 'This baby will live, Lisbet.'

'And will I?'

His thick eyebrows knit. 'You must.'

'I must,' she agrees. 'To be a mother. There is naught else, is there?'

'You will still be Lisbet,' he says. 'You will still walk in the forest with Ulf, be a wife, tend the bees.'

'Perhaps,' she says.

'You must fight for it.' Eren leans towards her, his body close enough to touch. 'I fought my mother, to be a musician. A musician who knows his letters is a waste, but still that is what I am.'

'And I am a women who knows her bees,' she smiles.

'Precisely.' He stretches out his legs. 'Should you not return to them?'

'Do you wish me to?'

He looks at her, full into her eyes and her breath catches. 'Shall I light the fire?'

She nods, unable to speak even after his gaze moves from her face and becomes intent on his new task of coaxing the embers into flame. She watches his lips purse, his breath bringing the fire to life, and a prickle of heat traces the place he had sucked the splinter from her.

What would it be, to be Eren's wife? This thought she allows in fully, sitting in the expanding dark, watching his face in the growing firelight. There would be many nights like this, spent under stars, following the constant shift and pull of work. There would be the lack of it, too, and no stability or control over where the work took them, but would she mind?

She allows her thoughts to reach further, into another world where it was Eren she met that night at the dance, his lute set at the heart centre of himself, Eren's fingers in hers, Eren's breath on her neck, Eren's baby inside her, Eren's promise of another possible life. And it would be different, truly. Not without its hardships, but it would be a new kind of existence, marginal. A bee outside the hive. She thinks, watching him, that maybe the priests are wrong: the opposite of order is not chaos. Maybe it is freedom.

'There,' he says, sitting back on his heels, the fire reaching to his shoulders. 'I'll fetch more water. Will you be all right?'

She nods, grateful he makes no more mention of her returning to the farm. Perhaps he needs this as much as she, this escape. It is as though they are together balanced on a precipice, delaying the moment of falling. She feels safe even alone, even when Ulf traitorously follows at Eren's heels to the river. She rises in the effortful way she always must after too long sat, and takes the steps to the platform.

It is swept largely clean by Eren, the candles Nethe stole from Sophey stacked, and his things are arranged as neatly as they had been in the bedroom at the house. His lute is laid crosswise across his pillow, like a sleeping lover. She thinks of him watching his father, the attention he must have paid to his fingers, the same devotion she had when she watched him play. What must it be like, to be a man and learn such a skill? In a woman's hands it would be witchcraft, to have such a power.

'Lisbet?'

She relishes the worry in his tone as she leans over the railing in mimicry of her first sighting of him, and waves. 'Up here.'

Eren lifts up his hands. He is carrying the kettle hung over one arm, and has rolled up his sleeves, showing his knotted forearms. His hands are full of mushrooms. Beside him Ulf carries yet another stick, evidently as proud of his efforts as Eren is of his own.

'I'll come and prepare them,' she begins, but he shakes his head, kneeling.

'Stay, it will take time to cook.'

She lowers herself so she can sit with her legs over the edge of the platform to watch him work, feeling like a girl despite her enormous belly, her swollen joints, the mild fear of falling. He cleans the mushrooms with his knife, peeling away the dirtied outer layers and slicing them one at a time into the kettle, already set over the fire to boil. He twists the garlic and places that inside too, then replaces the lid and brushes down his hands. She senses he is performing for her, as she did for him in the kitchen of the farm, taking extra care over each action. When it is done he rises and without looking at her, circles the trunk. She hears the creak of the stairs, the sink of the wooden planks as he lowers himself beside her, leaning forwards to rest his bare forearms on the painted railing.

For a while they sit in companiable silence, watching Ulf chew on his stick, his lips pulled back from his gums.

'He will miss you,' says Lisbet, finally. *I will miss you*, she thinks.

'I will miss him.'

'Do you not get lonely, on your travels?'

'Are you offering me Ulf?'

She wants to say, *Myself, only*. She shrugs. 'Have you never wished to marry again?'

She asks it as though she cares nothing for the answer, but he sees through it. She can tell in the glance he gives her now. 'This is no life for a woman.'

The scent of wild garlic reaches them, and Eren descends the tree to bring the kettle to her wrapped in a shirt. Together they blow upon it, and she pours it direct from the spout into her mouth. It is almost spicy with strength, the mushrooms tasting like meat. It fills her, warm and salty, the perfect counterpoint to her days of honey.

'It is good,' she says as he drinks.

'You sound surprised,' he says, wiping his mouth. 'I am not only a musician.'

'Who knows his letters,' she teases.

He inclines his head in a mock-bow.

'Will you play for me?'

They look at each other, then, and the whole world narrows to a point, to the channel of invisible energy from him to her and back again, the thread she longs to spool close and join them forever. It cannot be love she feels, she knows. Love is a lifetime's work. But still it is a lifetime's worth of something that passes now between them, an understanding. He feels it too, she knows it.

She knows, too, that he will not close the distance. But he does set aside the kettle and lie flat down and stretch out his arm for the lute, exposing the softly furred flesh of his lower belly. He sits up again and shuffles away from the railing, cross-legged, and brings the instrument gentle to his lap like a babe in arms, cradled close.

She turns awkwardly to sit opposite, as though they are about to play a clapping game. Still he looks at her, as his fingers find their place on the instrument's strings, as he calls them into voice. He plays the tune he played the last time at the dance tree, an elegy, a parting song. And all the while he does not look away, does not close his eyes to hear the music as he did in the market square, as though by drinking her in he can play better.

She feels the music stretch and arch over their heads,

becoming almost visible, golden and shining in the long dusk, the long farewell to day, the notes weaving into the branches, twining with her babies' ribbons, shaking loose the memories of past music and bringing all the weight of loss and forgetting down on their heads. He plays them into darkness, into the stars coming strong through the leaves. He plays her into calm, the whole forest lulled by him. She is crying, she feels the tears hot on her cheeks, and his eyes shine too.

When he at last stills his fingers, stopping the tune in full throat, and sets aside the lute, she knows his mind. He reaches out, his fingers still marked by the strings, and brushes her tears from her chin, her lips. His fingertips are rough with calluses, but his touch is soft, exquisite soft. He traces down to her wrist, and rubs his rough thumb at the tender skin there, his hand so dark against her she might have melted away into the night.

He kneels up and into the space between them, and he kisses her once on each cheek. He kisses her again on her forehead, firm and slow, as though smoothing out creases. And finally she tilts up her face to his, for him to complete the sign of the cross, the most holy gesture, as their lips meet gentle at first, and then hard.

There is no hesitation then. The time for that is long past, and when she lies back on the well-worn planks he comes with her, clasped to her side, their lips not lifting until his hand moves between her legs and she gasps. Even then, there is no pause, no moment of uncertainty or shyness as his fingers part her and find her slick and open.

She grasps for his shirt, to feel his skin against her skin, and there is no thought but want as she rolls to her side and he pushes inside her, her back pressed close to his chest, his heartbeat hers and hers his, no words but each other's names, repeated like prayers, like blessings, as though they are new, the first ones ever to speak each other truly, as pure and clean as beeswax fresh pulled from the hive of the first garden, at the beginning of everything.

None dancing

The city reels. It feels enormous and empty, like a heavy cape draped around Daniel Lehmann's shoulders. He does not pray so much as he should, but he does pray for Hilde, on her way to the shrine, with all his might.

He climbs atop the empty stage, the canvas stained brown with piss and blood, the wood beneath cracked by hundreds of feet. The dancers have left such wreckage behind. Fifteen people a day died, Herr Plater said with relish, lifting a cup of spirits to the heavens as he swayed on his feet, and in this heat Daniel is not surprised. They are buried in mass graves, trenches dug alongside the city walls. He shudders. Thanks be to God Hilde was taken to the shrine. The blessings are already falling on them.

The plague is done, and he is glad and saddened by it. But there is more he must do. He has a purpose now, as Herr Plater's man. A calling. In return, Plater has promised salve for Hilde's feet, beets and honey for their table, milk for Gunne and beer for the rest. More than that, prayers, and a place in Heaven for all who serve him, for they are serving the Twenty-One, and so God.

Daniel is beginning to wrap his mind around the ways of

the world. Not the petty struggles he sees in the almshouses, in the taverns and on the streets. The true power at the heart of everything. God sits over all, of course, but there are ways to approach His hem, to carve a place for himself and his brothers, his sister. He can care for them all, if he cleaves close to Plater.

There is a dark thought though, in his throat. It crouches there like a tumour. Doubt. He tries to swallow it down, but it is difficult to ignore. The kicks his master aims at stray dogs. The delight he took in dragging his wife to the gaol. The way he has turned lately to drink, sending Daniel between mill and tavern to fetch beer and genever, stuff that smells strong enough to burn. The anger that glows in his misting-over eyes. Better not to think on it. Better to place his trust in Herr Plater, and so in God. It cannot be wrong if he says it is not.

How must it be, to be so anointed? Daniel feels a shiver of anticipation, of fear, that maybe he could be like Herr Plater one day. A shark swimming among fishes, a king bee.

His stings have ceased to itch thanks to Frau Wiler's ministrations. He must not think on that, either. Herr Plater is expecting him with more beer, more news of the effigy. He says they do God's work. And Daniel Lehmann, for whom life has been a warren of difficult choices, believes him.

Twenty-One

Lisbet wakes to the smell of smoke, as familiar as her own hands and as out of place as Eren's arm across her. She lifts her head, remembering herself in that odd way she must each morning, her body larger and heavier, and more tired than she'd felt before sleep. A sharp pain lances up her side where the thin sheets Eren laid out have not offered enough protection from the rough wood of the platform.

She pushes herself up. She waits, a hand on her belly, the thin shell between her baby and the world, and waits for the shame to come. But she feels only joy.

She turns to look at Eren. He is childlike in sleep, the arm that had covered her now drawn up under his chin. His beautiful mouth is parted, and she resists the cumbersome action it would take to lean down and kiss it. There are decisions, not far off, decisions she never considered before last night but in her wildest, most dangerous imaginings. He will have her, she knows it, her and the baby both. He whispered it in her ear as he lay behind her, filling her, whispered that he loves her.

The dawn is only just broken, cracking through the scattering of leaves above them, the sky already a chaotic, unrelenting blue. The forest is noisy, crackling, expanding under the heat of another day of this endless summer. Ulf barks, and Lisbet is drawn back to why she woke in the first place. Smoke. She crawls slowly to the railing, to check the fire Eren had surely doused last night. Ulf is there, alert and facing into the forest. The fire is ash. He barks again.

'Lisbet?'

She turns to see Eren's eyes small with sleep, his hair mussed as a boy's. Her heart lifts at the sight of him, the memory of his body so warm and precise against her, his hot breath in her ear.

'Are you all right?'

'Can you smell that?' she asks. Eren sniffs the air, doglike. 'Is the fire still going?'

'No,' says Lisbet, and makes to stand, her legs stiff and whole body aching. She will never again curse a bed however ill-stuffed.

Eren leaps up and is beside her, helping her carefully to her feet. He rubs her upper arms and she leans momentarily against him, his lips again on her forehead. Ulf barks twice, louder and more urgent.

Eren's body tenses. 'Can you hear that?'

Lisbet listens, drawing away from him slightly so her desire and his heartbeat don't muddy her listening. Beyond Ulf, she can hear the forest shifting—

'No birds,' she says.

'And that.' Eren holds up a finger, his musician's ear picking out a strand of sound that slowly comes to Lisbet, the crackling she heard earlier, but resolving now, becoming like water, the low rumble of an approaching wave.

'Fire,' says Eren. 'Not far off.'

He grasps her hand, drags her towards the steps. 'We have to go to the river.'

'Eren,' she says, her throat very dry. 'Eren, it's coming from the farm.'

She can hear it now her ears have latched onto the sound, knows it is coming from their land. When they reach the bottom of the steps, Ulf circles her once in a panic, then shoots toward home.

'Ulf!' she calls.

'You go to the river. I'll fetch the miller and the children.'

She starts to argue, but he pushes her bodily in the direction of the river. 'I'll meet you there.'

He takes off running, and though Lisbet knows she should obey him, instead she follows.

He is already out of sight. Soon she has no fear he will hear her, for all the sound is roaring, and hissing, fire swallowing and strengthening. She cannot run, not with her belly and her legs still aching, but she goes as fast as she can, and soon she is at the forest boundary.

There is no mistaking the heat. Lisbet is suddenly afraid, though she should have been always, should have been since she went with Eren to the clearing. She shouldn't have believed him, shouldn't have believed she could be free of the rot, of all she is. Even her mother's sacrifice couldn't save her, so why did she believe his words could?

Then there is smoke over her head, filling the gaps between the trees with blackness. Dread-filled she goes, until at last she sees it, not a wall of flame engulfing the trees and making them impassable, not even the farmhouse ablaze like a pyre—

The skeps. The skeps are small heaps of flame, contained each to each in precise, burning mounds. The smoke is sickening sweet. Bees are flying from them, little sparks, chaoses of light, and their buzzing rises to such a pitch it is all she can hear.

They are burning to death, and she gives a weak cry, useless anguish, as she stumbles closer. Black smoke gathers over it all like storm clouds, and still the buzzing rises, rises.

Where is Eren, where are the children? Lisbet struggles closer, but she must take a wide circle, the heat beating her back. Sweat and tears pour down her face, her eyes blind with smoke, her body racking.

It is not until she is beneath it that she knows. Not until she is beneath the smoke, blotting out the blue with black Hellfire. That it is not only smoke, blocking the sun. That it has breath.

The bees that have survived are swarming, and it is exactly like a flock of birds, twisting the air, miring it with wings. She trips back, away from the swarm, and as she does her gaze falls groundward, and she sees more bees there, another, smaller swarm that has taken the form of a man, a man black and crawling with bees, and she knows it is the Devil, at last come to her.

She falls to her knees as he rears up, his voice a deep bellow. Ulf runs from between the burning skeps, his fur singed and eyes wide with pain, runs full at the Devil and sends the bees lifting in a furious and shapeless mass toward the sky. It is only a man, bloated with stings, wailing. He stumbles towards her, and she sees it is Plater.

'Frau Wiler!'

It is a girl's voice, but she does not stop to see who speaks, who pulls at her skirts, because there is movement deeper in the flaming hives. Eren is in there, Eren is amongst the burning skeps.

She knocks Plater to the ground, plunges into the smoke and swarms. She feels the bees, made mad by their terror, piercing her neck, her hands as she claws through them, smoke made solid and stinging, but she does not care, she must fetch out Eren.

Coughing, not hers. There. She noses towards it, eyes blocked and streaming with smoke, her lungs becoming heavy. Her baby. She cannot remain here but she cannot leave. There, again.

'Eren!' She chokes on his name, but there he is, he has hold of her, pulling her back.

'Away,' he calls, his strong hands on her, voice clear in her ear. It is all confusion, all stink and terror, and all that holds her tethered is Eren, Eren's hands holding tight—

Then, there. Plater. He is suddenly before them, filling her vision, bees crawling over burnt and stung skin. He is full of venom and smoke, he grunts in pain and anger, and she knows as he stands and wraps his hands around her throat what he intends.

'Bitch,' he grunts, his breath thick with alcohol. 'See now who I am. See what I can do.'

He speaks, she is certain, not only to her. He speaks to Ida, to Nethe, to every woman who defied him with her happiness. She knows, as red gold sparks pop behind her eyes, that he means to murder her. But she is not only her. She is her, and her boy. Her child, who has survived nearly nine months inside her. Fury surges as breath leaves her. Plater will not take him from this world.

She hears Eren's cry of shock, and grasps at him, her fingers finding his belt, the hilt of his knife. Her vision is black smoke and bees, and red, red anger. She raises her hand, and as Plater's fingers tighten and stars shoot across her vision, she brings it down with all her might.

There is a grunt, a gasp. Plater's hands are suddenly loose as rotted rope. They break open, and she would lose her balance but for other hands on her again. Eren holds her up and through streaming eyes, she sees the knife, buried in Plater's neck.

Pain twists and rips her apart. She looks down, expecting a knife in her own gut, but there are only Eren's arms.

'The Turk!' shouts another voice. 'It's the Turk!'

She sees, suddenly, how it looks. Plater dead, with Eren's knife in his neck.

She peels Eren's hands from her. 'Go,' she gasps. 'Go.'

The pain comes again, and Lisbet falls to her knees. She falls through the ground, away from the smoke, away from the skeps, away from Eren, and off the edge of the world.

•

It is only pain then, pain in her belly and her back and her heart and her head, pain beyond bearing, and Ulf is still running desperate rings around the yard, and the bees above are swarming thicker than smoke, and a small cool hand grasps hers, pulls her away and into the shelter of the trees, and as they close over her so does the dark, and all she can see is the black-gold flash of her agony.

•

More hands on her then, hands on her temples and raking through her hair, and most of all a fist opening and closing inside her. The Devil grips her between the legs and sucks, bites with teeth, and the ground splits and swallows her.

•

There are leaves beneath her, she knows them to be so, and she grasps great handfuls of them. She is not yet damned. She must hold tight. But somewhere there are snakes hissing, thousands of snakes twisting and striking out along the endless forest floor to meet her. Water is poured down her throat and she retches, and more comes. She drinks, sinks.

•

They have her on a rack. Her belly is splitting, she is certain. If she looks down she will see her guts, her workings neat like the purples and reds and blacks of the bees, the pure gold she saw when Eren entered her, her lids closed against the dance tree's ribbons. Still there are too many hands on her, and she fights them, bites them back, and a root is placed between her teeth and fills her mouth with splinters.

•

She is floating now, and people are speaking a language she is sure she knows but has forgotten. She has no use for words, her tongue is caught under the strap of leather that replaced the stick, and there is a roof above her, a roof with notched beams she has counted a thousand times, the whorls in that wood as she lay awake and waited for motherhood or blood. It has her now, and there is no use fighting.

'Push, Frau Wiler.'

Please God, my baby.

'Push, Frau Wiler.'

Please, God? My baby.

They pour acid down her throat. It stings like a thousand cuts, a thousand precise slices, and they follow it with honey so it is like she has swallowed the stem of a rose. She gags on the vinegar and honey both, but they bring her to the room. She is forced upright against the wall, the mattress beneath her sodden and her belly writhing like a sack of snakes. The pain knocks her sideways, and strangers hold her upright. She is pinned, screams like a fox in a trap. She will gnaw off her leg to be free.

Her body breaks with the sound of honeycomb: wet and splitting. Sweetness floods her mouth and all her fingertips buzz. She is a swarm, one and many, and she flies from the bed and over the forest, she is winged and enormous, and when she crashes back onto straw she weeps with all she saw.

'Not long now.'

Nothing like her mother's voice, no matter how she wills it.

'Lisbet, push.'

Nethe.

Lisbet strives towards her voice like a mole seeking safe passage through the dark earth of her agony. Nethe speaks to her again, softly and with love. There is a wave of fire inside her now. It ripples, the whole world narrowing to her centre. Her legs are drawn back and her spine is split and her mouth is open but she cannot scream.

'Push.'

She pushes.

•

There is a spoon, sweetened with honey. It is cool between her lips. There is a cloth on her forehead, and someone is crying but it is not her.

'Henne's son.' Sophey, far away. 'Henne's boy.'

Lisbet's eyes are shut, her arms heavy at her sides. Now something is laid across her, slick and shockingly warm, a boiled frog. But it moves beneath its swaddling. It is not one of her dead babies. It kicks and mewls.

'Your boy.' Nethe's breath is sweet with honey too. She wraps Lisbet's arms around the child, and though Lisbet is so tired she knows she could simply sink and leave and stop living, she grips tight and opens her eyes.

He is red and bloodied and beautiful. His eyelids flutter: she sees black pupils, the purest white of his eyes. Does he see her? Does he know her, as she knows him? Does he know that they are each other's? That she has walked through fire and loss, so much loss, so that it would be him, all along?

All the chambers of Lisbet's heart swell and flood. She smells blood and burning, hears the cord that bound them dissolving on the fire. Her son's mouth finds her breast, and it is sharp and painful and right.

At last, Lisbet finds her arms are left full.

Twenty-Two

Those first days are milk and blood. The smoke has scoured Lisbet's throat and dulled her thoughts, so it is only the ecstasy of holding her son that rouses her. Blessedly, Nethe is charged with her care while Sophey deals with the aftermath of the fire. For days the whole house stinks of honey and smoke, like a church. It is quiet as a church too, with Mathias and the children returned home after Plater's death. *His murder.* She closes the doors of her mind to the memory. She killed him so she could survive. Not only her, but her son, too. It does not cleanse her conscience, but it salves it enough to allow herself the joy of her boy.

She thinks instead of Ilse in Ida's arms, Rolf at Ida's breast. Why has her friend not visited her? She longs to throw open the windows but they must be closed until she is churched, to avoid her bloods rising.

This and other things are ordered by an empiric, who comes at some indeterminate time of the day or night to pull Sophey's tooth and stitch Lisbet together, wash her with more vinegar, check the baby is rightly swaddled. Lisbet is still so weak she faints through his visit. She wakes to hear Sophey and Nethe arguing, knows it is because of her somehow, and she cannot muster the energy to care.

Her mind is addled. Lisbet does not know how to sort through all the bliss and pain of it, pleasure and agony set sharp and jagged against each other, both with teeth, both violent and tearing. The love is exhausting, closer to fear in its intensity. It is days before she can do more than just feel it, before she can speak or do anything but take her son's weight and feed him, but it is enough. It is enough to breathe him in and forget for minutes at a time all that occurred.

Nethe barely speaks either. There is some deep stillness, some deep quiet to her. For the first few days Lisbet finds it soothing, but as she comes more and more to herself, she notices how Nethe watches her as she feeds, looking away as soon as Lisbet tries to return her gaze. Nethe has come back from the spring grey-skinned and serious-eyed, her hair grown enough to brush the tips of her ears. It is astonishing to Lisbet how recently she came to know Nethe, how quickly she came to love her. She wants to reach across the silence and tell her it is all right, that her son is born and there can be nothing more important. But Nethe's quiet gives her pause. It takes all her courage, on the fourth day of her son's life, to catch her sister's wrist as she passes her the baby.

'Sit here,' she says, and Nethe perches on the bed. Lisbet manoeuvres herself closer to the wall, and shrugs her shift over her shoulder. She stretches out her arm as her son begins to suckle. 'Come.'

But Nethe does not move. Her eyes are fixed on the closed door, beyond which Sophey scrubs and scrubs at the table, the bench, the floor, as though to scour all traces of recent events from history.

'Nethe,' says Lisbet softly. 'Whatever it is, you do not have to carry it alone. What has happened? Are you . . . are you still condemned?'

'Pardoned,' she says on an exhale. 'The Twenty-One offered clemency to all the dancers, and to all who falsified dancing. It came by Papal decree, that the dance was penance enough. And Plater never named us sodomites. He made sure no one knew him to be a cuckold.'

'But that is news of the best sort,' says Lisbet. 'You are free, you and Ida both.'

A tiny sound, a swallowed sob.

'Nethe?' Lisbet reaches out her hand again, and Nethe flinches from it. 'What has happened?'

Nethe looks at her, for the first time since sitting, and Lisbet reads it in her face, in the utter anguish written there. Suddenly she does not want to hear, does not want her right mind back, does not want her son in her arms, something so pure and lovely beside something so wretched.

'Ida,' she says. 'She is dead?'

Nethe's face crumples. She throws herself down beside Lisbet, and Lisbet gathers her in, feeling her shake, her hot tears falling on her shoulder. Between gasps, Nethe tells her how she came to herself on the cart, a day into their journey. How Ida was beside her, her breathing shallow, as though winded. How her eyes were black and unseeing, but how she seemed to know her. How Nethe held her as her heart slowed, and then stopped. How Nethe fitted herself along Ida's length until she felt her body cool and forgot where her skin ended. How they buried her in the graveyard at St Vitus' shrine, and she was given every blessing owed to her.

'I do not understand,' moans Nethe. 'Is it God's punishment? Why did He take her?'

Lisbet knows it was not God, but poppy. The poppy Karl gave her, that Ida swallowed in anticipation of drowning, to save herself the pain. The poppy that clenched her heart and sank her, just as it had Mutti. She cannot tell Nethe, how close she came to happiness. How cruelly it all has ended, despite.

'No,' she says. 'It was the dancing. Better that than drowning, Agnethe. You saved her from it.'

'I thought I would be caught,' she says. 'I thought only to show her I was there. I thought we would be drowned together. Then the dancers started screaming, and it was not me that moved my feet. I was elsewhere. I was flying.'

'I saw it,' nods Lisbet. 'You were no falsifier. It was true abandon.'

'She is dead. Oh God, how can she be dead?'

'But you are alive, and she did not have to go without you by her side.'

Lisbet twines her fingers through Nethe's and presses her cheek hard to hers. Her grief is soft and her son's mouth is sharp as it sucks on her. Lying there, with her newborn son and newfound sister, she feels more whole than she ever has. She thinks Ida would forgive her that.

There is more to learn, more loss. Dear, sweet Ulf is dead, his burns too painful for him to be allowed to live. The bees are burned or else fled to the forest. Eren is vanished, wanted for Plater's murder. Lisbet tries to tell Nethe, many times, that he is wrongly accused, but she stops her.

'Don't speak it, Bet.' And Lisbet finds she does not need to. So long as Eren stays gone, she need not protect him. Because she cannot cry openly for Eren she cries for the dog, and Sophey calls her soft and feeds her more vinegar.

Beside all these devastations, she also knows: her son is born and safe in the world. What else? Also that the hand she felt on her skirts was Ilse trying to prevent her entering the fire. That the hand on her wrist was Daniel's, that it was him who came to her aid and accused Eren. That he alongside Mathias tended her for a full day before Sophey and Nethe arrived and kicked him out.

'They had him in Nethe's room. He made a sty of it,' sniffs Sophey, rocking the baby so violently Lisbet doubts he sleeps but is rather rendered unconscious by her ministrations. 'Thank goodness I hid my marriage silks.'

Nethe and Lisbet exchange glances, and laugh with the hysteria of those who have encountered great disaster, and survived.

•

Henne returns when their son is a week old, bringing word the dancing plague is over. He is so tall, so broad he could block out the sun.

'They say hundreds died, and I can believe it. The stages are dented by their feet. But never mind all that. Lisbet,' he says, and his voice is made strange by their time apart. 'Thank you for my boy.'

My boy, thinks Lisbet.

He comes closer to the bed, and takes her hand, and his face is so bluntly carved she almost flinches. How had she not noticed the brutish jut of his forehead before, the lasciviousness of his mouth, the ghostliness of his blond hair and beard. He let Plater beat Nethe nearly to death. He kisses her hand and she cringes, disguises it as a wince of pain.

'I have named him Heinrich.' He beams, and she feels already the snapping of the threads that she has been building with the boy, the gossamer times when he is suckling and she watches him, waiting for a name to arrive and fit him perfect as he fits her arms. Here Henne has come, and brushed them aside. Here Henne has come, and swallowed their child entire into his ownership.

Her husband – for this is what he is, she reminds herself – misreads her wince, squeezes her hand. She had forgot his lack of care. He is holding too tight, her fingers moths disintegrating.

'You mustn't worry, Lisbet. We have come to an agreement, about the bees.' He kisses her hand again, and throws it from himself, stands to stretch. He fills the whole room until there is no space for her. She dreads the day they must share a bed again. How will she let him touch her, after Eren?

'Heidelberg was a waste of time. They were never going to allow us to keep the bees, not with the monastery so near. Really the Moor did us a favour, clearing the land. We have a new enterprise now.'

She has faded from the room. The Moor? He must mean Eren. She stops him, speaks over him as he rattles on about his plans to turn the skep yard into a beet field, to set Sophey, Nethe, and she to furrowing the land the very next month.

'Wait. What about E—' She swallows his name. 'What of the Turk?'

'Have you not listened? I thought Nethe told you all.' He sighs. 'He burnt the hives.'

'No,' she says. 'Not him. I know it was not.'

'The boy saw it all, the one who pulled you from the fire. He saw the Moor, or Turk, or whatever godforsaken creature he was, light it and pull you into the pyre. You are lucky to live. He murdered Plater besides.' Henne crosses himself, but he does not look reverent in the least. 'They are hunting him now.'

They will not find him, Lisbet thinks. *The Black Forest has swallowed Joss Fritz. It will offer the same shelter to Eren.*

'Henne, it was not him.' She struggles upright, her stitches pulling. 'The fire nor the murder. Plater—'

'No.' Henne takes her hand again. 'The Church will allow us more land for planting, Lisbet. Beets, onions, cabbages. The crops of my father and your father both. It is the best we can hope for.'

'Henne, you are not listening.'

'You must listen to me, wife.' He is hurting her now, his hand a vice. He knows, she realises. He knows it was not Eren. Has even perhaps guessed at Plater's responsibility. But who can take up a charge against the Twenty-One's man?

He is looking at her intently, warning in his eyes, and she nods only so he will let loose her hand. She tucks it under her armpit, her breasts sore, heavy. Soon her boy will be returned to her and he will drink, and she can be rid of Henne and be alone with her son.

'I don't know what Mutti was thinking, letting a Turk sleep here. In this bed!' He shudders, and Lisbet closes her eyes to keep the tears from sight. 'If I were here, I should have run him through.'

'You would murder a man,' says Lisbet faintly, though she knows he witnessed the near-murder of his sister.

'They are not men, Lisbet,' says Henne. 'The Church itself says to kill such a beast is only malecide, only the defeat of evil. It is in the service of God to do such a thing. I have been assured of it. It is not murder when you cast out a devil.'

She wants to throw herself upon him, bite and scratch and tear. She wants to tell him he is the Devil, he and Plater both, for what they did to Nethe, to Ida. She wants to say, I love him, the Turk you hate. But even if she could, he would not give her space to speak. Henne charges on.

'Fifty skeps, burned! At least all the wax was farmed, and we have six buckets of honey.'

That Lisbet collected. She knows then she is the same as the poor bees, that all his sadness is for their value, all the grief is for what they gave. If she had died and left the child living, would he care? The answer is obvious, and it breaks what is left of her heart. Only the boy when he is brought to her breast, and Nethe who carries him, begin to mend it.

Twenty-Three

When at last she is churched, and their son blessed, Henne allows Ida's children to visit. Ilse seems older already, her cheeks thinner, and she looks more like her mother than ever. She cries into the baby's swaddling, and Lisbet whispers to her that she, too, lost her mother. That Ida is in Heaven, and watches her, and is proud. That Ilse has a friend in Lisbet, in Nethe, that they will make sure she never feels alone, or anything less than loved. The younger children are only bewildered, and Rolf will bear no damage from it at all – Lisbet promises herself she will make sure of it. She feeds him what milk her boy leaves spare. Sometimes she brings both babies to her breasts and lets them twine fingers like twins as they drink. She will keep Ida alive for all of them, hold them in the sort of safety Ida bestowed upon Lisbet.

With Henne busy sowing the soil, Daniel Lehmann assisting him, Lisbet and Sophey and Nethe have hours in each other's company. Though Sophey is not softened by the events of the summer, she is smoothed, and the beginnings of friendship form between them, perhaps even love. But it is Nethe who Lisbet cleaves to, who gets her through those impossible early days of grief and pain and ecstasy. It is Nethe who saves her, day after day, and it seems to Lisbet that slowly they are learning to carry their pain and their love between them, growing it large enough, strong enough, to bear all else.

They take to sharing a bed. Henne grumbles when the baby cries, and seems relieved when Lisbet suggest she moves to Nethe's room. They wake in an exhausted cycle together, sleeping when the baby sleeps, talking when he feeds. Lisbet tells Nethe everything: about Eren, about her mother, even about the river. Nethe shares her and Ida's earliest days, and their last hours, and they laugh and cry until their skin is raw.

It is one such night, the boy asleep at her breast, when Lisbet smells rain. Her senses are still heightened, and she feels a creeping pressure in her skull, scents that beautiful, clear bloom of an approaching downpour.

'Open the shutters,' she whispers, and Nethe throws them wide. The night sky is clouded, and Nethe holds her hand out.

'Oh,' she says, and comes to Lisbet, her palm outstretched. On it balances a drop of water. She smears it over Lisbet's forehead, an anointment.

'Here,' says Lisbet, and holds out Heinrich. Nethe takes him, walks him to the window to show him the starting rain. Lisbet slides her legs from beneath the sheets. She has barely moved at the empiric's orders, and feels her stitches pull. But there is not pain, only a dim ache. When Nethe turns she is already on her feet.

She exclaims in surprise. 'Careful, Bet!'

Behind her, the rain catches some distant light and shimmers. Nethe holds out her arm to guide Lisbet towards the window, but she shakes her head, moving instead towards the door. Nethe mouths warningly at her, but Lisbet feels light, giddy.

They move through the dark house, Heinrich held tight to

Nethe's chest. Lisbet eases the outer door open, and they see Fluh running joyously in the gathering rain. Beyond her, Lisbet spies the absence of the skeps, levelled and planted. She steps barefoot into the yard. Those first cooling drops are like a blessing, and she feels transformed by them, sanctified. They give her the courage to approach the furrowed ground. There is where the first skep she wove stood. There is where she homed the wild bees she led from the dance tree. There is where she planted herself, and calmed the swarming bees. This is where she killed a man, to save her son. The rain begins to fall in earnest, hammering the parched ground, and she tilts back her head and drinks.

'Are you all right, Bet?'

When Lisbet says *yes*, it is the truth. She takes her boy, takes Nethe's hand once more. She does not need to stand there any longer. There is somewhere else to be.

•

A hundred or more years ago, an impossible time, the Pope forbade miracles: prohibited starvers, healers, the raising of the dead. There had been too many wonders, the marvels wreaking havoc. But here she is carrying her own, through the driving rain, and Lisbet wants to laugh for joy.

Nethe does not need to ask where they are going. They listen to the thrumming of the forest, coming alive under the clouds. The river will fill and swell, make clean the harrowed streets. Lisbet shifts her son in her arms. He is perfect. He is divine, an angel – these things she feels truly and without reservation. That she has made something good and pure and holy. Now his eyes are open and they are the darkest blue. She loves him so deeply it is to make the word hollow – her love for him sucks the marrow from her bones.

The dance tree is as she left it. There are her babies' ribbons, their sacrifices made so her son might live. Nethe takes Heinrich so Lisbet can climb, passes him up before following.

The rain makes a drumming sound on the leaves overhead, but barely a drop reaches them. The platform feels vast and solid beneath her feet. There is Eren's kettle, his mother's sole inheritance. There is Eren's lute. Lisbet hovers her hand over the silent strings. He didn't come back for it – a wise choice, but her heart aches for all he has left. Here is where they kissed and lay together, where she thought her life might grow larger than any she had ever planned for or imagined. Eren's music comes to her, the slow lilt of the tune he played on their night together.

Lisbet leans out, careful with her child in her arms, to the branch she led the bees from. Gently, she dislodges the wadding of tarred sticks, and lets them fall to the ground. Maybe they will come back, her bees. Maybe they will share this place, her babies and the bees, both.

There is a tearing sound, and Lisbet turns to see Nethe ripping a length of cloth from the hem of her dress. She looks to Lisbet for permission, then reaches up and ties it around the branch. From her pocket she pulls the ribbon, the silken twist of Ida's hair Lisbet had found in her pillow all those weeks ago, and loops it around the torn cloth so it hangs like an ornament.

'For Ida.'

'For all of us,' says Lisbet.

She begins to hum, bringing music to her as though the lute is not dumb at their feet but being played, dark nimble fingers plucking its strings. Nethe joins in, tunelessly, and wraps her arms around Lisbet and Heinrich. Beneath the thrumming branches, both holding and held, Lisbet hums louder. In the dark cave of her sister's chest, she smiles, her son's body hot against hers. He is here. There is a whole life ahead. She and Nethe begin to dance.

Author's Note

In July 1518, in the midst of the hottest summer Central Europe had ever known, a woman whose name is recorded as Frau Troffea began to dance in the streets of Strasbourg. This was no ordinary dance – it was unrelenting, closer to a trance than a celebration. She danced for days, any attempts to make her rest thwarted, until it drew the attention of the Twenty-One, the city's council, and she was taken to the shrine of St Vitus, patron saint of dancers and musicians. After being bathed in the spring there, she stopped dancing.

But it was too late. Already, the dancing plague had spread, and it lasted two sweltering, frenzied months. At its height, up to four hundred people danced, with claims that up to fifteen people a day died. It is the biggest outbreak of such a mania ever recorded.

But it was not an isolated incident. Between the fourteenth and the seventeenth centuries, dancing plagues, or choreomania, occurred regularly. Sometimes they were contained and concentrated around the feast day of St Vitus. Sometimes they involved only children, sometimes mainly women. Often, the dancers were society's most vulnerable, whether through class, age, race, or gender.

Because of these characteristics, one of the most popular explanations, both now and then, was a religious mania. God and the Devil were not ideas to be debated in medieval times – they were facts, as real as weather or hunger. Indeed, weather was sent by God, and so too was drought and famine. The sixteenth century was especially plagued by extreme weather events, and though these are now easily explained by science, at the time there was only one explanation for the endless ruined harvests, the excruciatingly hot summers, and the winters so cold people froze to death in the streets. God was punishing the human race, and they must atone.

At the very end of the fifteenth century, He had sent a warning: a comet that many notorious preachers such as Johann Geiler von Kaysersberg, who is a favourite of Sophey's in *The Dance Tree*, pointed to as a sign of damnation. It threw the Alsace region, a much-disputed area between France and Germany, into a state of panic, heightened by war at the borders between the Holy Roman Empire and the advancing Ottoman Empire, as well as by two decades of floods and drought that decimated crops. Those closest to poverty were forced to borrow from the Church, who seemed to be more a business than representatives of God.

The rancour between ordinary people and the Church intensified to such a point that serf-led rebellions became a regular occurrence and constant threat. Starving farmers took up arms against their creditors and landowners, and were summarily hanged. The anger increased. More starvation, more revolts, more hangings. And all the time the Holy Roman Empire was coming apart at the seams as the Ottomans grew their reach. The fear of these brown-skinned invaders was transformed into rabid hatred by pamphlets that painted them as demons walking the earth, gruesome words replicated with ease by the printing press, which originated in Strasbourg.

It was amidst this disorientating time that Frau Troffea took up her dance. Life for a working-class woman was especially fraught, being that they were chattel and held no legal power in church, state, society or at home. Perhaps she felt assailed by the doom spoken around her, and lost her mind. Perhaps she ate poor-quality bread made with rye tainted by ergot, a fungus that causes nerve contractions and the sensation of fire in the limbs. Perhaps she could not afford bread, and searched the Black Forest for mushrooms to sate her hunger, and fell into the grip of a hallucinogen.

All of these have been offered as explanations, but it is John Waller in his exceptional book *A Time to Dance, A Time to Die* (2009) who creates the most compelling case for this being no simple madness, nor poisoning, but a mass religious trance instigated by the unique pressures and beliefs of the time. It is difficult for contemporary readers to understand the absolute role of religion in medieval life, how fully it informed every-thing from medicine to punishment, tax to sex. *The Dance Tree* owes an enormous debt to John Waller's research, although I have taken great liberties in my work of fiction. Anyone wanting to read more about the dancing plague of 1518 must seek out his book.

As with any story, I have learnt so much by writing *The Dance Tree*. It's easy to draw lines from then to now in attitudes to the LGBT+ community, to immigrants, to class. We have come so far, and not nearly far enough. The power structures we operate under are no longer titled 'God' but they are still very much in existence. The world-at-large remains too often a hostile place for people who live, look, or love a different way. In *The Dance Tree*, I wanted to offer my characters a place to be safe and themselves. I am only sorry that the outside world found its way in.

Finally and on a personal note, having experienced our

contemporary pandemic through the lens of recurrent pregnancy loss, I wanted to depict that experience in my novel. I haven't yet found enough stories that explore this particular pain and love, though it affects one in one hundred people, and miscarriages occur in one in three pregnancies.

Lisbet is my attempt to offer a mirror to anyone else struggling to see themselves, and a window to those who might need the insight. I hope you don't begrudge her her ending.

Kiran Millwood Hargrave, November 2021

Acknowledgements

All novels contain a part of your heart: *The Dance Tree* has all the broken pieces of mine. Thank you to the people who supported me through this, the hardest of processes.

My editor, Sophie Jonathan, who helped me find the right words and the right path. My agent, Hellie Ogden, for telling me to take time to heal. To all at Picador, from proofreaders to typesetters, copyeditors to marketing teams, publicists to sales reps. To the wonderful people at Janklow and Nesbit, US and UK. To Kirby Kim, for his utter belief. To Rakesh Satyal and all at HarperOne.

To booksellers, librarians, and readers everywhere.

To Katie Ellis-Brown, for early guidance. To Elizabeth Macneal, for earlier guidance. To Sarvat Hasin and Daisy Johnson, for the earliest guidance.

To my family, my in-laws, my friends. Especially to my mother, Andrea, sisters-in-law Miranda, Madi, and Milli, and to Katie Webber. To my beloved cousins, nieces and nephews, to the babies born and growing while I wrote this story — miracles all.

To the people who help us live through disaster. To Dr Ingrid Granne, Ginny Mounce, Emily Carson, and Zoe Seargeant.

To the babies we lost. To all the people who know what that feels like.

To my husband, Tom. I love you.